advanc

"In Brandes' thriller, a young woman must come to terms with her father's violent past and reconcile with her role in it. This hard-to-define novel tugs at the heartstrings and shocks the senses in equal measure. Brandes writes in a gentle, descriptive style, filled with the glories of nature and the darkness of a lonely, isolated life. Tilly's fierce intelligence and perseverance suggest shades of Delia Owens' *Where the Crawdads Sing* and Harper Lee's *To Kill a Mockingbird*. Readers will feel deeply for her during her long, arduous emotional journey, but Brandes' skill also makes it possible to feel empathy for Frank and his cause, even if readers deplore his actions. Ultimately, this is a novel about finding a balance between loving someone and recognizing that sometimes love can be misplaced. A moving coming-of-age novel that blends thrills and heartfelt familial drama."

—*Kirkus Reviews*

"Simmering with suspense and brimming with heart, this beautiful story of heartache and resilience will linger long after its final pages."

—Kimi Cunningham Grant, USA TODAY
bestselling author of *These Silent Woods*

"Kate Brandes writes with a kindness and generosity rare in contemporary fiction. The story is well told and dramatic, but it's her careful elaboration of the people and the natural world of Stone Creek, that stay with us. In this communion with every living thing, with the forces of creation, not destruction, *Stone Creek* can stand alongside the novels of Barbara Kingsolver and Wendell Berry."

—Anna Kodama, poet and author of
Lit Only By a Few Thousand Stars

"In *Stone Creek*, author Kate Brandes considers the emotional as well as environmental fallout of sabotage, no matter how well intended. A beautiful coming-of-age story."

—JoeAnn Hart, author of *Arroyo Circle* and
Highwire Act & Other Tales of Survival

"Through the specific and timely lens of ecoterrorism, Kate Brandes has created a moving story of a woman who still needs her father's love, yet who fears that his infamy will threaten the secure if lonely life she's built without him on the shaky foundation of their off-the-grid, anarchist past. From constantly building tension to exploding dams, book clubs will love discussing its many evocative layers."

— Kathryn Craft, Award-winning author
of *The Far End of Happy* and *The Art of Falling*

"Brandes's keenly observed, loving descriptions of the natural world—the birds, trees, and wildflowers of Stone Creek—make a reader understand why her characters are willing to fight to protect it. A well-plotted tale exploring the choices we make to care for the places and people we love, this novel is sure to be a book club favorite."

—Jenn Rossmann, author of
The Place You're Supposed to Laugh

stone creek

kate brandes

—— *a novel* ——

Kate Brandes

Wyatt-MacKenzie Publishing

DEADWOOD, OREGON

Stone Creek
Kate Brandes

ISBN: 978-1-942545-52-2
Library of Congress Control Number: on file

Wyatt-MacKenzie Publishing
DEADWOOD, OREGON

Wyatt-MacKenzie Publishing, Inc.
www.WyattMacKenzie.com
Contact us: info@wyattmackenzie.com

dedication

To my loves: D, O, and S

september 2023

chapter one

Tilly Stone lay in bed that Friday, watching dust motes swirl slowly in the morning light. The day had finally come and with it a mix of anticipation and dread bottled up and shaken to the point of bursting. All night she'd barely slept, listening for any sounds in the house. Probably he wasn't coming. It would be better in so many ways if he stayed away. She had to remember that. It had been seventeen years, for god's sake.

Still, she'd left her backdoor open the night before and now imagined Frank, her father, right at that moment waiting for her in the kitchen down the hall.

Tilly got out of bed and stood for a long moment staring at the painting hanging on the wall: Henry's portrait of her at thirteen. She'd moved the painting years ago from the old place up on the mountain behind her house and hung it by her bed to remind herself of who she'd been before Frank left and before she'd built her home and business and tried to forge a life that hadn't worked out quite how she'd imagined.

She put on jeans and a flannel and pulled her hair into a ponytail. Then went down the hallway and peeked slowly around the corner into the kitchen. But the only thing there was the untouched blackberry pie she made every year on the eve of their shared birthdays. Only this was *the* birthday that marked her thirtieth year and Frank's fiftieth—the day he'd said he'd come back.

2

The kitchen suddenly felt too small. Too close. She went outside, fleeing an overwhelming sense of disappointment.

It had cooled some overnight. Nighthawks flew in long twisty loops searching the overcast sky for insects above Stone Creek that ran beside her house. A mild, humid wind dimpled the creek as a yellowed leaf from a towering walnut landed on the slow-running water, backed up by the dam sitting just below Tilly's home.

The same dam that had triggered Frank to blow up all the others.

Tilly looked back at her house and her woodshop next door. Both stood between the base of Short Mountain and the edge of town. She wondered if the FBI was watching her property, waiting for Frank like she was.

Behind the house an old, long forgotten footpath wove through the woods that went up the mountain to the cabin where she and Frank once lived. In front of her house lay the small town of Cottersville sitting along the Delaware River, which separated Pennsylvania from New Jersey. Just like her life, her home was caught somewhere between the wild, unknowable mountain of her past and the domesticated but equally inscrutable town of her present.

She turned back to her front door, but decided not to go in there, not right now. Instead, she went to her shop, turned on the lights, and checked the cork board for the next furniture order. She might as well get some work done. Maybe that would help get her mind off Frank. The shop phone rang. It was early for a call. Tilly hesitated, wondering if it could be Frank. Longing and trepidation thrummed in her chest as she answered.

"Tilly, it's Greg Roberts."

The mayor had never called her before. She relaxed some. She could not continue on like this. Frank was gone.

"I've only got a minute but figured you'd want to know the town council is meeting about the dam on Monday night. They're thinking of finally taking it out. Figured you'd want to be there."

This was a surprise. For years she'd tried everything to convince the town to remove the dam. All her efforts seemed to be for nothing when town council made the decision to keep it three years ago. But maybe now they were about to change their tune. "Thanks for letting me know."

She hung up and a noise from the back of the shop made her turn.

That's when Frank stepped out of the shadows.

chapter two

It was his jacket that stirred feelings she'd only imagined the iceberg tip of. The same navy blue with the yellow bird insignia on the upper arm, now worn thin and riddled with holes. "You came."

"I promised I would."

His voice was more gravely than she remembered. His eyes, more watery than before, gave him a dreamy look he'd never had. His beard was streaked with white, and a tooth was missing from the front of his mouth. She took a step toward him but froze when she caught the scent of old sweat and a body that hadn't been washed in a long time. Bits of grass clung to his hair on one side. He'd grown more feral in his body, and, she sensed, in his mind, too, given the rumors she'd heard. Or perhaps she'd become too tame.

"There's a lot to say," he said.

"Yeah." She wiped away tears she could feel on her cheeks. He was her dad and she still loved him. She couldn't deny that now. This was true even though she saw him for who he was much more clearly than she could have as a child. Yet, their connection ran even deeper than she'd understood.

He took two long steps toward her and reached for her hand. She braced herself, unsure of him. His skin was chapped and rough, but his touch warm and gentle.

"You're all grown up. Of course, you are." He stared at her like he couldn't quite believe it. "And look at what you made of this place." He looked all around the shop. "You built a whole life." His voice was full of the admiration she craved from him, still. "I've missed you. You have no idea."

He let go of her hand and ran his fingers over the table she'd just made. "You built this, too?"

She wanted to say so many things. She wanted him to be impressed, even as she also wished it didn't matter to her. Knew it shouldn't.

The sound of gravel against tire made them both turn to the window facing her house. Tilly recognized the black car pulling up behind her red pick-up, its headlight beams sparkling against the drizzle now falling outside.

"That's FBI Agent Mac Stevens." She suspected Frank already knew this. "He visits every year on this day. He's been trying to track you down since you left."

Mac got out of his car, took a long drag, and blew smoke over his shoulder.

Frank stepped toward the shop's back door, now skittish as a wild animal. "I know you have questions. But I want you to know whatever it looked like, I didn't hurt anyone. I think you know that."

Except she didn't know.

"I need your help with the dam."

Of course he'd ask this of her. And yet it came as a cold surprise.

Frank's eyes were trained on Mac as he knocked on the front door of her house.

"I've wondered—" she said, thinking of the Cotters, "—what really happened, where you've been? I thought you might have died. Why did you leave?"

Mac had given up on Tilly's front door and was headed toward the shop.

Frank, eyes still on Mac, nodded his head toward the window that looked out over Stone Creek. "Come to the dam tonight. At midnight. I'll be at the edge of the woods. We'll talk then." He slipped out the back door and disappeared into the trees.

Mac came to the shop's front door seconds later and Tilly opened it for him.

chapter three

Mac was looking at her too closely. Tilly could still smell Frank's sweat in the air and wondered if Mac could, too.

"This isn't an easy day for you, I know," he said gently.

Mac's concern for her wellbeing still came as a surprise. She picked up a piece of sandpaper and busied herself with smoothing off the edge of a board so he wouldn't get the idea he should hug her or something. He stopped by on her birthday every year but they both knew this one was different.

He ran his hand over his short afro, wet from the rain. He took off his raincoat, shaking off beads of water and hung it on the back of a chair where it dripped into a puddle. It didn't occur to him that she might mind the water on her floor. Mac was messy in his dress and habits, often wrinkled with crumbs and stains down his shirt. So the puddle on the floor was just him and he meant no disrespect.

"I have some news that might be hard to hear," he said.

She stopped sanding and quickly started again, hoping Mac hadn't noticed. If he had a chance of catching Frank, it would be through her. That was the other thing they both knew. "What news?"

"An anonymous tip came in by email directing me to the last dam Frank bombed. The one on the Umbra Creek."

"Oh?" Tilly had a feeling in her chest of having crossed a line past which she could breathe normally. The air around her had

8

suddenly grown thin and useless, like she couldn't get enough of it into her lungs. The Umbra Dam was the last one she and Frank had done together.

Mac handed her his phone. "I took this photo yesterday when I went there."

The image showed a tree marked with a yellow bird on the trunk. The shape and color of the bird matched the one on Frank's jacket. "And I found this tacked to the tree." He handed her a sheet of paper that said: *I'll be back when I'm fifty.*

She glanced at the back door.

"No fingerprints, of course. And we couldn't trace the email. But I wanted to warn you that somehow news of this is already making the rounds on social media, at least among the Frank crowd. You need to be prepared for the possibility this could go mainstream. Reporters might show up. Especially given the timing with the birthday." Mac's phone rang. He slipped his hand into his pocket and checked the screen. "It's my wife. I'll just step outside a minute."

Mac had described the "Frank Crowd" to Tilly before as a fringe online group disgusted with the modern world's hyperconsumerism and ecological destruction. They wanted to do away with modern systems and return to pre-industrial ways of living. Some of them were inspired by the writings of Ted Kaczynski, but also Frank to some degree. Ironically this group gathered online on tech platforms like Discord and Twitter or X—whatever it was called now. Tilly had never seen any of these posts. She stayed far away from all social media. The last thing she needed was more ways for people to harass her about Frank.

Even with the shop door closed between them Tilly could hear Mac's side of the phone conversation.

"Let me talk to our little sweetheart." After a pause he said, "You have bear-bear ready for the trip? Uh-huh." He listened for a moment and then made kissing noises into the phone.

"I'm taking my granddaughter to the zoo tomorrow," Mac told her when he came back inside.

"How old is she?"

"Three, and she's the brightest star."

Tilly had always liked the family side of Mac. In the seventeen years they'd known each other she'd come to think of him as a good man, despite that he was hunting Frank.

Mac patted his coat for cigarettes and pulled one out. He wouldn't smoke it in the shop but liked having it in his mouth to talk around. "There's more than what I found at the Umbra Dam."

"What do you mean?" She felt too warm all of a sudden and wished she could go outside into the cooler air.

"*The Philadelphia Inquirer* received an op-ed with Frank's by-line this morning, submitted by mail." He handed her a copy. "They wanted to print it but contacted us first. We've asked them not to run it. It's typed. No fingerprints."

She scanned it. Unspoiled landscapes, thinking outside boundaries created by government and industry, the industrial machine—that all sounded like Frank. But it was the last paragraph she read twice.

> *These last years I've lived outside of rules and ex-pectations. I've breathed clean, life-giving air, swum in snowmelt, and walked the forests. I've rested and reawakened. Now I'm raising an army.*

Tilly pictured what she'd heard about Frank most recently from the strangers who occasionally showed up at her door claiming to have spent time with him. According to their stories Frank had been moving among a series of far-flung cabins and tents deep in the woods where people were drawn into his worldview, even as he kept them in the dark about who he was. According to these accounts Frank saw himself now as some kind of anarchist prophet, whose mission was to inspire people to rebel against the poisons of western civilization, industry, and technology. She hadn't quite believed the stories. People said a lot of things about Frank that weren't true. But maybe this time was different.

She handed the paper back to Mac, the one person interested in the real Frank—not the anarchist legend crap. Mac had inter-viewed countless people, studied Frank's op-eds and journals, and followed up on every lead since Frank's disappearance. He understood Frank almost as well as she did, although he considered Frank a terrorist and wanted to put him in jail. Tilly didn't trust Frank, but jail was a cruelty he didn't deserve. Unless he'd done something worse than she thought him capable of, which, she had to admit, was possible.

"What do you make of that op-ed?" Mac asked.

She shrugged, trying to keep her face blank. "Was there a postmark?"

"It was mailed from a small town in upstate New York, near the Umbra Creek."

"Any other papers get it?"

"Probably. Most will dismiss it as nutball stuff. No one knows Frank Stone outside this local area and small corners of the internet, unless they remember you and he were once national news. But that was a long time ago now. The press around here will be interested though. And some won't bother to contact us before printing or posting. You need to be ready. I think you should hire a PR person in case this thing gets too big too fast."

She couldn't afford a PR person. And she wasn't ready for any of this.

Mac cleared his throat. "And you need to call me right away if Frank makes contact."

She gave him a quick nod.

"We'll be patrolling the area over the next few days to keep an eye out."

summer 2006

chapter four

JUNE

It was night—the only time they worked.

Frank drove a stolen Ford pickup they'd burn later. Tilly cranked her window all the way down to feel the honey-suckled June air on her face as they went along the remote, windy road through upstate New York.

She switched on her handheld transistor and sang along to what was playing. Frank had gotten her the small SONY the year before when she'd turned twelve so she could keep up with current events. But mostly she listened to music and imagined other people listening and humming along to the same song.

Frank tapped the steering wheel with two fingers, not to the music, but because this is what he did when he had something to tell her she wouldn't like. "I've been thinking," he said.

"Uh-oh."

His quick smile didn't match his eyes. "We need to change location right after we're done with this job."

She kicked the dash. "But we only just unpacked."

He stared straight ahead, lips pressed into a thin line. He hated it when she complained. But this was insane. Moving every two weeks was bad enough, but this time they'd rolled out the sleeping bags an hour ago.

His foot eased on the gas and the truck slowed. "The Feds are on our tail. And they don't have enough imagination to understand the significance of our work. You know that."

This was Frank's FBI speech. She'd long pictured the FBI as an army of identical wiry men dressed in suits, standing in long rows as though produced by a factory. In her mind, they each carried a briefcase containing photos and recordings of innocent people, guns at the ready.

Still, she'd never seen an agent. Neither had Frank as far as she knew.

But Frank liked to talk about Ted Kaczynski's arrest in 1996 as though it had just happened yesterday. She wondered if he was about to launch into that now. She'd read Ted K.'s manifesto, all 232 numbered sections about why he'd mailed bombs to people. How industry and technology caused psychological suffering while it also damaged the natural world. And about corporations having too much say in people's lives. Ted, like Frank, spent all his time thinking about how to fight the system. Tilly realized after reading the manifesto that Ted talked like Frank or Frank talked like him, more like. Tilly didn't understand why Frank thought so much of Ted K. because Ted would write things like: *I will kill but I will make at least some effort to avoid detection, so that I can kill again.*

She and Frank blew up dams, not people. A statement against big industry and ecological destruction and a fight against complacency, Frank said. They worked to inspire a revolution, but not to kill. Never to kill.

Even so, Tilly was tired of moving around. She wanted a regular life where she could listen to songs with other people in the same room. She most definitely did not want to pack up all their shit again and drive somewhere else in the middle of the night.

"Listen," Frank said, sitting higher in his seat, "you'll like this new plan."

She spit a bad taste out the window.

"What I've been thinking is we move once more and then stay put. Hide in plain sight. We'll do this last dam and start fresh. What about that?"

She stared at the side of his face, trying to figure out what he was really saying. They'd never stayed in one place longer than a few weeks. "What do you mean?"

"If we don't leave a trail, the Feds can't track us. They don't know Frank Stone from nobody. They don't know Tilly Stone. We can live where we want if we stop the work."

She tried to figure out what he was aiming at because it couldn't be that simple. "Why would we stop now?"

"You've wanted a more normal life. I promised myself when you got old enough I'd give you that. You're almost thirteen, so maybe it's the right time—that's what I'm saying."

The night was so black she could see nothing beyond the reach of the headlights. It was hard to imagine living another way even if that's what she wanted.

"You should have a real home. For a while anyway," he said.

"Where would we go?"

He hit the brakes, stopped the truck right in the middle of the road and faced her. "I was thinking about the family cabin."

Now he was talking. She threw her arms around his neck. This was Frank's childhood home. He'd told her so many stories about Cottersville. Could he really mean it? She squeezed him harder, hoping to seal the deal.

"All right, all right, Tilly-bell." He laughed as he hugged her back. "But we need to talk serious for a minute."

She sat back in her seat but couldn't stop smiling. This was better than ten Christmases.

"I need to tell you right now," he said in his dad voice, "all the old rules apply."

She pressed her lips together in an effort to look more serious. "I know the rules."

Frank insisted she speak like an "educated person." He was constantly harping about proper English and forced her to read way too many books. And they went to plenty of movies, which typically brought on another lecture: "See what the actors do, the mask they put on for the part they're playing? That's what you have to do. Disappear into the situation you're in. You want to be the person in the background playing the bit part. The one no one sees."

She'd blended in fine with other kids in the library. In fact, she did it better than Frank. Ladies noticed him too much. But she could sit in a restaurant, go to the post office, the store, a gas station without anyone looking twice. Still, none of that was real. Now, Frank was talking about living a real, regular life.

"We still keep to ourselves. Do for ourselves. That's how we stay free. It's how we stay together."

If they lived in one place, she'd make friends and belong somewhere. Maybe she could even go to school.

"No promises we can stay, either," he said. "The first sign of trouble and we're out of there. No complaints if it goes that way. You understand?"

She nodded. "Can I meet other kids? I mean ... later if we're careful and everything goes right?"

A glimmer of a grin crept in as he hit the gas. "One thing at a time, girl."

Even though she knew that was supposed to be the end of the conversation, she couldn't help herself. "Cottersville is where you met my mother, right?" His grin turned downward.

There'd been just one time, about a month ago when he'd had more beers than usual, that he'd said her name: Helen. Tilly'd figured out a long time ago her mother had died during childbirth. That's why he never talked about her. But since he'd told Tilly her name, she liked to imagine her, Helen, living in a house in Cottersville, where she and Frank might visit and decide to stay. Frank told her she got her dark wavy hair from her mother, like she got the blue eyes from him.

The truck came to a hard sudden stop. Frank got out without a word and went around to the front. Tilly got out, too. There on the blacktop three baby opossums sat next to their dead mother. Two of the babies were still trying to nurse.

"Jesus," Frank said. "Look at that."

Frank often made decisions based on signs that appeared to him. Surely this was a sign, but of what Tilly couldn't tell. She just hoped it wouldn't change his mind about going to Cottersville.

He took off his jacket, the navy-blue one with the yellow bird stitched into the upper arm, and scooped up the littlest opossum, which seemed even smaller in his big hands. He wrapped it loosely in his jacket. "Hand me the other two."

Frank had rules about wildlife. If there was the possibility the animal could fend for itself then nature knew better than people. But sometimes, like in this case when the opossums were so young, they could help them.

"There's a wildlife rehab place not far from here. We'll drop them there when we're done."

Back in the truck Tilly held the opossums on her lap, thinking of things Frank had mentioned about Cottersville: the cabin; the herons flying to and from the nearby rookery; the little town where everyone knew each other; and Stone Creek, named for their family. It was also the place where Frank's dad had been in a bad accident at the Cottersville Dam, which is why they did their work.

Frank switched off the headlights and drove the last mile or so in the dark, coming to a stop next to the Umbra Dam. They sat waiting, to make sure they hadn't been followed. But Tilly was eager to get this job done so they could start this new life. "We haven't seen a soul over the last three days of scouting around here," she said. "We aren't going to see anyone now, not in the middle of the night."

"I just don't want anyone to get—"

"—hurt. I know. But no one's out here."

"Fine." Frank thumbed over his shoulder at the box in the back of the truck. "You're up then."

She handed him his jacket with the opossums, got out and double checked that each stick of dynamite was tied with a primer cord and the fuse blasting cap was taped correctly.

Any prints or other trace she left on the bomb material couldn't be linked to them. She'd been born at home since Frank hated Big Pharma. *Hospitals pump people with poison.* There was no birth certificate. With no records of any kind, she was no one to the government and they were kept safe this way. So safe, Tilly now realized, they could live in Cottersville and no one would know the difference.

She wrestled the box out of the truck bed and, struggling under its weight, carried it to the edge of the dam, then set the charges. She unspooled the fuse as she walked back toward the truck.

On a tree close to the dam, she spray-painted the trunk with the same yellow bird insignia on Frank's jacket, taking time to make sure the wings tapered and spread at the edges, so it photographed well when the news crews showed up later.

Back at the truck, she pulled a lighter from her shirt pocket, flicked it, and held the flame to the fuse, maybe for the last time.

When the burn crept steadily along the fuse, making its way toward the box, Tilly climbed into the truck, and they drove off. The firebomb behind them lit the night in one sudden white flash so bright it burned her eyes. The truck jumped with the thud of the explosion and her forehead hit the rear cab window hard enough to bruise. She knew from experience to keep more distance between her head and the glass, but she was preoccupied thinking about Cottersville.

Down the road, the smell of smoke became as faint as the sirens in the distance. And above them, the stars shone bright.

chapter five

On the last leg of the journey to the family cabin, they hiked across the shoulder of Short Mountain through a uniformly dim, gray-green oak forest.

Frank had quieted over the last day, probably thinking about returning to the place that haunted him because of what had happened to his dad.

She'd pieced together the tragic story over a long period of time. He'd been a boy when his pop worked for Cotter Paper, the paper mill in Cottersville. Paul Cotter, who owned the mill then, wanted Frank's pop to fix a crack in the old mill dam, used by the company in its earliest days to power the first mill. Frank's pop hadn't wanted to make the repair. He didn't think the dam was good for the fish. Felt it disrupted the natural flow of things. Frank liked to say his pop was one of the world's first environ-mentalists. He'd wanted to get rid of the dam so Stone Creek could run free, the way it was supposed to. And anyway, by that time, the paper company had moved their manufacturing oper-ation just across the river in New Jersey and didn't need the dam anymore. It was an artifact of the paper company's beginnings. But Paul Cotter insisted on the repair and if Frank's pop wanted his job, he had to fix the dam.

It took a backhoe to do it. Frank was ten at the time and it was his birthday so he'd been allowed to stay home from school so he could watch his dad operate the big machine. At first it had been exciting watching his pop, who'd even shown off a little to wow young Frank by spinning the big machine around and raising and lowering the scoop. But then the backhoe slipped on the muddy embankment and rolled into the water, taking Frank's pop under, pinning him by his jacket.

The only time Tilly had seen Frank cry was when he'd described to her how full of hope his pop's eyes had been when Frank first jumped into the water and tried cutting him free with the pocketknife he carried. But the jacket was thick and unwieldy. Frank kept at it, cutting as best he could. But hope slowly faded from his pop's eyes as despair took over. Then his pop passed out and went lifeless in front of his eyes while Frank kept trying to free him, even as his own air supply grew thin. He couldn't stop. Wouldn't leave, even when everything faded and turned black.

Frank came to on the streambank. The men beside him were trying to tell him something. He scanned around for his father but couldn't find him. He tried to go back into the water, but the men held him even as he kicked and bit them, fighting to get free with everything he had until two men came out of the creek carrying his father's limp body.

He was alive, but he'd been under too long. There was brain damage.

After the accident, his mom had to quit her job to take care of his pop because Paul Cotter and the company didn't lift a finger to help. The family lost their house in town and had to move to the family hunting cabin up on the mountain. They lived there for years away from everyone else. His mother, who'd finally had enough one day, left Frank to take care of his dad on his own.

And so as Tilly and Frank now walked through the woods headed for that same cabin on Short Mountain, Frank was probably reliving it all.

It started to rain. Beads of water rolled down Tilly's back and she wondered how it would be between her and Frank now that they wouldn't have their work. Their lives had revolved around a way of life they'd developed together as a team. He scoped out remote dams and made sure no one came around much. Then he'd get a truck and supplies while she built the bombs based on calculations for fire power and spacing. Frank wrote op-eds to coincide with the bombings. Those op-eds, written for the small paper local to wherever they happened to be, were the most important part to Frank. The bomb was the hook he needed to get people to read.

Their work was what they talked about. It's what they did together. They'd made a real difference in the world. They'd had a purpose that gave Tilly a sense of importance, even if she didn't always like the way they had to live. So, it was hard now to envision anything different for their lives.

Daylight faded as they picked their way, more slowly now, through a thorny section of raspberry cane and greenbrier. Over the last hours a numbness had set into Tilly's legs. They moved on their own, like they weren't even part of her. The discomfort didn't bother her so much as the possibility Frank might change his mind before they got there. Because there was a pattern. After each bombing a period of calm would give way to whatever drove Frank from the inside pushing them onto the next dam. She didn't know what would happen when the pressure started to build again.

Tilly wondered how much further they had to walk when the outline of the cabin finally appeared against the dusky June sky. Frank held up his hand. She stopped and waited while he scouted ahead. She crossed fingers on both hands hoping someone hadn't claimed the place in Frank's absence. Water dripped from her nose, and she looked back at the thick undergrowth they'd just walked through. The worst thing would be having to turn around.

She waited and waited, long enough that she grew worried something had happened. When he finally made the screech-owl call, their "coast is clear" signal, she hurried toward him, eager to finally see the cabin.

Tall pale-green grass, coming into its full height, surrounded the place. There was no road or sign of anything around except more forest. Frank had told her before you could only get there on foot. No power or running water, but they were used to that. At least a small outhouse sat in back.

Two sides of the porch railing were broken off and the remaining one leaned heavily to one side. Treading carefully over the rickety porch floor, so it didn't give way, Tilly came to stand beside Frank in the doorway. Inside the one-room cabin, black mold fanned upward from the bottom of the walls. Water dripped from a hole in the roof onto the rotted floor. A sharp musty smell tickled her nose, making her eyes water. Cobwebs, mice droppings, dead flies and thick dust lay everywhere. Wasp nests clung to the walls, ceiling and along the cracked window-panes.

"It's worse off than I figured," Frank said quietly.

Tilly looked around for signs of their family. "How long since Grandmom and Grandpop lived here?"

"Mom left right after I graduated high school. I stayed to take care of Pop until he died about a year later."

"And then you left?"

He stepped inside. "I was here a little longer. In fact," he stamped the floor lightly with his foot, "you were born right here."

He bent down and tugged on a tarp covering something along one wall acting as though he'd said nothing out of the or-dinary. She stood in the doorway stock still, taking in this new piece of her history. She wasn't sure what surprised her more: what Frank had said or that he'd said it. Maybe he was in the mood to say more. "So how did you meet my mom back then?"

He looked up from the tarp.

"Well," he said, straightening up, "Pop had just died. I was pissed all over again at Cotter Paper. After dark I'd go down there to the mill operation across the river and slash tires, spray paint the buildings, that kind of thing. Anyway, this went on for a few weeks and your mom, who was still in high school and had re-cently started the school newspaper, decided to stake the place out so she could interview me." He smiled thinking about it. "It was your mother, not the police, who caught me in the act. That's how we met."

Tilly leaned down to help him with the tarp, pulling on her end while he got the other.

"And did she get the interview?"

"Not at first. But she was persistent. And persuasive. Never met anyone like her before or since. And, you know, one thing led to another."

Then, Tilly thought, I was born, and Helen died. That's probably why Frank had finally left Cottersville. He couldn't take any more death of the people he loved. Still, knowing now that she'd been born right here in this place reinforced the connection she'd felt to Cottersville all her life. She could almost feel the taproot extending from her feet right through the cabin floor, nestling deep into the soil and rock below.

Frank watched her face, seeming satisfied what he'd said meant something to her.

They pulled the tarp away to uncover a worn wooden table, three chairs, and aluminum-framed cots. "Same ones I grew up with." There wasn't a sense of nostalgia in his voice, but instead something that didn't entirely sit well.

They righted the table, and Tilly ran her hand over the coarse white paint trying to imagine her grandparents and a younger Frank eating dinner around it. Frank's face had a sad look of remembering. Seeing his old home in this state couldn't be easy.

"It won't take much to patch the roof," she said. "Soap and water will make a huge difference. We can replace the bad part of the floor and dry everything out."

"So, you're not disappointed?"

"No."

He gave a quick, decisive nod and unzipped his pack, pulling out their tent. "Set this up outside. That'll be more comfortable until we get this place cleaned up. I'm gonna sleep in here." He handed her the tent.

"Can't I sleep in here, too?"

He shook his head. "I need time on my own, just for a night or two. This place brings back memories. Pop and I were close, like you and me. It was hard seeing him like he was after the accident."

Outside the cabin it was windier than when they'd arrived. The wind gusts yanked the grass this way and that. The rain had stopped, but the thick, heavy clouds overhead promised more soon. She tamped down a circle of grass and set up the tent. She crawled inside and watched as the trees flapped their branches in the wind like swimmers against a strong current. Lightning splayed through the sky while it thundered and started to pour.

She slipped on a jacket. Between booms of thunder, she listened for cars and other sounds of Cottersville a couple miles down the mountain, as she tried to imagine a life there.

chapter six

The next morning when Tilly unzipped the tent, the sun came through the trees in a fan of light. The rain-soaked June soil smelled rich and fertile and wood thrush trilled from their nests. A great blue heron flew overhead, and she watched it land about a quarter mile away, probably in the rookery Frank had told her about.

Inside the cabin Frank was emptying his backpack, setting the contents on the table. "Good morning." He grinned easily enough. Maybe his first night hadn't been so hard.

She jumped at the sound of a sudden loud siren coming from down the mountain.

Frank laughed. "Fire whistle. Tells the volunteers they're needed for an emergency."

Tilly thought about this. "They hear that and come help?"

"Yep."

She'd heard distant fire whistles before, after their bombs went off. Those people must have been volunteers, too, awakened in the middle of the night. She'd never thought about that before. Those sirens didn't always mean police. Sometimes they were regular people coming to help.

Frank took a thick notebook out of his pack and laid it on the table. She picked it up and opened it to blank pages. "What's this?"

"I'm planning to write while we're here." He met her eyes. "A private diary."

She put the notebook down and pushed it aside.

Frank shouldered his pack. "I'm going to town for some oil paper, nails, and tarps so we can patch that hole in the roof. I'll pick up candles and a couple flashlights. Wasp spray, too. You search for firewood. When I get back, we'll clean out the wood-stove and see if it still works."

"What about the smoke? Won't people see?"

"We're hiding in plain sight, remember?" He winked at her.

"Can I go with you? You'll need help carrying all that stuff."

"I'll manage." He stepped toward the door but turned back. "When you're done with the wood, there's a bucket by the out-house and a scrub brush under the counter. The spring's a little ways past the outhouse. Start cleaning. If you get bored, have a look around. The rookery's about a quarter mile over that way." He pointed over her shoulder. "But don't go beyond there."

Why did she have to stay put if they were hiding in plain sight?

Frank scratched something off the back of his neck and peered at it. "Once things settle, I'll take you to town. But Tilly ..." he waited until she looked at him, "don't go exploring beyond what I've told you is okay until I say the time is right. You hear me?"

"Yeah."

"Cottersville's a small place. A tiny town cut out of the woods. The paper mill owns the bottom of Short Mountain next to town so no one ever comes up here, since that would be trespassing. People aren't going to bother us and that's what we want. At least until I can get some things worked out."

september 2023

chapter seven

Tilly checked at her watch: 11:15PM. From her kitchen window she scanned the tree line next to the dam. She didn't see any sign of Frank, but he had said midnight. Part of her still couldn't quite believe she'd seen Frank in the flesh that morning. It had been so quick she almost didn't trust it had happened. It felt impossible now to sit in the house and wait and she didn't want to draw undo attention by standing out there, so she decided to walk through town until it was time.

The moon was almost full as Tilly went past the Hart house, which was quiet at this hour, with only John and Mary living there now that their kids were grown. She walked on through the cemetery thinking of the phone call she'd gotten from the mayor about the meeting about the dam on Monday night. It was just occurring to her that the timing of his phone call and Frank's arrival was a little disturbing.

She noticed Henry's lit kitchen window. Maybe he or Finn had forgotten to turn off a light since they usually went to bed early. Or else Henry was preoccupied with the same thing she was: Frank's promise to return on his fiftieth birthday. Probably the whole town felt on edge, at least to some degree.

She wished for the thousandth time that she didn't care about Frank. He could very well jeopardize the life she'd built for herself, and she wanted to protect Cottersville from him. It also

28

wasn't lost on her that keeping her life open enough for him meant keeping it closed off to most everyone else.

But Frank, the constant ghost in her life, showed up in the form of emails and people at her door asking about him or claiming to have seen him. That had been truer in the last few years as Frank had become more of a focus, at least among a certain anarchist subculture largely inspired by TV and movies about Ted K. over the last decade.

A great-horned owl called as she approached Henry's kitchen window. Tilly heard it as a warning. She kept to deep shadows as she stood looking in from the outside, surprised to see Finn, Henry's eleven-year-old, at their kitchen table. He was sketching something. The glass of milk beside him and the open door of the microwave suggested he couldn't sleep.

She and Finn had met when he'd been about four. She'd been feeling restless that night, too, and took a walk through the cemetery. Finn and his mother were there. "He won't sleep," she'd said. "Insisted we come out here." Finn had gazed up at Tilly, like he'd been waiting for her to arrive. Then he'd reached out and taken her hand. This was before the divorce, before Finn's mother had moved six hours away to start a new life with a new man.

After that first meeting Finn started leaving his house when no one was watching and showing up at her shop door. It took only a few weeks of this before his parents gave up trying to stop him since he was so determined. Henry made a deal with Finn that if he stopped running away, Henry would walk him to Tilly's shop on Saturdays for a regular weekly visit. Henry'd done this, waiting on the edge of her lawn until Finn reached her shop door, before starting his mail route. This pattern had continued for the last seven years, only now Finn was old enough to come to her shop on his own.

If Henry saw Tilly right now watching through his window, that would likely end her relationship with Finn, the one thing Tilly couldn't bear. Yet she needed to see their kitchen with its pale-yellow walls and white curtains and the stocked fruit bowl next to the dishes left to dry on the counter. Finn's homework and books scattered across the kitchen table, next to his socks on the floor spoke of a lived-in, loving home. Even the basket of neatly-folded laundry, sitting at the base of the stairs helped Tilly feel more peaceful. Finn sipped his warm milk and she wondered if he'd tell her in the morning about what had kept him awake.

She stepped away from the house and surveyed the town, taking in the tidy houses containing families that all knew each other. People here lived for neighborly chat. Growing up with Frank, it hadn't been important to know who was marrying who, or who'd just had a baby, or gotten a new job. But it turned out this is what filled people's lives. This community had long ago woven together a kind of invisible curtain between themselves and outsiders. Neighbors fought occasionally amongst themselves about loud noises, pets, and property lines, sometimes fueled by differences in politics, but even so, there was a kind of baseline acceptance if those neighbors had lived here long enough. An acceptance that wasn't extended to those who weren't born and raised. It wasn't personal exactly, just a natural form of protection for a community that was more like a large family. For outsiders, there was a surface level politeness over a layered complex of history and relationships that had been messed with, in part, by Frank. Most people wished Tilly hadn't settled in town. But some folks didn't seem to mind. Like John Hart, for one. Ruth and Ada from the library. And Finn, of course.

The fire whistle went off for some emergency. She looked at her watch. Ten minutes until midnight. She walked toward the dam listening to truck doors slamming shut as people got up from bed, dressed, and readied themselves. Pickups would arrive at the firehall moments from now and then the fire truck, lights and siren on, would leave on the way to some waiting crisis she hoped had nothing to do with Frank.

chapter eight

Tilly waited near the tree line at the dam as the hum of tree crickets rose and fell in the darkness around her. She checked her watch again. Twenty past midnight. Apparently, Frank wasn't going to show. At least she'd seen the fire trucks return to the station shortly after leaving. That usually meant a fire alarm had been tripped for some reason other than a fire.

Her shirt clung uncomfortably. The night air had grown more humid and made everything feel too close. A black car drove slowly past the front of the house and parked in the church lot next to the cemetery and across from Tilly's place on the other side of the creek. No way that was Frank. Maybe Mac? But hadn't he been headed back to Philadelphia to take his granddaughter to the zoo?

She held her breath, listening for breaking twigs or rustling of leaves in the woods, but there was only the old tire stuck in the spillway sloshing around as it churned in the water. The disappointment was painfully familiar, only cranked up by years of let downs. Like when the phone rang, and it turned out not to be him. Or when she'd been convinced she'd seen him around Cottersville again and it had been someone else. Every piece of mail that wasn't from him, every email, and knock on the door. And people wondered why she wasn't on social media. That would have truly sent her over the edge.

So now when she thought she heard her name, faintly, from the shadows of the woods, she dismissed it as another trick of her mind conjured by cumulative moments of letdown.

But there it was again. "Tilly."

She glanced at the black car parked at the church. The driver hadn't moved, so she slowly stepped closer to the edge of the woods, eyes to the dam, in case they were being watched.

"That car at the church is FBI," Frank said. "They're coming by every hour or so."

Tilly hadn't noticed, although Mac had mentioned as much.

"We don't have much time," he said. "I need to know if you can help me. With the dam, I mean."

She couldn't look at him even though she wanted to. Not if the FBI really was watching. "I'm not blowing up anything."

"Good, cause it has to stay where it is."

She turned her head slightly in his direction. "What?"

"The dam has to stay."

She thought again about the call from the mayor about the meeting on Monday. How would it look if she suddenly stood up in front of town council and asked them to keep the dam where it was when she'd been fighting for its removal all these years. And more importantly what was Frank up to?

Someone stepped out of the car at the church. The person, a man, was peering in their direction, but she could tell it wasn't Mac. This man was too tall and slim.

She wished she could see Frank's eyes. But she didn't dare look at him. She felt irritated by the mystery and lack of straight answers. That hadn't changed.

The man at the church didn't walk across the bridge, but instead to the other side of the streambank about two hundred feet from where they stood. "Ms. Stone? I'm FBI Agent Willy Sharp," he called out. "I'm working with Agent Stevens. Everything okay?" He fumbled with something. A flashlight, she thought. He swore softly, thumping it against his hand.

"I'll come back," Frank whispered.

"Wait. Where have you been?" She kept her voice low but had to risk asking this now because she needed to know that badly and she was reasonably confident the sound of the water would cover their voices.

"Getting people together. But something's gone wrong. I'll tell you about it later."

She wanted to ask about the Cotters. To see if he knew what had happened to them, but Agent Sharp flipped on the flashlight and Frank stepped back into the darkness as Sharp swept his light over her and into the trees where Frank had just been standing. "Ms. Stone, everything all right?" Mac had never had a partner before, at least not one she'd seen. "Were you talking to someone?"

"Just checking out the creek. That's not against the law, is it?"

He gave her an unpleasant look for a long moment and then turned back to his car.

She remained where she was, wondering what Frank had been about to say and noticing how strongly the air smelled of woodsmoke, a scent that always made her think of the cabin up on the mountain.

Summer 2006

chapter nine

JUNE

In the mornings, the scent of woodsmoke in the cabin was intense. Even during the warming June days, Tilly kept the stove lit for as long as she could stand, trying to dry the place out.

It took weeks to scrape away the last of the mud wasp nests and scrub down the walls and floor. She emptied bucket after bucket of dirty water outside, having to walk to the spring each time she needed more water. Tilly found a few snake skins in different crevices of the cabin, but luckily no sign of snakes.

Each morning Frank disappeared through a small band of hemlock trees and headed down the mountain to Cottersville. He spent hours in town getting supplies and looking for work. More hours than seemed necessary, and Tilly suspected he was doing things he wasn't telling her about. But that was nothing new. At least that gave her time to search the cabin for clues about their family. She discovered a moldy stack of romance novels crammed into the back of one cupboard. They were from the Cottersville Library and had been checked out fourteen years ago to Max Stone. Max, short for Maxine, was her Grandmom's name.

At the back of a kitchen drawer lay Frank's report card from ninth grade. Mostly Cs and two Ds. His teacher had written: *Frank is exceptionally smart. However, he doesn't follow direction. If he could put his mind to his schoolwork, he could easily have a perfect report card.*

But he's looking out the window too much and thinks he knows better than his teacher.

In another drawer, Tilly found a receipt for milk, baking soda, soap, and oatmeal from Fredrick's, the store in town. Underneath the receipt lay a scorecard from a card game with *FRANK* and *MOM* written in Max's block lettering. There was no *DAD*.

Tilly imagined Frank as a boy living in the cabin with his father, the one who'd been his favorite parent, before the accident at least. What had it been like then, when his pop had become someone who no longer spoke or fed himself or even looked Frank in the eye?

Frank had told her that on the morning of the accident, his pop had left him a birthday present on the kitchen table that Frank found later, after his dad had almost drowned. It was a novel by Edward Abbey called, *The Monkey Wrench Gang*. The book was about a group of people who fought industry in defense of nature. A note for Frank in the book said: "Wish I could live this way." Frank had seen these last words from his father as a sign for what he should do with his life. Tilly had asked Frank many times over the years to bring her a copy of the book from the library, but he never had. She searched for that novel in every nook and cranny of the cabin, but it wasn't there.

When Frank was home in the evenings they worked on the cabin. The last project had been to clean out the old cistern, which was just a faded plastic barrel outside. Once it filled with rainwater captured from the cabin roof, Tilly wouldn't have to go to the spring every time she needed water.

They'd also fixed the floor and patched the roof with oil paper before covering it with a blue tarp. "Next summer we can replace the whole thing," Frank promised.

Now they worked on the windows. Frank concentrated on every measurement, sometimes asking her advice, wanting to get it right. One, two, three weeks passed with no sign they were leaving.

When they finished the windows, he came home with white linen fabric printed with lemons. "Thought this would make nice curtains."

Tilly stayed up late for a week, measuring and cutting, lining up those lemons along the seams and stitching small and evenly. There'd been enough extra fabric to make a small matching cloth to cover the peeling white paint on their table. They hung the curtains after breakfast on a Saturday when Frank was home all day. The sun shone through the linen in a muted light making the interior cozy and inviting.

From the woods, Tilly cut wild geranium, bee balm, and pink lady's slippers, and placed them in old glass bottles she'd found in the garbage dump next to the outhouse. These bouquets lined the windowsills and scented the cabin with delicate sweetness. Before dinner one night she put the cloth she'd made on the table and Frank stood back inspecting the cabin before he sat down. "You've made a real home here, Tilly."

Frank liked to say that Tilly already knew more than most college students, but she didn't think that could be true. She did notice that, like the places they'd been before, the library books he brought home weren't stamped out to him, and she wondered when he planned to get a library card.

He'd most recently brought her a copy of Anna Karenina and a book on the history of colonialism. He'd also gotten her a couple books in the Foxfire Series, full of how-tos on the home life of old-time Appalachian people. There was a section on cabin building that Tilly read first. While Frank was in town during the day, she made notes and drawings on cabins she wanted to build. Then she started building models out of wood scraps.

On the weekend, she helped Frank plant asters near the front porch. "They won't bloom until September," he said. That would be after the school year started. When he bought pillows and blankets for their cots that matched the yellow in the curtains, she figured he really did mean for them to stay.

Tilly took time to collect and make food he enjoyed. Bowls of juneberries from the woods, dinners of oyster mushrooms, dandelion greens and pasta, salads of wild onion, purslane, and violets, along with jugs of spearmint tea made with cold spring water to wash it all down. The woodstove had a flat top for cooking and a small oven inside. Baking was tricky with the oven right beside the firebox, but as long as she turned whatever was in there often enough, she could keep bread and pies from scorching.

Frank made a fuss over the dinners and filled her in on what he'd seen in Cottersville, although with never enough detail.

"When do I get to go to town?" she finally had to ask.

He stopped eating. "Well, not yet. And I thought I already explained if we want to stay, I have to lay the groundwork. That's going to take time."

She'd been doing everything he'd asked. And they'd come here to start over. "I know how to keep my mouth shut. I don't understand why I have to stay hidden away."

He put down his fork and pushed his plate away. "Let me put it to you this way: You disobey me on this and we're out of here."

chapter ten

With the cabin in good shape and Frank now gone to a regular handyman job that kept him in town each weekday from nine to five, Tilly started making daily trips to the heron rookery. The raucous birds, with their deep hoarse croaking calls, flew in and out of nests clustered high in the trees. At least they were a kind of company during the long days.

To pass the time, she decided to try building a little cabin of her own under the rookery using some of the techniques she'd read about in the Foxfire Book. Frank had seemed impressed with the models she'd made from the wood scraps. Maybe she could show him what she was really capable of by building a whole structure on her own. She'd build it in secret and surprise him with it later. It was something to do anyway while she waited for Frank to "lay the groundwork."

She chose a spot near the rookery that was hidden by thick brush and tall ostrich ferns, marking the borders of the foundation with stakes and string. She dug six holes, three on each side along the wall lines, and in each hole, she stacked pillars of flat rocks gathered from a nearby abandoned quarry pit. Any extra spaces were packed with creek stones to make the pillars stable. Tilly dragged small trees back to the rookery with a rope tied around one end. Once she had enough logs, she stripped the bark with an axe. She used these logs to build the base, hewing them flat and fitting the bottoms over the stone pillars. The physical effort this took at least helped put her frustration with Frank to good use.

When she got tired of working, she rested on a nearby low-slung tree branch that reached out almost horizontally, dipping toward the ground in a U-shape so wide she could lie back, spine balanced on the limb, and watch the birds above without hurting her neck.

Tilly was lying on this limb when a heron flew in close to her, landing next to Stone Creek, which began at the spring behind the cabin and ran through the rookery before heading down Stone Mountain toward Cottersville. The blue-gray heron positioned itself, still as a statue at the edge of the creek, next to a big white pine. She'd seen plenty of great blues before, but this was the first one up close. The bird was huge, with long legs and a graceful sinuous neck, at the end of which was a long, dagger-like bill. The heron suddenly sensed Tilly and took off with a great whoosh of her feathers. But the next day the heron came back to that same place and this time seemed to watch both Tilly and the water, staying for a while before she headed for the trees above. Tilly began lying on the tree limb very still while the heron was in its spot. As days passed, they grew used to each other's company.

When the heron was there Tilly tried to take on the bird's stillness when it was hunting. She even felt at times like their breaths were matched. When the heron would snatch a fish, lightning fast, part of Tilly doubted the bird had moved because she hadn't moved. But then the heron's throat would bulge as she swallowed the fish.

When the big bird took off it seemed like a miracle each time when her heavy body lifted in the most unlikely, graceful way as she carried herself with slow, deep wingbeats that pumped the air with complete faith. Tilly decided to call her Marvel and, in her mind, she told Marvel about the life she and Frank used to have and the one they were trying out now. Tilly told her how lonely she was with Frank gone so much and how she thought by now she'd have friends, but lately Frank changed the subject every time she brought up going to town.

Near the end of June, while Tilly rested on her tree limb waiting for Marvel, something came crashing through the woods toward the rookery. She jumped up and hid behind a large rock
just as a boy, close to her age, with dark hair and glasses, emerged
from the thickets. Binoculars hung around his neck. He wore a
white t-shirt and cutoffs. Fresh scratches marked his arms and
legs. He brought the binocs up and trained them on a heron
landing in a nest above. After watching the bird for a long moment, he let the binocs dangle around his neck and took a seat
on her tree limb a few feet from where she hid. He opened his
backpack and stuffed half a sandwich into his mouth with no ev-
ident table manners, crumbs flying. Then he guzzled a whole bottle of water, some of it spilling down the front of his shirt.

She thought about saying hello. She and Frank were supposed to be hiding in plain sight. Frank had said not to go to
town, but he'd never told her not to talk to people she might
meet, accidently. And if they planned to stay in Cottersville then
at some point she needed to make friends. Frank thought it important for her to know how to blend with other people. That's
why he'd taken her out in public before. And she'd been able to
talk to kids just fine during those times when she and Frank went
out to the library or a playground when she'd been younger. Tilly
wondered what she might say to this boy now. People on the
radio talked about the new Pirates of the Caribbean movie. She
hadn't seen any of those movies since Frank only took her to sad,
serious ones so they'd have the theatre to themselves.

A feather fell from a nest above and rocked its way downward, landing at the boy's feet. He picked it up and slipped it behind his ear. She took this as a sign and came out from behind
the boulder.

chapter eleven

The boy jumped when he saw Tilly and dropped his water bottle on the ground. She picked it up, brushed off most of the dirt and held it out. He eyeballed her and she realized she wasn't dressed for this. Her hair had been stuck in the same ponytail since the day before and her overalls were dirty. She had other clothes, ones for public, but they were still in her backpack.

She took a seat on the tree limb deciding to play it cool. "I've been working. That's why I look like this."

"Working where?'

"On my cabin."

"You don't live around here."

He said this with such finality that Tilly lost her words for a moment. She gestured vaguely in the opposite direction of the cabin. "I just moved." His eyelashes, longer than hers, framed deep brown eyes. "What's your name?"

He tilted his head, deciding whether to tell her. "Henry."

They were hiding in plain sight, she told herself, offering her hand. "I'm Tilly."

He shook quickly and then picked up his binoculars to inspect the nests above. "You've got rough hands for a girl."

She decided to let this go. "You like birds?"

He nodded. "So does my grandpa." He gave her a swift side glance and then sat next to her.

"Does your grandpa live around here?"

"Yeah. He's like my dad since my parents died when I was a baby."

So, he was missing both parents, not just a mother. She tried to think of what to say next. "Have you seen that new Pirates of the Caribbean movie?"

He gave her a strange face and she realized it was an odd question or asked at the wrong time maybe. She should have asked about his parents.

"I don't really like movies," he said. "Especially not that kind. They're too loud. Grandpa thinks I'm old-fashioned."

"Because you think movies are loud?"

The boy adjusted his glasses. "Cause I'd rather be reading or drawing or being outside, or"—he lifted his binoculars—"bird watching."

He watched a heron fly over, its neck curled into a tight S shape, wings broad and rounded, with its legs trailing behind. He rubbed at red bites on his legs, that were in addition to the scratches she'd already seen.

She jumped up and snapped off green stems of jewelweed growing nearby. "Here," she said, offering them to him.

He scratched hard at his leg again, leaving trails of welted red skin behind. "What am I supposed to do with those?"

She bent down and rubbed the watery ends of the stems over his legs.

"Hey!" He scooted away from her. "Stop that!"

She stood up. "Does it still itch?"

He thought about it and looked at her a little more closely. "No?"

"Jewelweed's good for poison-ivy and bites. Plus, it won't make your scratches sting."

"Jewelweed?"

"You know how the water beads on the leaves like it's covered in diamonds. Like jewels?" She swung her hand around at all the plants right in front of them along the creek. "Grows near water."

He was confused. She silently repeated to herself what she'd said, trying to figure out where she'd gone wrong again.

Tilly was relieved when another heron took off, drawing his attention away.

"Grandpa sees the herons that fish the dam fly this way in the evenings. I've been trying to follow them for a week. Finally kept sight of one long enough to make it here. But I had to run through the woods to do it. That's how I scratched up my legs. Then the mosquitos got me. Probably smelled the blood."

He'd mentioned "the dam." There couldn't be more than one in Cottersville.

"Hey, look at that bird." He pointed to Marvel standing at her usual spot near the base of the white pine.

She tried to get off the ground, flapping her wings oddly, struggling in a way that made Tilly's chest ache. She saw then that her wing was bent.

"What's wrong with it?" Henry said.

She'd die if she couldn't fly, couldn't eat. But then as though to prove Tilly wrong, she settled down and hopped over to her usual spot at the edge of the creek and became still, eyes to the water.

"Should we take it to the vet?"

Frank wouldn't interfere if Marvel might make it on her own. She wasn't a defenseless baby without a mother like those opossums they'd found on the road. "Look," she whispered, nodding toward Marvel, poised over the water. "She's hunting. I think she can take care of herself."

Marvel quick-speared a fish and gobbled it down.

"Check it out," Henry said, impressed.

"Her name's Marvel."

He shot her a raised eyebrow. "Like the comic books?"

She had no idea what he was talking about. "Like a miracle."

He peered through his binoculars like he might be able to find evidence of this. "How do you know it's a girl?"

"I just do."

"She's missing a toe on her left foot, same side as the hurt wing. What do you think happened?" His words were slow, like he thought about each one.

"Flew into something most likely or maybe someone shot her. Hard to say."

He stood putting the remains of his lunch and water bottle into his bag. "Will you be here tomorrow so we can check on her?"

She liked the idea of him coming back. He seemed easy to talk to. "I'm always here around mid-morning." But what if he left and forgot about her and Marvel? "Before you go, come see what I'm building."

He swung his bag onto one shoulder. "Okay."

She led him through the tall ostrich ferns and stepped over the low walls inside the footprint of the foundation. He didn't follow but stayed outside staring and saying nothing. The place wasn't much yet. Maybe it had been a mistake to show it to him so soon.

"*Cool fort!*" He'd finally come through where the door would be to touch the rough timber base. "You made this *by yourself*?"

"Yep." She liked the idea of calling it a fort.

"So that's why your hands are so rough." He sounded impressed now.

"I could use some help." She pulled two pieces of jerky from her shirt pocket and offered him one. She sat on one of the tree stump seats she'd made, and he took the other, biting into the jerky and chewing thoughtfully. "Never had this kind before."

"Made it from a deer I shot last year."

He spit it out.

"Hey!" Frank had sold their rifle before they'd come to Cottersville, so she didn't know the next time she'd make more.

Henry eyed the remaining piece in his hand. "Sorry. Just never had homemade. I was surprised is all."

A small piece of green yarn stuck out from a bag she'd tucked into the corner of the fort. Tilly edged her stump seat over a few inches to hide it from view. She hadn't even told Frank she was making a scarf. He'd mentioned nothing more about her mother, but maybe her grave was in Cottersville. Tilly wanted to lay a scarf there to give to her mother something personal. Keeping this to herself made Tilly feel like she was keeping to at least some of Frank's rules.

"I'm gonna build the walls next," she said, testing the waters.

His eyes looked shy and bold at the same time. "Can I help?"

"It'll take us awhile."

"That's okay. We have all summer before school starts again. And I've always wanted to build a fort, but Grandpa's too busy with work. And with his wife now, too."

"You mean your grandmom?" She wondered if Henry's grandparents might have known Max or her Grandpop before his accident. Maybe they even knew Frank when he was younger.

"No. I mean she is my grandma, I guess, technically. But they just got married a year ago and she wouldn't want me to call her that. She's younger."

"Oh." Tilly was having a hard time following this.

"But she's a nice person. And anyway, I could definitely help when Grandpa's at the mill and she's at work. No one will even know I'm gone."

The mill. The dam. Goosebumps broke out on the back of her neck. "Your grandpa works at the paper mill?"

"Owns it. He's Paul Cotter."

She turned away, busying herself with stacking a few rocks in the corner so he wouldn't see her face. Frank would not want her talking with Paul Cotter's grandson. Still, Tilly thought, there might be a reason for their meeting at this moment. Maybe now that she and Frank lived near Cottersville, Frank was figuring out what was just occurring to her: If they stayed, they'd have to live in the same town with the Cotters. And not every person in the Cotter family could be bad. Henry seemed nice. He liked herons and wanted to help build the fort. It wasn't his fault his parents had died and now he had to live with Paul Cotter. Maybe, in fact, they were meant to be friends to help heal what happened a long time ago now. And even if Frank didn't have any of these thoughts, that didn't mean she and Henry shouldn't be friends. She just wouldn't tell Frank. Not yet anyway. "I have plenty of nails and an extra hammer. Lots of trees around here, too."

"Great!" He clasped his hands together in front of his chest. "I'll come back tomorrow then."

"There's just one thing ...."

"Yeah?" He picked up a hammer and turned it over as though he'd never held one.

She took it from him, set it down, and turned his shoulders

so they were eye to eye. "I'll get in a lot of trouble if you tell anyone about this place, or me. You can't bring your grandpa or anyone else to see the rookery. And you can only visit when my dad's not home, so only during weekday work hours. Don't even think about starting up the mountain before nine thirty and you'll have to be on your way every day by three. Understand?"

He scratched at his temple. "I guess. But why?"

"My dad's super private. And you can see," she gestured to her clothes, "we don't have much. He's embarrassed about being poor. And you must have everything you need since your grandpa owns the whole mill." Henry nodded. "That's why you need to keep our friendship secret. It's really the only way we can build the fort together. Otherwise, my dad will forbid it."

Henry had a solemn look. She knew he was taking this seriously.

"I'm not kidding around." She used the same tone Frank used with her when he wasn't kidding around.

Henry met her eyes. "Okay." He appeared both excited and scared, which she took as a sign of his commitment.

"So never tell anyone about me or this place. And I won't say anything about you. No matter what."

"No matter what."

"Swear on your grandpa's life."

He put his hand to his heart and closed his eyes. "I swear."

chapter twelve

On the last Saturday in June, Frank and Tilly ate their breakfast without one word between them. Even though she and Henry had only known each other a week, Tilly couldn't stop thinking about him. After that first day, she was sure Frank would notice the difference in her. That he'd smell Henry on her somehow. Or see evidence of him in her face. She felt that changed.

But Frank didn't seem to know. And she'd realized over the last day she would have to tell him about Henry because that was the only way to have both him and Frank in her life. She couldn't take the chance of accidently saying the wrong thing, which meant she didn't say much. Not that Frank seemed to notice. In order to tell Frank, she was going to have to get to Cottersville. Then she could explain she and Henry had met there.

She put her fork aside. "When do I get to go to town?"

Frank glanced up, chewing his eggs, giving her an impenetrable look. With his fork he pushed the last of his breakfast into a small pile on his plate, considering his options. "Tell you what. I'll take you to a lookout not too far from here." He said this as though the idea of it made him tired. "You can see most of the town from there." He stood, scraped the remains of his eggs into the garbage and put the plate on the counter. "I promise we'll go soon enough. But I'm still sorting some things."

This was better than nothing. Frank slipped on his backpack and she jammed her feet into boots before he changed his mind.

Frank led the way through the stand of hemlocks next to the cabin, down over the hill where she'd never been. About a half mile through the woods, they came to a lichen-crusted rock surrounded by rhododendrons in full pink flower. This cliff offered a clear view of the Cottersville she'd pictured in her mind.

She could see now that the town was indeed small. She couldn't even see a traffic light. There had to be bigger towns nearby for shopping and the movies, but from this overlook there was nothing but Cottersville, adjacent fields, and more forest.

She recognized the old brick building directly below them as the Cotter Paper Mill offices where Henry's grandpa worked. She hadn't realized until now that you had to cross a small bridge over Stone Creek to get to the office. The creek ran in front of the office building with the small dam just downstream of the bridge. That was where Frank's dad had had his accident.

Beyond the creek lay the Cottersville cemetery surrounded by a low stone wall. Farther to the west were squared and striped fields, all with a low wooded, mountain backdrop. To the east, the Delaware River wound through the landscape, sparkling in the sun so brightly she had to squint. Across the river, she could see the paper factory operations where they now stood in New Jersey, built after the original mill operations moved, leaving only the office building remaining in Cottersville. The smokestack across the river, printed with "Cotter Paper" at the top, pumped smoke drifting toward them in a diffuse low line. Frank had told her that they'd rebuilt the plant to make recycled paper out of wastepaper. They did this to stay competitive in the global market and it was why they were still operating.

Frank let out a long whistle as he looked out over the valley. "Haven't been to this spot in years." He was quiet for a moment. "Seeing it from up here reminds me of why I always thought of Cottersville as a place of intersections."

Wispy clouds overhead made shadows drift around the valley below. "Intersections?"

He tipped his head toward the dam. "Remnants of the town's industrial past intersecting with the natural world. For other towns, it's steel or lumber or old silk factories. Hardly anyone even remembers how blue-collar things once were. And see there?" He pointed along the river, where a path or road of some kind ran parallel. "That's the old rail bed, now a state park. Trains have been replaced by bikers and runners. And there—" He motioned to the hillside where an opening in the trees made an odd straight line. "That's where the trolley used to run. This land went from wild to rural to industrial when the paper mill operated at full capacity. And now all that industry is on its last breath, and Cottersville, just like everywhere, is headed toward something new, and maybe worse with the way people are more and more controlled by technology." He looked down at her and then back over the valley again. "The river, the roads, the old railroad, trolley tracks, people's lives, family history— all kinds of paths cross here."

"Does my mom's family still live here?" she tried to sound casual, as though she wasn't really that interested.

Frank took a seat on the rock, and she sat beside him, hoping he would tell her some things.

"Not anymore. They all passed." He smiled in a sad way. She waited for him to say more, but he was lost in thoughts he kept to himself. He looked up at the sky. "It's not easy being back. I'm trying to do the right thing."

She hoped he wasn't about to change his mind about staying.

"I have to see that mill every day. And the dam."

She turned away, suddenly uncomfortable and feeling guilty. The last weeks she'd pictured Frank carefully reintroducing himself to friends and old acquaintances in town so one day soon he could introduce her. But she wondered now if he knew about her and Henry? If that's why he'd been so quiet lately? Maybe it was why he'd brought up the paper mill just now?

Frank's arm went around her shoulder, and she relaxed some. "Even though it might not seem like it, I do have a plan. It's just taking time. That's why I haven't taken you to town yet. I hope you can be a little more patient."

She didn't like all the smoke and mirrors.

"See Stone Creek," Frank pointed to where it flowed into the Delaware. "The Cotters might have the town named after them, but we've got the creek and it's been running over this land for many thousands of years, shaping this limestone valley. I like to think about that. How our family's creek carved out the bedrock the town is built on. That's how deep we run in this place." He didn't hide the flare of pride in his voice. It might be hard for him to be back, but he also loved things about Cottersville.

"Where do the Cotters live?"

He pointed to the other side of the cemetery where a white house with blue shutters stood in a row of similar houses.

So that was Henry's home. She'd expected something bigger, more fitting the rich and powerful notions she had of Paul Cotter. "You lived in town once, too, right? Before the accident?" She wanted to understand more about the family's past and how people in Cottersville might feel about the Stone family. What would Henry think when he found out her last name?

Frank picked up a small rock and tossed it over the edge. It hit once with a sharp plink and again as it tumbled over the cliff. In the distance a car drove past the mill offices, horn beeping, and they watched it recede.

Frank stared after it, maybe gearing up for whatever it was he had to say. "The house was over there beside the store." He pointed in the direction the car went, but trees blocked the view. "It's changed a lot. I don't even recognize it now."

"How did you move all the stuff from the house to the cabin since there's no road? Did people in town help?"

"Yeah. That's about all they did."

She was asking too many questions. She knew that but couldn't stop herself. "How was it living at the cabin back then?"

He glanced at her. "It was hell, at least at first. But after being there a while, away from the people that turned out not to care much anyway, I realized I liked living outside the social cog. I saw the value in it. And by that time I was coming to understand that my dad had been a visionary. These days we know dams block fish from migrating. They change the water levels, the flow and temperature, which changes the ecosystem. It's a ripple effect.

One thing that's not the way it should be sets off a chain reaction. That's how Pop thought about it. He wanted that dam gone. And instead he died because he was forced to fix it. So I started to think maybe what happened to Pop happened for a reason; like maybe it was a message to me about what to do with my life. That I needed to take a real stand against the kind of systems that put Pop in that position."

Frank leaned back on his hands, face to the sky, and Tilly sensed he was about to get on his soapbox.

"There are thousands of those dams on creeks all over the northeast built for early industry. That was the beginning of industrial disregard for the environment and ordinary working people. It was the evil of too much power." He squinted into the distance. "Pop wanted that dam gone for reasons most any environmental scientist nowadays would tell you are valid, like I said. And no one listened to him because Paul Cotter and Cotter Paper were more important than he was. A company more important than a human being. Think about that." He turned to look at her, trying to keep an upbeat tone and hold tight to the present moment. But his eyes welled up. "Then when you were born on my birthday, the date of his death, it was him telling me again to do something that mattered."

Tilly sat very still, arranging it all in her mind. She'd heard some of this before but not enough to put it all together.

Thinking back seemed to sharpen Frank's sadness into anger. "Ted K. may have gotten a lot of things wrong, but he was right about how people's lives have been bent and twisted by industry to fit the system. And that, Tilly, is the root of all problems. People, like nature, aren't made to be part of an industrial complex."

He had her full attention and she wanted more than ever to agree.

"The work we've done together was a political statement against unchecked power. Those dams were just the beginning of a problem that's only grown worse. They symbolize what happens when power means more than humanity. People all over the world are forced to do things they don't want to do because of power and money in the hands of a few. Every time you and I blew up a dam, we made a statement against that. Every op-ed I ever wrote carried that message."

He was charged up, deflecting the bad with the good. It was like he needed to justify all their years before this. Like he needed to defend his choices. But Tilly had the feeling these were things he wanted to say to someone else because she'd heard this part before.

In the field beyond, a tractor rumbled patiently back and forth, leaving clipped alfalfa behind in a neat row in front of a long-abandoned tractor, grown over with weeds.

"We've had to be deliberatively provocative to wake people up," he was saying. "Because more than ever people are asleep to the disrespect and corruption permeating every part of modern society."

"Why didn't we ever blow up the Cottersville dam?"

He blinked rapidly, like he was trying to get her back into focus. He turned to stare at the dam. "I'd like to blow it to bits. I've dreamed of it. But there's too many people around. And we can't blow our cover now, can we?"

The wind blew pink petals from the rhododendron all around them and Frank pulled a couple from her hair. "You know I'm working as a handyman, for Cotter Paper."

She went cold. "What?" She knew about the job, but not who he'd been working for.

He sat back. "They're still the only place hiring. Even if they are a shadow of what they once were."

"Why would you work for them?"

"It's part of the plan."

Whatever he was up to, he'd also just said he wasn't going to blow up the dam.

He turned her face to his. "The thing you have to ask yourself is this: How bright will you burn? What's the source of your fire? What are you going to do with your life that means something?"

His eyes bore into hers. She was supposed to have learned a lesson from what he'd told her and now say something profound. She pulled away and brought her knees to her chest, hugging them. She couldn't think of a big enough answer. She only wanted to stay in Cottersville, be friends with Henry, and understand more about her mother. But she couldn't say any of that. Her throat went dry and she could only shake her head.

The disappointed hiss of empty silence stood between them. Tilly wished now she'd stayed back at the cabin. Clouds billowed on the horizon, and she kept her eyes on them, afraid to look at him. After what seemed like a long time, he finally pointed to a small horse farm beside the mill office. "See that place." His voice had thawed, and, in that way, he let her know he was ready to talk again.

She nodded, not yet trusting her voice to be steady.

"The Harts used to live there. I grew up with John Hart. Pretty sure that's him with those horses."

She could see he was a big man, but they were too far away to make out anything more.

"John's one of the good ones. Despite what I said about the Cotters, this was mostly a good place to grow up. I wouldn't have brought you here otherwise."

He got to his feet and put on his backpack. "I'll be back in a while. You go on to the cabin."

As she watched him leave, she thought about what she now understood. She would have to end things with Henry. There was just no way Frank could ever understand they were friends.

chapter thirteen

JULY

On the first morning of July the bright sun poured golden light into the woods surrounding the rookery. The ferns, backlit, glowed like stained glass. It was as though the conversation with Frank and the realization she and Henry couldn't be friends anymore had never happened. Still, Tilly rehearsed in her head what to say to Henry. Only she couldn't come up with good reasons for ending things. He'd followed the rules, coming and going at the times they'd agreed to, and he'd proven himself steady. Every weekday at ten-thirty, he met her in the fort and worked hard. She decided to tell him Frank had forbidden her from seeing him anymore, which would have been true if she'd told Frank about Henry.

When she heard Henry coming, she decided to speak to him right away, so she didn't lose her nerve. He came striding through the ferns, holding something squarish out in front of him. He grinned when he saw her, turning what he carried toward her. It was a painting, of her.

"Did it from memory." He angled it back toward him, looking at it, then turned it back. "Not bad, huh?"

He'd painted her prettier, and somehow, wiser. It was something about the way he'd done her eyes.

"Can we hang it in the fort when we're finished?"

She couldn't stop staring at the painting.

"Unless you don't like it."

She reached for it to take a closer look. It wasn't just a good likeness or even that she looked better than in real life. It was something else. He saw her this way. Like she was powerful, opposite of the way she'd felt with Frank the day before when he'd asked her what the source of her fire was and she hadn't been able to think of anything good enough. Henry had captured something she now recognized in herself but didn't know was there before.

"I love it." She looked up at him and decided he had nothing to do with the dam or the past and she needed him in her life. She would just have to come up with a way to explain this to Frank.

chapter fourteen

Henry and Tilly spent most of July hauling and cutting wood to build the fort. As they dragged logs from the forest, Tilly made sure they kept within the allowable boundary Frank had set for her, by making the argument to Henry that wood was easier to haul if they were pulling downslope. And there was no shortage of fallen limbs. They sorted the logs by size to figure out the sequence they'd use them: biggest ones first. Tilly showed Henry how to cut the trunks to length and hew off the sides before notching the ends, so they'd fit together.

The mechanics of building and Marvel's welfare made up most of the conversation between them and in this way Tilly avoided having to say much about Frank. If talk did turn to other things, she tried to keep it on the news coming over the radio, which Henry seemed happy enough to chat about.

When the walls were over their heads, they made a ramp by leaning several extra-long logs against the top of one wall. Then they rolled logs up the ramp to set them in place so they could finish the walls. The work turned Henry's body strong and tanned and Tilly found herself staring at the muscles in his arms as they set logs into place.

"Your dad teach you how to build stuff?" Henry asked one day.

"We've fixed up a lot of places together." That was true. And Frank had taught her basic skills. But most of what they were doing with the fort Tilly'd learned on her own.

When the walls were finished, they worked on the roof next using a range of log sizes for the gables held in place with a few straight logs. They cut a couple felled cedars into pieces small enough to split into half-inch shakes for the roof. Even though they'd been at it for weeks, the work never felt long or boring.

Tilly was faster at making shakes, so she did that while Henry nailed them onto the roof. They were about halfway done when Henry seemed to lose interest in talking about the fort or the news and pushed conversation more stubbornly toward the personal. Tilly tried keeping him talking about his grandpa, wanting to learn what she could about Paul Cotter. Although the more Henry told her about him, the more impossible it seemed that Paul could be the same person who'd ruined her family. He'd taken care of Henry since he was four months old. And it wasn't just making sure he was fed and clothed. There was real love between them. Henry spoke of long hikes, nightly dinners together, fishing trips, birds they'd seen, museums in the city and birthdays with homemade cake.

"He'd rather be painting than running the mill," Henry said, as he brought down his hammer.

"So, you get your talent from him?"

Henry rested his hammer on his knee. "I guess. But I don't wish I could paint all the time. Not like he does."

"Why doesn't he paint all the time, if that's his main interest?" She didn't know what she was asking exactly, except she did want Paul Cotter to have an understandable reason for what happened to Frank's pop. Even if that reason meant he wasn't a good boss because he wasn't suited for the work.

Henry gave a quick hitch of his shoulders. "The mill takes a lot of energy. Grandpa says he keeps it going for me since my uncle doesn't have any interest."

"Your uncle?"

"Yeah. He's a science teacher at the high school."

"You see him much?"

"Sometimes. I mean we get along. He's got his own life though. He and my grandpa don't talk. It's because Grandpa has a lot of pride in the company. He feels the Cotter family helped build Cottersville and sees the mill as part of town history." The hammer slipped from Henry's hand and hit the ground with a hard thump.

Tilly picked it up, climbed to the roof and handed it back to him. "Do you want to work at the mill when you get older?"

Henry pulled a couple nails from his shirt pocket. "Nah. But I'm not telling Grandpa that." He wiped his brow. "None of it might matter for long anyway."

"How come?"

"I hear Grandpa talking about bankruptcy after he thinks I'm asleep."

Did Frank know about this? "What do you mean, bankruptcy?"

"There's too much competition now in the recycled paper market. That's what Grandpa says. I wish he wouldn't take it so hard. It's not like he has any control over any of it. But that company has been his whole life."

"Maybe if he doesn't have to work so hard, he'd be able to paint more." Tilly could see now the whole problem was really the company. If it were gone, Frank could forget about whatever plan he'd concocted, Paul Cotter could paint like he really wanted, and Frank could know she and Henry were friends.

"It's the people who work for the company grandpa worries about. Like what they'll do for money when the factory's gone. He's takes it to heart. Hasn't been himself lately. The last few weeks he's had trouble sleeping. I don't think he's really told anyone at work about the company going under."

Tilly climbed back to the ground, wondering again what Frank knew and whether any of this might be part of his mysterious plan.

"What about you?" Henry said. "You never say anything about your dad."

Tilly stuffed a bunch of shakes into a bag and climbed back to the roof. She handed the bag to Henry, thinking the whole time about how to keep him from circling too close. "My dad's really private, remember?"

"Is he hiding something?" Henry grinned but the curiosity in his eyes made her heart thump wildly.

"We're poor. That's what he's hiding."

"Lots of people don't have money."

"Well, except you." She wondered if this could still be true given the bankruptcy. "I can't even tell my dad we know each other because you're a Cotter. You've kept your promise, right? About keeping me a secret?"

"Yeah." He brushed away sawdust and it caught the wind and drifted. Tilly climbed down, wanting to end the conversation. She hoped Henry understood there were things she couldn't say. She chopped at the cedar again.

"Where do you even live, anyway?"

"Over there." She waved her hand around, not looking at him.

"How come you don't ever come to town?" He floated this like he already knew it wasn't possible but wanted to check his theory.

"Don't feel like it."

"Don't you get lonely up here seeing just me and your dad?"

"No." She switched on the radio and whistled along to the Dixie Chicks. Maybe he'd take the hint they weren't going to talk about this anymore.

He kept working, not saying anything. She switched off the radio during a long commercial break.

"Thank God," he said.

She glared up at him, ready for a fight. "If the radio was bothering you, why didn't you tell me to turn it off?"

"Because you're mad at me."

"I am not."

He raised an eyebrow.

"You just don't like music."

"Not that crap, I don't."

"Well, what kind do you like? Nerdy stuff?"

Henry laughed, not reacting to her bad temper like Frank would have. "My grandpa plays the blues. I like that."

Tilly chipped off shingles at a fast clip. "Never heard of it."

Henry started singing:

"When we first met, I felt deep in my heart
That you were for me
And I was for you, baby.
But we were too young
And it wasn't our time, darlin',
It wasn't our time. Oh, no, baby, it wasn't our time."

He smiled down at her until he saw her face. "I can't sing it like they do on the record. Obviously."

"I guess not." She was joking but he didn't laugh. She wanted to put things right between them. She went into the fort and got the scarf she'd been knitting. She held it up so he could see it. "I'm making this for my mother."

Henry peered down at her, put down his hammer, and climbed to the ground. She stretched the scarf out when he touched the knitting. "You haven't mentioned your mother."

"She died when I was born. But I'm making this to put on her grave, so she has something from me." Telling Henry this, something she hadn't yet told Frank, made her feel closer to him than to Frank, and this thought startled her.

Henry was studying her now in a way that made her heart speed up, but differently than before.

"Why don't we take a break and see how Marvel's doing," he said.

They sat together on the tree limb, waiting until Marvel showed up as she did on most days. She still couldn't fly, but her wing had healed enough to get off the ground a few feet, maybe enough to get out of harm's way. Henry quietly took Tilly's hand in his. He kept his eyes on Marvel, as though nothing had happened. "Where do you think she goes at night?" he asked.

"Don't know. But I'm glad she comes back every day."

He squeezed her hand.

September 2023

chapter fifteen

FRIDAY **SATURDAY** SUNDAY MONDAY TUESDAY WEDNESDAY THURSDAY FRIDAY SATURDAY SUNDAY

Tilly stood at the workbench sharpening a saw blade, thinking about that last good day when Henry had reached for her hand while they'd been waiting for Marvel. That had been just before everything turned upside down. If only she'd known what was coming, maybe she could have warned Henry somehow or been more prepared herself.

Through the shop window, she saw Finn, Henry's son, coming. Behind him the goldenrod at the edges of the fields in the distance was backlit by the morning sun, still low in the sky.

Finn came in the shop after checking behind him, as though someone might be watching. He held a card at his side. It was the day after Tilly's—and Frank's—birthday, but she and Finn only saw each other on Saturdays.

On the front of the card Finn had drawn the two of them sitting together on a blanket in the woods having a picnic. He was quite a skilled artist, even at eleven. In the drawing, they were deep in conversation, which made her smile. Inside the card was one giant heart. No words.

The term *selective mutism* made it sound as though Finn had a choice. He'd described it to her once as a kind of stage fright, where if he was anxious, the words got stuck. The anxiety could be caused by many things, including someone close by who he didn't know well. This was true no matter how much he wanted or needed to talk. On most days he sounded like any kid as long as he was with his dad, his mom, or Tilly. But when there were other people around and his voice left him, people saw a boy who couldn't or, in their view, wouldn't speak. His condition was made worse by people's reactions: asking question after question he couldn't answer, speaking for him or over him. People even wondered sometimes aloud and in front of him if his mutism was due to trauma, emotional or physical. It wasn't. Unless anxiety could be counted as a trauma and for Finn, it did. According to his doctor, he would grow out of this, although that day had not yet come.

But on Saturdays it was hard to remember Finn suffered from anything when he was in Tilly's shop and perfectly relaxed. Whatever might have been keeping him awake the night before when Tilly had seen him sitting in his kitchen, now seemed a distant memory. Finn went to his desk in the corner of the shop and began a pencil sketch for a new painting. Tilly filled a jar with water and set it in front of him. "Thanks for the card. I love it."

Burnt, Tilly's cat—Finn's cat really—hopped onto Finn's lap and purred like a truck. Tilly polished the table she'd just finished; the same one Frank had admired.

Finn whistled softly to One Direction's *Drag Me Down* playing on Tilly's old radio sitting on the shelf above him. His shoulder bones stood out against his shirt as he moved his paintbrush across the paper to the rhythm. *Nobody, nobody* ... this boy, who struck Tilly as mostly feathers and heartbeat, was slight for his age. People often took him for years younger than eleven, which helped when he couldn't answer their questions. They'd give him a pass for being shy or too young, rather than judging him as rude or spoiled.

Finn ran his hand over Burnt's back and the cat rolled over and grabbed playfully at his wrist. Finn looked up at Tilly with his father's brown eyes, watching as she ran a rag soaked with linseed oil and beeswax over the tabletop. His eyebrows knitted together as though something was just coming to him. "Where's that table going?"

"Alberta, Canada."

"Where's that?"

"North of Montana."

"How come people out there don't buy a table from somewhere closer?"

She ran her rag around the outside edge of the table. "Guess they like mine more than anything close by."

He squinted at her as though trying to figure out what made this table special. "Where'd you learn to make furniture anyway?"

"When I was thirteen, I went to live with someone my dad knew. He taught me."

"You mean after your dad left?"

She tried not to look surprised. "Yeah." Of course, Finn would have heard the story by now. Probably from Henry. She and Finn had just never talked about it. She put down the rag, filled a kettle with water and put it on the wood stove, hoping he might let this subject drop.

"Why didn't your dad take you with him?"

She added a log to the stove. "Not sure."

Finn gave a puzzled face and she was relieved when he went back to his painting. She tried rubbing the ache out of her neck and noticed Finn looking at her again, his wheels still turning. "How long were you with that person who taught you to make furniture?"

"Until he died, when I was about eighteen."

"Then you came back here?"

"Yep." She tapped a packet of hot chocolate mix against the counter and poured the contents into a mug. She added hot water from the kettle, stirred it and handed the mug to Finn.

He blew across the top before taking a tentative sip. He put the cup down and pointed out the window. "There's Dad."

Henry, in his postal uniform, stuffed mail into the slot of the front door of her house. His hair was longer these days, brushing the top of his collar, which along with his dark rimmed glasses made him look like some poet-type.

She always waited until he was well on his way to John's place before retrieving her mail. This was just one of the ways she avoided him with a level of dedication she tried to hide from Finn, who was now throwing her a mischievous glance. "I think Dad should start dating."

She laughed, mostly out of surprise.

Finn frowned. "It's not funny."

"I'm sorry." She cleared her throat.

"It's been three years since mom left. He needs a relationship."

Had Finn been secretly building up some far-fetched hope she and Henry might get together? Is that what he was getting at? And he mentions this when Frank had just walked back into her life. She tried not to see this as a sign as she glanced at Henry on his way now toward John's house, his mailbag heavy on his shoulder. They lived in this town together but had separate lives.

"Dad talks about that summer he met you." Finn gave her a slant-wise glance. "Or at least he does until he remembers you aren't supposed to be friends."

Finn stared at her, waiting for a response for so long she decided he didn't blink enough. "We've had our differences over the dam. I think you know that." Maybe Finn's questions had to do with the meeting on Monday night the mayor had phoned her about. The mayor would have called Henry, too. Maybe Finn was trying to head off the inevitable conflict the dam's removal brought up between her and his father.

"Why does Dad want the dam to stay so bad and you want it gone?"

Answers to that question probably seemed like they should be simple when you were eleven years old. "It's complicated, Finn."

He looked at her like she'd just said the most boring, predictable thing and packed up his things. She didn't want him to go, didn't want to be left with the whole day ahead waiting for whatever Frank would do next. But, of course, that wasn't Finn's problem. And it was probably better that he go.

After he left, the wind gusted outside and rattled the door. The golden morning light had given way to something dull and unflattering against a mottled yellow and purple sky that reminded her of an old bruise.

chapter sixteen

Tilly only half heard Burnt's angry meow as she stood at the shop counter unpacking supplies and wondering what Frank had to tell her. Burnt yowled again and she realized it was way past the cat's breakfast hour. As she poured food into his dish, he threw her a reproachful look, then ate quickly, making soft growling noises.

She checked her phone, scanning for news about what Mac had seen at the Umbra Dam. Then she searched for Frank's Op-ed, checking if any local papers had printed it. She didn't see anything yet, thank god. Still, googling Frank's name brought up plenty and she clicked on a YouTube video of a woman talking about him, one Tilly'd watched before: Dr. Anna Birch, Professor of American Studies. She was maybe early-forties, attractive and put together in a professional way, but with the surprise of a tiny diamond stud in her nose. Tilly unmuted her phone.

"... Frank Stone loved the Northeast as Thoreau did and spent his time trying to save it. He's an anarchist, but not a violent one. He harnessed his anger to make positive change. That's why he's a popular figure today. An icon, really."

These were things Tilly might have said about Frank. Well, except the icon part. Anna Birch was one of Frank's old flames who was now writing a biography about him she planned to publish this year to coincide with his fiftieth birthday.

She'd first contacted Tilly six months ago about an interview she wanted for the book. That's when Tilly'd read what she could find on her and discovered the website about Frank that she'd created, as well as the Facebook, Twitter, and Instagram accounts. Anna taught courses on pop culture and the media at a small college in upstate New York. She specialized in anarchists and Frank seemed to be of particular interest. She even authored a substack newsletter called "The Fringe," which Tilly hadn't read.

She put her phone down on the workbench, tired of thinking about Frank. She slid small pieces of cardboard under the legs of the table she'd just finished and pushed it over to the side of the shop. Charlie, who sold her furniture at his gallery in New York, had arranged for the shipping company to pick it up later that day.

Her cell phone buzzed and she checked the screen. It was a reporter from the local paper, one who'd called her before about stories related to Frank. He probably wanted to talk to her about what had happened at the Umbra Dam. She didn't pick up. She had to focus on her work and acting normal until she could have a real conversation with Frank. Then he could go and she could get on with her life.

The next item on the docket was for someone from New Paltz, New York who'd ordered many things over the years by email through Charlie's gallery and always paid cash. When Tilly asked about the buyer, Charlie said they wanted to remain anonymous. Tilly had made this person a desk, bookcases, and a dining room table. This time they wanted a sideboard to match the table.

Tilly went through her supply of boards ordered first by wood type and then by source. Luckily, she still had enough boards from the original maple she'd used for the table.

She carried the wood to the shop counter and with a pencil marked the first rough cuts for the top, back, and side pieces. When she could, she used trees that had blown down, as long as the wood was in good shape. Giving a fallen tree new life was something she felt called to do.

A soft knock on the door made Tilly look up. Henry Cotter stood outside. He never came to the shop. Maybe something had happened to Finn. She rushed to open the door and stood face to face with him, feeling some underground river of emotion surface unexpectedly. Maybe it was seeing him up close so soon after Frank.

"I'm here about Finn," he said. She took a step back so he could come in.

They had a polite relationship, although not a close one. She'd kept her distance when she'd gotten back to Cottersville, given that he was married at the time. And then when he'd divorced, they were used to avoiding each other. She didn't want to intrude on his life anymore, not while Frank was still out there. She'd tried to make amends for the past through Finn since their friendship seemed to matter to Henry, given how few people Finn had in his life. And Finn hadn't been part of her life with Frank, so in her mind he was protected from all of that.

But that left much undiscussed between her and Henry. They'd never talked about what she'd withheld from him about Frank. He'd never told anyone what he knew about Helen and Frank. Tilly knew this because Mac had asked her nothing about it.

"Is something the matter with Finn?" Tilly asked.

"Yeah."

She brought her hand to her throat. "What's happened?"

"You tell me." He crossed his arms. "And you can start by explaining how you convinced town council to hold *another* meeting about the dam tomorrow night."

She brushed sawdust from the counter to the floor, trying not to react. "The mayor called and invited me. I had nothing to do with setting up the meeting."

His eyes narrowed. "The timing with Frank's 50th doesn't seem like a coincidence. If you didn't have anything to do with it, then who did?"

Tilly took a step back from him. "The town council?"

He looked doubtful and Tilly couldn't blame him. The timing was weird.

Still, Henry's insistence the dam stay where it was had never made sense to her. Why did he care about it so much? She'd worked with conservation organizations and government officials for eight years to take it out. She cared about the migratory fish and water quality benefits she spelled out in the grant and permit applications. And the spillway of the dam was a dangerous trap, especially in high water. But what Henry didn't know, what no one knew, including Frank, was her main reasons for wanting the dam out of there were personal. She saw it as a representation of her past with Frank that held her captive just like the dam held back the water in Stone Creek. It wasn't rational and she certainly couldn't tell anyone this, but if the dam was gone, she might be able to put Frank behind her and start fresh.

And she'd chosen to do things right, working within the law. She'd wanted people to see she wasn't like Frank. She'd worked for years to convince the town to take it out, but when in the end they'd said no to the removal, she'd respected that decision. She hadn't imposed her will. Although no one had ever recognized this, not even Henry.

"Tell me about Finn." Tilly nudged Burnt off the stool and invited Henry to sit.

He took a seat with his feet braced, as though expecting this wouldn't go well and he might need to make a fast exit. Tilly poured half of her freshly made coffee into another mug and handed him a spoon along with packets of dry cream and sugar. She wondered if Henry still liked old-fashioned things like bird watching and blues records. Did he still hate loud movies?

He stirred in sugar, staring into the swirling liquid. Burnt jumped into his lap and Henry automatically stroked his fur in a gentle, sure way that made the cat purr as loudly as he did for Finn.

"Finn's talked more about this cat than he's talked about anything, at least before ..." Henry turned toward his son's corner in the shop, with the picture of Tilly and Finn tacked to the wall, along with the birthday card Finn had just given her.

"Before what?"

"Before he stopped talking."

"He seemed fine when he was here yesterday."

Henry glanced at her. "And he was fine when he came home, but then something happened because he hasn't said a word since last night. Not even to me." He let out a shaky breath. "He's got that stone-faced expression he used to have only at school or with complete strangers."

Henry took a sip of coffee, regarding her across the mug. "And he's painting some things over the last day ..."

"What?"

He gazed out the window across the cemetery toward his house. "The same scene over and over. It's the dam and the mill office back when it was still here. The details ..." He put his head in his hands. "I haven't handled it well."

"He's not saying anything at all?"

"I don't think he can. He's trying to paint whatever this is. I think it must be related to this meeting about the dam. But even that wouldn't explain ..." Henry put his coffee cup down and pushed it away.

Tilly wondered if Frank had involved Finn somehow in whatever he was doing. But that would cross boundaries even Frank had to respect.

Henry sat back. "You've always been able to figure out what Finn's trying to say with his paintings. I'm keeping him home from school, until I know what's going on. Can you come to the house later this morning and take a look at the paintings?"

chapter seventeen

Like most homes in Cottersville, Henry's smallish two-story sat on a narrow lot. An old barn behind the house that once sheltered horses now served as the garage. The antique blue shutters and white exterior were exactly as they had been when Henry'd lived there as a boy. He'd repainted the whole place a summer ago with the colors chosen by the Cotters before him.

As Tilly knocked, something moved in the window of the house next door. Crystal Booker waved to her from an upstairs window. Tilly could almost hear the questions popping through the windowpane.

Crystal let the curtain fall. Tilly knocked again, with more urgency. But there was no answer. Crystal stepped out onto her porch with a broom.

"Hello, Tilly," she called out.

There was no avoiding this. "How've you been?"

Crystal remembered the broom in her hands and made a few sweeping motions. "Volunteering a lot, you know, since my retirement. I like to make myself useful." She said all of this in a brisk, nose-up tone that implied she was a positive force in the world. Unlike some people. "And there's my new grandchild."

That would be Roy's baby. Of course she would bring that up.

Roy and Tilly had once dated years ago, and Crystal would never let her forget how badly that had gone.

Henry came from around the corner of the house wearing thick gloves and a protective veil, bees circling his head. He took off the gloves and hat, tucking them under his arm. He tilted his head in the direction of the two hives stacked in the side yard. "Either of you interested in honey?"

"You know I don't like the taste," Crystal sniffed.

Tilly took this as her cue. "I'll take some."

Henry opened his door and just like that they were in his kitchen and out of Crystal's sight.

"Stay out there and she keeps talking," he said. "Lives there by herself and Roy doesn't visit much. I think she drives him a little crazy."

On the kitchen island sat baking soda, a canister of flour and other makings of the chocolate chip cookies Tilly could still smell. A dusting of flour had been wiped from the floor, but not quite all the way.

"I made coffee not too long ago. I'll get you some." He reached for a mug and pulled a small pitcher of cream from the fridge. The efficient way he moved in the kitchen suggested he could cook, and Tilly looked longingly at the plate of cookies she could now see sitting on the counter.

"I'm just here to see Finn. I don't need anything."

"How about a cookie?"

"No thanks."

"Okay, well, Finn's in his room." Henry pointed upstairs. "When I told him you were coming, he made eye contact with me for the first time since last night." Henry reached out a hand. "Let me take your jacket."

She hurried out of it so he wouldn't try to help her and hung it on a peg next to his mailbag slung beside a dusty pair of binoculars. She wondered if those were the same ones he'd used as a teenager.

Upstairs, Finn stood in front of an easel in the center of his room, next to a small table covered with tubes of paint, trays, and brushes. There was a bed, a small desk, and a shelf loaded with books, games, and large sketchpads. A flashing light drew her eye to an old answering machine sitting on the desk. Finn had once told her his mother left messages for him there since he didn't have his own phone yet. Plus she'd given up her cell phone because the new boyfriend was a spiritual type and they were pursuing some phone-free way to enlightenment or something.

Finn turned to Tilly and offered her a small smile. He was the only one she gave a Christmas present to. The one person she talked to on a regular basis. Still, she'd never wanted him to feel an unfair obligation toward her. He came and went from her shop as he wished. So this visit to his room where she'd never been—one he hadn't asked for—felt odd, like an overreach on her part, a violation of some unspoken agreement between them.

She stepped closer and Finn switched on the lamp next to his easel revealing the details of his painting, perhaps not minding she was there after all. Like Henry had described, it was the old Cotter Paper Mill building next to the mill dam, where her house now sat. In the painting, Stone Creek ran high and foamy, almost over its bank. And someone was sitting in a car next to the mill building. Henry hadn't mentioned that.

Finn peered up at her, expecting her to make sense of this, like she had when he'd started first grade and painted pictures of himself in the classroom where he sat alone and without a mouth, surrounded by kids talking in groups. That and another self-portrait where Finn had butterflies in his throat, unable to escape his closed lips, had helped lead to his diagnosis after she'd spoken to his mother.

Then there was the time, maybe a year later, when he'd been about seven and he'd drawn himself holding an orange cat. His mother was allergic and still lived with Henry and Finn at the time. When an orange kitten appeared at Tilly's shop door, she'd kept him. Finn named him Burnt after a paint color he favored at the time, Burnt Orange.

So now Finn expected her to understand this painting. He dipped his brush in red paint and added some small detail, then looked at her. The hope in his eyes was terribly intimidating. She didn't immediately know what to make of what she was seeing. He was painting this scene at home, so maybe this was mostly a message for Henry. Finn needed to tell him something and since Finn seemed to be okay with her seeing the painting, too, maybe he also wanted her to understand the same thing.

The landline in the corner of the room rang in a loud shrill, making Tilly jump. Finn's body stilled, his hand poised above the painting in mid-stroke, as he stared straight ahead. He made no move to answer the phone and instead let it ring until the old answering machine took the call. A voice came over the machine and as soon as the person asked for money to support breast cancer survivors, Finn relaxed and began painting again. Weird. Finn and his mom got along well. But maybe there was some tension with the boyfriend? Although Finn had seemed to like him well enough before.

Tilly leaned in to study the details of his painting. Underneath the long branch of the old walnut tree reaching over the width of Stone Creek, there was someone in the water. She hadn't seen that before. The person, submerged except for the head and shoulders, wore a blue jacket with a hint of yellow gold on the upper arm.

The nape of her neck prickled as she trawled her mind for explanations of why Finn had painted Frank. Maybe Henry was right about this being related to the meeting about the dam. The last time she and Henry had argued about the dam in public, Finn had been eight. The past wasn't a secret and people talked. Finn knew more now that he was older. But why was Frank in the water and who was sitting in the car?

Henry came into the room carrying a basket of laundry. He set it on the floor and went to the window without even glancing at the painting.

"Maybe we should go for a bike ride later, Finn? What do you think?"

Finn pointed to his easel. Henry's eyes flicked only briefly in that direction.

"How about lunch?" Henry offered. "I could make you a sandwich?"

There was that quick jerk of the shoulders Finn kept at the ready to answer questions. He took his painting from the easel and taped it to the wall beside others he'd already painted. Tilly walked past them, studying each one. There were slight variations, but Frank and the person in the car were always present and positioned the same way.

Tilly had a powerful need to know right then what was going on in Finn's head. She took a paper and pencil from his easel and handed it to him. "Can you write out what you're trying to say?" It felt important she and Henry understand what this was about. Writing thoughts and feelings was often even harder for Finn than talking, but she had to ask.

Finn held the pencil, hand trembling. He touched the pencil to the paper, concentrating, trying, but only made scribbles. He dropped the pencil to the ground with a tightly wound misery in his face she'd never seen there before.

"I'm sorry," she said quickly, ashamed for pushing him to do something he clearly couldn't. "I know you're trying to tell us something. I just thought ... listen, the meeting about the dam is tomorrow night. You worried about that?"

He held up his wrist with the bracelet she'd made for him years ago. It was lined with a row of wooden beads carved with simple words—YES, NO, PLEASE, THANK YOU. He touched YES. Tilly and Henry looked at each other.

"You don't need to worry," Henry said. "Tilly and I disagree about what should happen, but the decision's up to the town council."

Finn prepared his easel for another painting.

Tilly looked again at the ones on the wall but could make no more sense of the scene. "Finn, remember how you've told me sometimes you need to walk away from a painting to see where it's going?"

He gave a sharp nod.

"I think your dad and I need to do that. We'll take another look later and figure this out." She hoped that was true.

Finn, disappointed, and done with them for right now, picked up his brush and started sketching another version of the same thing.

Downstairs, Tilly retrieved her coat and stepped outside, just as a great blue heron flew overhead. Henry was right behind her, and she wondered if he'd seen the bird. If he had he didn't give any indication. The wind blew and yellowed leaves fell around them in a great whirl.

"Finn probably got ideas for those paintings from the library," she said. It was the only logical explanation she could come up with if Frank hadn't been involved and she desperately wanted to believe he hadn't. "He goes there on his own sometimes, right? He knows about the meeting, so he went looking for information." Finn had mentioned before he sometimes went to the library for schoolwork since there was no computer at home.

Henry leaned back against the house, arms crossed. "But what's your take on what he's painting?"

She cocked her head. "I don't know why he's got Frank in the water. Or who's in the car."

Henry dropped his eyes from hers.

"Finn knows we disagree about the dam," she said. "He's probably trying to work that out."

He scratched his nose. "That doesn't explain everything."

"Like?"

He shrugged.

"The past isn't a secret. There are plenty of photos of the mill buildings. Photos of Frank, too. Maybe this is Finn's way of trying to get us to stop arguing about the dam. Or he's trying to tell you he's on your side."

"You could stop insisting the dam come out. That would solve the problem—if we were both on the same side."

Tilly, suddenly frustrated, walked away and left him standing there. Why did it always have to be about the dam with him?

"See you tomorrow at the meeting," Henry called after her as she walked off through the cemetery.

chapter eighteen

Tilly walked home from Henry's, listening to the ever-present scold of crows and flickers across the cornfield next to the cemetery.

It was a reminder of how little Cottersville had changed since Frank had last seen it. All the old buildings and houses were still around, except the mill office. Really there wasn't much new, beyond her house and the shop. The same abandoned tractor stood on the side of the dirt road on the hillside in the field next to wild blackberries brambling in the hedgerows, all of it surrounded by woods beginning to turn toward reds and golds. This landscape was one of the few things that hadn't let her down.

Church bells rang and people poured out of the chapel. There'd been a wedding. Ruth and Ada were there, standing in the shade talking to a couple people in the library's book club. The owners of Fredrick's, the small store in town, chatted with Roy Booker, who cradled his new baby as his wife stood smiling beside him.

It seemed ages ago now when she and Roy dated after she'd first returned to Cottersville. That had been right after she'd learned Henry had gotten married with a baby on the way. Roy had had no idea of the steep ridges and valleys carved into her heart, ones she herself still didn't understand. She'd pretended

to be someone who loved him since she thought that would ensure he wouldn't leave. But then she'd left him after realizing she
didn't want to fool him or herself any longer. Ever since then her
love life had been carried out in bars and one-night stands in
places outside of Cottersville, at least when she got lonely
enough. She was glad to see Roy happy now at least.

A flock of starlings landed in a couple trees near the old Stone
family plot. They were having some long, complicated conversation until suddenly the birds flushed all at once in a scatter of
black before regrouping in the same tree.

Tilly bent over the usual pile of stuff littering the ground near
the graves of her grandpop and great-grandparents: cards and
long letters to Frank; drawings of golden birds in flight; copies of
The Monkey Wrench Gang; pictures of fists raised in protest; photos
of Ted Kaczynski; peace signs in various forms; joints, mostly
smoked; copies of Frank's op-eds; photocopied pages of Frank's
journal; and an assortment of leaves, feathers, and candles, one
of which was still burning. People left things here for Frank,
which struck her as both morbid and invasive. It had been a while
since she'd last cleaned up. But there was a lot more here than
usual, probably because people had become even more interested in Frank since Ted K.'s suicide in June. She started gathering it all into the large plastic bag she'd stuffed in her pocket
before leaving the house that morning.

As she blew out the candle, someone touched her arm and
she jumped in surprise, dropping the bag and spilling what she'd
gathered.

"Tilly Stone?"

A woman stood over her. She was maybe in her late thirties.
Another glassy-eyed Frank-follower, this one with long straight
hair she cut herself by the looks of the crooked bangs. A wide tie-
dyed scarf was draped over her bare shoulders. She smiled at Tilly
with yellowed teeth that made Tilly wonder how long since she'd
seen a toothbrush.

Tilly got to her feet, wishing she was already safely inside her
house or shop. This was why she stayed home most of the time.
So she didn't have to deal with these stray people drifting in and
out of Cottersville looking for Frank.

This one smelled strongly of weed. Tilly checked around for anyone else, but those who'd been at the church had driven off, probably in a hurry to get to the reception.

"I need to find Frank," the woman said. "It's important."

"It always is."

The bloodshot eyes went wide. "Frank and I met in Oregon. I was talking to these people in a bar about how things need to change with people trashing the planet and stuff. They invited me to come camp with them. And this guy shows up, sits down and starts talking. I was just blown away." She put her hand to her heart.

Tilly considered which way to walk. She didn't want this nut following her home.

"He chose me, you know." She adjusted the scarf on her shoulders and her features rearranged as something dawned on her. "I guess that would be weird, right? Me talking about your dad like that."

Tilly resigned herself to listen to whatever tie-dye had to say. Maybe she'd go once she finished.

"His message should be blasted across the mainstream news. Like what he says about the tech giants and how they manipulate society so much that they make the real decisions for people now. He's right about destroying industrial society to regain our humanity. The future of the planet and its people is up to those willing to fight for what's right. Frank showed me that." She tapped her chest twice. "He wants us to take out the electric grid and the internet to drive people toward a freer way of life. That's the way to lead people out of the system."

Maybe the rumors were true. Maybe Frank really had spent these last years wandering around convening a bunch of lost souls to carry out his vision, although by the look of this one Tilly wasn't sure they would get very far. "I'm not interested, okay?"

Tie-dye blinked as though she had to have misunderstood. "But you're his daughter. You know what I'm talking about. He knows what's going on. He's the truth." Tie-dye raised her fist in solidarity.

Tilly glanced back toward Henry's place, but he wasn't around. This woman, like all of them, saw Frank as an irresistible combination of Earth warrior, revolutionary, and outlaw. She and plenty of others like her needed someone to follow, to obsess over. That's how Frank had gained status. That and the fact that the FBI had never caught him, which fueled his underdog persona. What Frank's followers never considered were the costs to those who helped or supported him along the way.

"Can't believe he came from this nothing little town, though." Tie-dye was looking in the direction of Tilly's house. "The dam's smaller than I figured."

That dam, small as it was, had haunted Frank, Tilly, and all of Cottersville.

"I need to talk to Frank because some people are planning things he won't like. They don't want to just attack infrastructure and property. They're talking online about hurting and killing. Frank may not realize this is going on. That's why I need to find him."

Tilly didn't know if she could believe anything this woman was saying. "I don't know where he is."

"Everything okay, Tilly?" It was John Hart's voice behind them. He was coming from the direction of the church, dressed in a coat and tie.

The woman walked off toward a VW van parked in the church lot and Tilly felt a sense of relief. This encounter reminded her that she'd installed a back door to her home and shop that opened into the woods, which allowed her to come and go virtually unseen if she wanted. She would use them more from now on.

Tilly and John watched the woman go and then John shot Tilly a sideways glance. "You know what I'm going to say."

"Don't."

"You need someone in your life, Tilly. That way people won't harass you like this. Or at least they'll think twice."

"I know that's what you think." John meant well, but he remembered what happened with Roy as well as she did. It was better for everyone if she just kept to herself.

John turned toward her, clasped his hands together, an idea coming to him. "You know what?"

She raised an eyebrow.

"My dog had puppies. You should see them." He smiled so wide his eyes almost closed. "This big." He held up his hands six inches apart. "Brown with white feet. Their little ears are pointed straight up." He put his hands to either side of his head to demonstrate. "A mix of terrier and something else. Something big because you should see the size of their paws. And they're smart, I can already tell."

"That's great." He was so excited it seemed rude to not try to express some interest.

"I'm gonna bring you one."

"What?"

"One of my pups."

"No."

"People love puppies. Puppies and babies. You've heard that, right?"

"I have a cat. One that wouldn't like a puppy. I would not like a puppy. And I have no plans for a baby either."

"Well, see there. Puppies help when you're looking for some-one—they open people up. Cats are for staying inside."

"I'm not looking for anyone."

He hitched up his jeans and grinned, undaunted. "You're going to change your mind when you see those little fur-babies."

She knew better than to argue with him. John, the loving husband of Mary, father of four, volunteer fire chief, roofer, town council member, vegetarian, was also the self-appointed Tilly Stone matchmaker.

He walked with her back to the Stone family plot and helped collect the bits of Frank's shrine that had fallen out of her bag. In the parking lot the VW van was finally leaving.

"It's still weird to me that people come all the way to Cottersville because Frank Stone grew up here," John said. "In my mind he's just a local boy."

Tilly stuffed the last of the cards and candles into the bag and watched the side of John's face, wanting to ask him questions she'd never dared voice aloud before. "I've been thinking about the past lately, John."

He turned to the tree behind him, still full of those noisy

starlings squawking about something new. He turned back. "The past?"

"What do you think happened to the Cotters all those years ago?" This question felt particularly difficult since Tilly assumed everyone figured Frank had done something to them, even if no one would dare say that to her.

John reached for some papers still scattered on the grass, which he handed to Tilly while giving her a careful look. "Not sure we'll ever know."

Tilly stood with the bag of stuff, ready to get back to her shop where things could be made to fit together nicely. "Thanks for showing up when you did."

John winked. "You bet."

On her way home she dropped the bag of Frank tributes into the cemetery trashcan thinking again about that woman and what she'd said about those people willing to hurt others for Frank's ideals. She hoped to god none of that had anything to do with Frank showing up now in Cottersville. But then again, he'd kept her in the dark before.

Summer 2006

chapter nineteen

AUGUST

Every day was the same. Frank went to work. He came home. Repeat.

He and Tilly discussed food and supplies but little else, each of them busy with their separate lives. He'd stopped mentioning even the smallest thing about Cottersville, so she passed the time at the dinner table, the only time she and Frank were idle together, thinking about Henry.

It was still strange that she and Frank now lived in different worlds. They'd been so connected in their old life, relying on each other in ways they no longer had to. She didn't want to go back to that time, but she did miss the closeness between them. The only real way to get that back was to tell Frank about Henry. Because her relationship with Henry had turned her into another person, one Frank didn't know anymore. But she was afraid Frank might not let her see Henry, or worse, he might decide they couldn't stay in Cottersville.

There were things she wanted to be able to ask Frank. Like how it was working for Paul Cotter. Had he changed his mind about him at all? Or about the Cotters in general? Did he know about the bankruptcy? She still wondered about her mother. Was her grave in Cottersville or somewhere else?

But Tilly couldn't see how to bring up the subject of Henry, so she worked hard instead to maintain the status quo, which meant keeping the cabin clean and having dinner ready. That wasn't hard aside from finding an occasional snakeskin she couldn't explain. She wasn't sure if that meant they still had mice, and therefore snakes, or those skins had fallen out of some crack she hadn't thoroughly scoured.

On a night in early August, Frank wanted to play poker and Tilly was happy for the chance to do something together. She decided if it felt right, she'd try to talk to him about Henry. Or at least ask about the possibility of school.

Frank lit some candles in the center of the table and dealt the cards. He set the mood and closed off any possibility of mentioning Henry by quizzing her about the escape plan they'd talked about back in early June, another lifetime ago. This was something he'd done regularly before they'd moved to the cabin, but not since.

"If we have to run and get separated, where do we meet up?"

She played along, hoping this would be short-lived. "Heron rookery, right?"

He dealt another hand. "And what if one of us is hurt too bad to move?"

"Leave. Don't get caught. We'll find each other later." She lay down a card and he slid her another before taking two for himself. "Why are we going over this?"

He stared at his cards. "To be ready."

"For what?"

"Probably nothing. But, you know, it's good to be prepared."

Later, after she'd gone to bed, she tried to tell herself Frank was just falling into old habits. That this was his way of keeping them safe. But as the last of the summer fireflies flashed outside the cabin window, she watched from her cot as Frank wrote in his journal like he was running out of time.

"What are you writing?" she asked a couple nights later when it was too hot to sleep and he was at it again.

He looked up, surprised to find her still awake. "Things other people need to hear." He closed the journal and stood. "Since you're awake, I have something for you. I was saving it, but there's no real reason for that."

Tilly sat up, wiping the sweat from her forehead.

With a candle in hand, he reached for a box under his cot and held it out. "Since you've been so patient, staying around the cabin like I asked, I thought you might like something new to wear when we go to town."

Inside the box lay the softest blue sweater she'd ever seen. She ran her hand over the knit and glanced at the tag: *Cashmere.* So, he'd been saving for this. And he really was planning to take her to Cottersville.

"It's too hot for a sweater now, of course." He laughed like he only now realized this. "But the weather will turn soon enough. I thought you should have something nice and that color matches your eyes."

She held it up to show him and he stared for a long moment, eyes bright. "Yeah. That'll do."

It was the middle of August when Henry handed Tilly the last cedar shake to finish the roof. She nailed it into place, and they climbed down and stood looking at what they'd made. He hugged her, awkwardly from the side until she turned toward him, and their bodies fit together as though they were meant to. This helped her keep from thinking too much about how it had been almost two weeks since Frank had given her that blue sweater and they still hadn't been to town.

When Henry left a short while later, she lay near the cabin in the tall grass threaded through with purple bergamot, Queen Anne's lace, and black-eyed Susans. While she waited for Frank to come home, a monarch floating through the wide blue sky above receded from view, fading into nothing. Frank walked right by her without noticing she was there.

She followed him inside the cabin and as soon as she saw his face, she knew something had gone terribly wrong. He tapped two fingers against the counter. He must have found out about Henry. But then he said nothing else the rest of the night.

The next morning cicadas buzzed in the hot, sticky August air while Tilly and Henry sat idle inside the fort. For the first time, conversation between them seemed hard. Henry left after only a couple hours.

The next day they sat outside the fort with even less to say. He seemed different, like he was thinking about other things.

"There's a lot going on with school starting next week," he finally said, as though he thought he should explain.

Tilly picked up a hammer and pounded in a nail sticking out of one wall. "What'll I need for school?"

"The regular stuff."

She didn't know what that was and didn't want to guess out of fear of getting it wrong. "What's regular around here?"

He swatted at a fly and lay back on the ground, hands behind his head. "Backpack, paper, pencils."

"And books?"

He gave her a funny look. "They give you books, of course." He got to his feet. "Listen, I gotta go. There's some stuff I have to take care of."

She tried not to seem disappointed. He probably did have a lot to do. Or maybe since the fort was finished, he wasn't as interested in being with her anymore. "Don't forget our picnic on Monday. You're in charge of dessert."

She watched him disappear down the mountain as a broad-winged hawk circled high above, repeating a shrill call that sounded like an alarm.

That evening Frank chopped wood until after dark like he was avoiding her, too. She tried to force herself to go out to the woodpile and tell him about Henry, but that felt even more impossible than before.

Over that rainy weekend she finished the scarf. On Monday, after Frank left for work, she made cheese sandwiches, sliced apples, and added mint to a jug of spring water. She put on her new sweater since the weather had finally turned cool. Henry was late and forgot to bring dessert, but when he came into the fort, he stopped short and stared at her. "You look pretty."

Her stomach did a little flip. She pointed to the wall where she'd hung his portrait. "The final touch. What do you think?"

He came to stand beside her in front of the painting but didn't say anything. She turned to look at him and found him staring at her. He touched her cheek and bent down to kiss her, long and warm, in a way that stole her breath and then gave it back.

chapter twenty

That kiss seemed to ensure everything would work out.

But in the last days of August, Frank talked about the FBI as though they were right around the corner. He now regularly questioned Tilly over poker games he insisted they play late into the night. As soon as the cards were dealt, he'd start in: "If the Feds come through the front door, what do you do?"

"Go out the back window. Head for the woods." She knew she sounded bored and irritable, but they'd been in Cottersville for almost three months, and no one had come looking. No one had ever looked for them as far as she knew.

He scrutinized her over his cards. "And if you're caught, what do you say?"

"Nothing about our life. Not where we've been. I can't re-member anything." She blew out a long breath, hoping he'd get the hint. But even though he'd still never taken her to town, he went through his old list of rules for public outings: No jaywalk-ing. No littering. No loitering. No stealing. Always present your-self neat and clean. Be agreeable. And never walk away fast.

"The way people see you is everything," he was saying. "It doesn't matter how you feel. People see a weakness and they'll go after it. You give them nothing." He lay his hand down on the table, fanning out the cards. Full house. He'd won, again.

He shuffled the cards and laid out another game. Tilly just wanted to go to sleep.

"You want to know the most dangerous threat?"

She shifted in her chair. Couldn't he see how tired she was?

"We are, to each other." His eyes were fixed on her to make sure she was paying attention. "People get at you through those you love. Ted K.'s brother got him locked up. That can't be us."

Her eyes were so heavy she could hardly see her cards anymore. She discarded three randomly, hoping this was their last hand.

Frank slid new cards over to her but held onto his, rearranging them. "The system is the worst kind of cage. If the Feds discover who we are and catch you, they'll watch you and never stop, until they have me, too. To be together, we have to have our freedom."

She nodded, automatically. There'd been too many of these late nights.

"You get our escape bags ready like I asked?"

"Yes." She'd stocked them with boots, clothes, food, water, and other supplies Frank had been collecting over the last weeks before stashing them under a rock overhang near the spring. She told herself it was just a precaution. That Frank wasn't really intending to use them.

He shifted his cards around again, still sermonizing. "Poker's good practice for life, Tilly. People think they know you based on what you show them. So, don't share your feelings or opinions. Let them fill all that in for you because they will. They'll make up a whole story having nothing to do with you."

She couldn't take it anymore. "Why does any of this matter now?"

He leaned in. "Because things change in an instant. What you must remember is to never show how you feel about your hand. If you have nothing, make me believe the opposite. If you have something, make me think you don't. The objective is to use everything you have to get your way and to survive. Use what you know to play the most strategic game. That's what matters."

They laid down their hands. She'd lost and now finally understood that Frank didn't want to stay in Cottersville. That's what this was about. But she couldn't go back to the way things were before. He had to see that. She stood up from the table. "I'm going to bed."

"Don't move." He said this with an odd intensity, like their lives depended on it. He wasn't even looking at her, but at the floor. She didn't want to play more cards or listen to his paranoid rambling. She turned away from the table and he stood so fast to grab her wrist that he knocked his chair back.

She pulled away, afraid of him for the first time. He pushed her hard enough that she fell to the floor, trembling from shock and anger. This had to be about Henry. But then Frank's boot came down on the head of a snake. A copperhead. One she'd been about to step on if he hadn't pushed her out of the way.

"Jesus, Tilly." He picked up the dead snake by the tail. "I told you not to move. You need to listen and do what I say." He opened the door and tossed the dead snake outside. He helped her up and hugged her too tightly, maybe scared because she'd been in danger. Or because she hadn't obeyed.

chapter twenty-one

Henry, his hair and glasses covered in drizzle, showed up at the fort the next morning much earlier than he was supposed to. Frank had left the cabin only a short time before. Henry didn't come inside, but stood in the rain, arms crossed, until Tilly came to the doorway.

"Saw your dad just now. And I've seen him in town," he said.

She was too surprised to react. Of course Henry would have seen him at the mill. But she'd kept him and Frank so separated in her mind she hadn't actually considered them meeting. That had been stupid.

Henry dug into the wet ground with the toe of his shoe, exposing the dark soil beneath. "I've watched your dad go up and down the mountain over the last week. Funny how I never saw him until I decided to look."

A seed of foreboding unfurled inside her and grew into something dark and formidable. "What do you know?" Her voice sounded detached and far away.

"I know what your dad's doing in town every day."

"He's working." She wanted that to be true, even though she knew it was more than that.

Henry stuffed his hands deep into his pockets. "Sometimes he works. But my grandpa doesn't know that. I doubt they've even met. Know why?"

She wanted him to stop. Why was he speaking to her like this?

"It's because he's working for my grandpa's wife. But most of the time he's doing other things with her. I've seen them."

He wanted her to ask what they'd been doing. She knew that. She rushed him and pushed as hard as she could. He stumbled back. She picked up a rock and threw it, hitting him in the middle of the chest with a dull thud that made them both wince.

He turned and strode away.

"You swore to keep our secret. Remember that!"

When she realized he was gone and not coming back, she checked the escape bags, filling water bottles and adding more food until it started to pour. She returned to the cabin and paced, waiting for Frank. Every minute felt like an hour. He would be angry of course. He had a right to be. They'd likely have to leave that night, even with the rain.

Frank finally came home well after dark. He was restless and in a sour mood, but he said nothing about Henry. The tension between them felt so thick she could say nothing. She had no idea what Frank was thinking anymore.

The rain, which had grown softer over the last hour, now pounded the roof.

chapter twenty-two

SEPTEMBER

Over the next few days when Henry didn't show, Tilly tried not to think about him. Instead, she sorted through her options.

Frank had not mentioned Henry, so she had to assume he didn't know. That or Frank was testing her. Either way, her only choice was to tell him the truth, which she should have done a long time ago.

On the third day of September, their shared birthday, Tilly made Frank's favorite, blackberry pie, hoping that would help soften him when she told him about Henry. She also had the scarf ready to show him. There couldn't be any more secrets between them, at least not on her end.

By evening, the day had grown edgy and blustery gray. Rain, that had been falling off and on for days, turned into another downpour. Frank walked into the cabin soaking wet, letting in with him a boggy odor of moss mixed with copper.

"Happy birthday." She held up the pie, forcing a cheerfulness that didn't fit the weather or the mood between them.

"Pie smells good." He took off his wet jacket and hung it on the back of the chair before going back outside. Water dripped from the sleeves and hem, puddling on the floor.

Frank returned with an armful of wood he dumped next to the stove. He wasn't even looking at her.

"Everything okay?" she asked.

"Yeah. Fine."

He was lying, again. "What do you do for Cotter Paper, exactly? You never said."

He gave her a quick glance before putting wood in the stove. "Whatever they need."

This non-answer, one of too many for too long, irritated her, fanning embers already burning white hot. "Can't you talk straight for once? You're not the only one who gets to have secrets, you know."

He laughed at her. "And what secrets do you have?"

It was his condescending tone that uncapped what she hadn't been able to say until now: "Henry Cotter and I've been seeing each other all summer. And I love him."

Frank stared at her in utter disbelief. So, he'd had no idea.

"Don't you have to register me for school? It already started and I want to go. I'm tired of always being stuck here."

He gaped at her as though she was very foolish. "They're not gonna let you in school unless you're injected with vaccines. Plus all they'll do is fill your head with useless information."

Did he even know anything that mattered to her? Did he care? "Why haven't you ever taken to me to town? We've been here for months!"

He gave her a wild-eyed look, like a cornered animal.

"I want to see my mother's grave. I deserve that at least." She held up the scarf. "I made this for her." Her voice cracked against her will. She didn't even care about her mother that much. She wanted to hurt Frank now. To get back at him. "She died, right? That's why you never say anything about her."

He turned his back to her, resting his hands on the counter. She could practically hear the buzz and crackle in his body.

Everything burning inside Tilly suddenly became quieter as she sensed she'd pushed past something she shouldn't have. But even so, she needed to know. "Why did we really come here?"

Frank opened his journal, which was sitting on the counter beside him. He ripped out a blank page and scrawled something across it before holding it out. "You and me ever get separated, I want you to go to this address. This is the person who taught me explosives. I trust him. And I think you could learn some things from him."

This, she hadn't seen coming. She didn't take the paper. She already knew everything she wanted to know about blowing things up. "What are you telling me right now?"

He dropped the page on the table and wouldn't look at her. "I've made mistakes. Things I can't undo. You can make it on your own if you have to."

She couldn't stop her head from shaking as she tried not to cry. "What are you talking about?"

"If we get split up, I'll come back for you." He ran a hand through his hair. "If the Feds find out who I am, I'll have to go under. Deep." He stared at the pie, thinking. "I'll come back on this day, our birthday. That's a date we can both remember." Some switch had flipped, and he was suddenly calm. Too calm. Like he'd gotten past what he'd been afraid to say. This idea of going away wasn't some off-the-cuff thing Frank had just dreamed up. "Worst case, let's say I'll be back for you by the time I turn fifty, okay? That's how old my dad was when the accident happened. So that feels like the right plan."

She almost laughed. Was he kidding? But she could see he wasn't. A violent, desperate feeling gave her no choice but to run out the door into the rain. She went to the fort and hugged her legs to her chest trying to stay warm. All she could think of was how Henry had turned away, too, and everything that had seemed good was breaking apart.

She stayed there for hours as the rain continued and the night grew colder. When the shivering got so bad she couldn't stop her teeth from chattering, she went back to the cabin. Frank was asleep or pretending to be. A note on the table sat next to the untouched pie: *All we have is each other.*

She changed into dry clothes and put her boots next to the cot.

chapter twenty-three

Frank dressed early the next morning, barely looking at Tilly before rushing out the door.

As soon as he left, she jumped out of bed and slipped her boots on. She followed him, keeping to the path he'd worn, taking care to stay far enough behind him—a precaution she probably didn't need given how fast and carelessly he was moving. When she reached the bottom of Short Mountain, early dawn had shifted to a still gray. Frank was just ahead, walking toward the front of the paper mill offices.

She waited until he rounded the corner and then crept to the side of the building. He was there with a woman. She assumed this was Henry's grandpa's wife. She was young, maybe Frank's age, and pretty, with a high-boned face. She and Frank were arguing, but Tilly could hear some of what they were saying over the growl of Stone Creek beside them, flowing muscular and treacherous from all the recent rain.

Frank turned slightly and she noticed the green scarf she'd knitted spilling out of his coat pocket. Why did he have that? The argument grew more heated, and their voices raised enough that Tilly could hear more, even above the noise of the water. "Look at it!" Frank yelled. He was trying to get her to take something from his hand.

"What right did you have?" she said.

A mouse scuttled across Tilly's foot but at first she thought it was another snake and screamed. Both Frank and the woman turned toward her.

Frank's eyes widened in alarm, but then, just as quickly, he seemed to resign himself to something. "You see, Helen." He pointed to Tilly. "There's our daughter."

All of Tilly's attention shifted from Frank to the woman. Helen. Helen, her mother? Helen, Paul Cotter's wife?

A car horn sounded, and they all turned to a blue car approaching the bridge leading to the mill offices.

"Tilly," Frank suddenly hissed. "Go home! We'll talk later."

She stayed put. That was her mother. She wasn't leaving.

"Tilly!" Frank stamped his foot. "Go. Now. Helen and I will come to the cabin very soon and explain everything. I promise! But you have leave at once."

Tilly didn't know who was in the car, but she sensed a confrontation was coming. The tone of Frank's voice and his promise of explanation made her turn and run back toward the forest. She looked back only once, wanting to see her mother again, but now the building stood between them.

She trudged straight up the mountain, not keeping to the path, walking through a patch of mud that stuck to the soles of her shoes, weighing them down. The gray cloud deck overhead darkened and there was not one bird in sight.

She'd seen Helen. She'd seen her mother. She was alive. Of course this was part of Frank's plan. Had he wanted to come back to Cottersville and bring their family together? But Helen and Frank had been fighting. And Frank had her scarf. To show her? But he'd also been trying to get Helen to look at something else in his hand. Why had he said nothing to her about Helen before?

Inside the cabin, a slow rain grew into a white roar on the roof. The wind blew so hard it sounded like a loud, sustained groan and Tilly could hear tree limbs occasionally crashing down in the forest around her. When she peered out the window looking for Helen and Frank, irregular flashes of lightning lit the sheet of water flowing like a curtain over the porch eave. In town, the fire whistle went off over and over again.

She waited, watching for them, but Frank and Helen didn't come.

At midnight she went out, instantly soaked as she stepped out from under the porch roof. She walked to the overlook, rain hammering every inch of her body while wind gusted from the east. The ground was so heavy with water, the earth had grown soft underneath, and couldn't be trusted.

At the overlook the valley below was completely black, as though it had disappeared. A single light winked on in the distance, followed by another. She struggled to make sense of what she was seeing and realized people were firing up generators. The power had gone out. Of course it had.

Back at the cabin Tilly lay awake, waiting all night, but Frank didn't show. Probably delayed because of the power outage or maybe something to do with the dam. Or he was so angry with her he'd chosen to stay with Helen instead of coming home.

September 2023

chapter twenty-four

Tilly removed the blade on the table saw to clean it, thinking of Helen. She'd never dared to ask anyone about Frank's relationship with her. She was too afraid of people making connections. Instead, she'd found out what she could on her own, by way of old yearbooks and everything she could find that Helen had written.

Her impressive writing career began with the high school newspaper. Tilly'd read Helen's early reports on Frank, which she found in the library when they'd finally gotten old local newspapers online. The *Bucks County Mirror* reprinted some of her high school paper news since Helen had essentially scooped them. Tilly had even found an op-ed from the principal of the high school and the editor of the *Bucks County Mirror* stating their intention to stand with Helen and her decision not to reveal the source of her information about the "vandalism" at Cotter Paper. Helen did more than just report on what she saw. She presented Frank as committing an act of protest in such a way that the reader couldn't help but side with Frank, at least a little.

Helen's reporting went on until the end of her senior year when she disappeared right after graduation. One news account, in which her parents made a public request for information about her, mentioned she'd left a note saying she was taking a road trip for several months. She'd taken her car. But her parents had felt it out of character.

Three months later she'd driven back to town. The news coverage of that had been no more than a paragraph or two. One reporter noted her dad saying she only had a few miles on the car since he'd last changed the oil, right before she'd disappeared. Meaning she hadn't gone on any road trip. Or if she had, she hadn't driven.

The date of her reappearance was right after Tilly's birthday. Tilly figured she and Frank had hidden her car and she'd gone to live at the cabin with Frank where he'd handled the delivery. Then Helen had returned to Cottersville because maybe she hadn't wanted a child?

Of course, Tilly couldn't ask anyone these questions. She'd had to sit with them until she could get the truth from Frank.

After Helen returned to Cottersville she'd worked full time at the *Bucks County Mirror*. She'd even been nominated for a Pulitzer Prize for local reporting on the widespread corruption in the small, cash-strapped Cottersville school district. She'd later done a long profile on Cotter Paper and what it meant to the community the year before she and Paul Cotter married. In the photo included as part of their wedding announcement, Paul gazed at her adoringly and she looked, Tilly thought, unsure.

Mac pulled into the driveway with, Tilly assumed, Agent Sharp, the man who'd interrupted her meeting with Frank at the dam.

"See you got a new partner," she said, when Mac came in alone.

He glanced over his shoulder. "That's Agent Sharp. The bureau thinks I need more supervision, at least when it comes to Frank's case."

Mac watched as Tilly sprayed cleaning fluid on the saw blade and scrubbed at the teeth with a small wire brush.

"You find a PR person yet?" he asked her.

"That really necessary?"

Mac leaned against the door and crossed his arms. "That op-ed I showed you is going to come out somewhere. All it takes is a slow news cycle for something to catch."

She considered this as she brushed dirt from the saw teeth, revealing the shiny metal beneath. The thought of reporters nosing into her life felt like wolves closing in. This was the reason she'd mostly stayed away from her cellphone since Mac had shown up with the news of Frank's calling card at the Umbra Dam. Only a few online outlets had reported on that so far, at least from what Tilly could find. They'd quoted Anna Birch who always seemed ready to speak about Frank, given her forthcoming biography.

Tilly had seen enough quotes from Anna Birch to know she was good at talking to the press. She gave them quotable sound bytes and knew Frank's history better than he probably remembered it himself. Anna had taken the heat off Tilly over the last days and for that she'd been grateful. But if Frank's story did grow as Mac suggested, the press might not be satisfied with speaking only to Anna.

Tilly reinstalled the blade and turned on the saw to test it. Mac winced at the loud whine of the machine Tilly let run a little longer than necessary before turning it off.

"Get yourself a PR person," he said. "Someone good and do it before tonight's meeting if possible." He buttoned his coat.

Tilly was surprised he'd mentioned the meeting. "Are you involved somehow?"

"I asked the town council to reconsider removal. After what happened at the Umbra Dam and Frank's interest in Cottersville, we're concerned the dam's a target. Plus—and this is important for you to know—there's evidence that a faction of Frank's followers have banded together with plans to use extreme violence. We're not sure how far they might be willing to go."

Tilly thought of that woman she'd met in the cemetery who'd mentioned this same thing. "What kind of violence?"

"Bombs with the intention to hurt people."

"Who's in this faction?"

"It's a small online group from what we can tell. No one's using real names and they're careful, so we're still trying to figure out who they are. But they share an interest in destruction of the modern way of life and a return to nature. A lot of them, it seems, were originally inspired by a show on TV about Ted Kaczynski called *Manhunt: Unabomber* that in some ways showed his ideals in a positive light. And since Frank is often associated with Kaczynski, they idolize him, too. These people were scattered all over the internet before. They're a mixed bag: some actually longing for some kind of apocalypse, some sick of mainstream political correctness, and some just talking shit. But anyway, one person rounded them up and brought them together online. We're not sure who that is. They talk about how the modern world drove Kaczynski to suicide last June and they've become more focused on Frank, because, you know, they think he's still out there. Based on what this group has been talking about most recently, we have reason to believe they'll come after the Cottersville Dam."

"Is Frank involved?"

"I don't know."

After Mac left, Tilly decided she needed to face her cellphone and found twenty new messages. She managed to listen only to the most recent one: "We're about to publish Frank Stone's op-ed. We'd like to do a companion story from your point of view."

If the press attention got bad enough, that might get in the way of her seeing Finn. And she'd promised to look at his paintings again. Tilly had to do something and she could think of only one place to turn.

"I'll be damned. You finally called back," Anna Birch said, when Tilly phoned her.

"There's a new op-ed coming out, apparently written by Frank."

"Is there?" Anna said, a little breathlessly.

Tilly realized this new attention on Frank would only be good for Anna's book sales. "I'll do the interview, but I have a condition."

"Name it."

"I've been warned by the FBI that this latest news about Frank has the potential to become a media circus. Can you be my spokesperson and deal with the press so I can live my life as normally as possible?"

"Absolutely. In fact, I'm already in town for the meeting tonight. Figured it might be important for the book."

"I don't have money to pay you, but I'll do the interview."

"Great. I'm staying at a local Airbnb for the next week to try to make as much progress as I can on the writing. I'll see you tomorrow morning bright and early. And at the meeting in just a few hours."

chapter twenty-five

Cottersville conducted its business on the first floor of the stone municipal building, under the library which occupied the second story.

Tilly stood outside the building, its parking lot full of cars, watching a lone star shine through the boughs of the old apple tree in the cemetery. Swallows crisscrossed overhead, reminding her of nights she and Frank spent watching the birds on the banks of one creek or another.

Aside from this meeting about the dam, she'd organized all the others. People had come to the first meeting years ago to speak their mind, mostly in opposition to the dam's removal, since people felt it was part of the town's identity. Henry certainly had. What no one ever said out loud was that even though both the Cotter and Stone families had a long history in Cottersville, the Cotters had built the town and the Stones had offered nothing but headaches. Probably to most people the dam seemed more a part of Cottersville than her family. In that first meeting the parking lot had been as crowded as it was this night, but at all the many subsequent meetings, the number of people had dwindled until it was mostly just her and Henry arguing with each other in front of the council every six months or so. This had gone on for years. At least up until three years ago when she thought the council had made their final decision to keep the dam where it was.

When she walked into the meeting room now, every folding chair was occupied. Some people were even standing. Of course word had gotten out that the FBI had called this meeting. The council members were at a table in the front. John Hart, as president, sat beside the mayor, flanked on both sides by the others.

Mac, who sat in the front of the room, looked, as usual, like he'd slept in his button down and khakis, especially beside the meticulous Agent Sharp. Next to him were Ruth and Ada, from the library. Crystal was on the other side of Mac. Henry sat in the back. Tilly stood against the wall a couple rows behind Anna Birch who she recognized from her YouTube videos.

Everyone from town seemed to be there chatting with the person next to them. Tilly tried to muster the familiar satisfaction of knowing more about the dam removal than anyone in the room and choosing to be quiet and on her own. But instead, she found herself staring too long at the floor, feeling self-conscious, wishing she'd gotten there early enough to get a seat.

She opened the folder she'd brought with her, scanning the notes she'd taken since the first dam meeting eight years ago. A legal dam removal, even a small one, took years. It also took money and a complicated stack of permits. She'd tried to do it the right way, working with a local conservation group to get a grant to study the effects of the removal.

After that they'd gotten the permitting applications approved. There'd been the first of many public meetings to discuss the removal with the community. That's when Henry had first spoken against it. Then over and over he'd rallied support for studies that took months or years: hydrologic analyses, flood impacts, fish-habitat changes, shellfish effects, sediment loads, endangered species assessments, pollution impacts, and archeological evaluations. When all those had been completed and he could come up with nothing else, he'd gathered so many signatures for petitions opposing the dam removal that, in the end, despite all the investigations supporting taking the dam out and a grant to pay for most of it, town council had voted against it.

The work had been agonizingly long and slow. Frank would

never have understood this approach to environmental protection. He'd hated organizations like the Sierra Club and Nature Conservancy because he claimed they worked within the system and didn't make any real change. He'd thought they were really only interested in helping to sustain the hyper-consumerism of Western ways of living, just like every other arm of the system. And Tilly had to admit there might be some truth to this. She could also see that Frank had taken out more dams using his methods than a hundred people would be capable of going about it the legal way.

But when she'd been young, Frank would go on about how powerful people put themselves first and considered nature a thing to be used to get what they wanted. Frank would complain about their ego-focused ways. But he could never see his own ways weren't much different. He thought he alone knew the answers. She shared his desire to protect water and land, but she would only do that in ways that were supported by the community. She wasn't interested in being part of some fringe group working outside of everyone else. She was interested in being part of Cottersville. It was not her decision alone whether the dam stayed. You couldn't just pull one thread and expect the whole thing not to unravel. She'd followed the law, even when that meant working slowly and failing to get what she wanted in the end. Still, maybe she hadn't failed, because here they were again, talking about the dam.

The room stood for the Pledge of Allegiance, everyone facing the flag in the front which hung above a row of Cotter Paper Mill photos that included a portrait of Paul Cotter. Tilly ran through all the old arguments she'd used over the years to defend against Henry's declaration that his family's defunct paper mill represented an "historical artifact," and the dam its only remaining structure. This was old habit and something she'd gone over in her mind when she thought she'd known what to expect from this meeting. But that was before she found out Mac had set it up. And before she'd learned Frank wanted the dam to stay.

The crowd quieted when the mayor started speaking. "We've reviewed all previous reports and petitions regarding the dam removal, submitted primarily by Ms. Stone and Mr. Cotter. We've gone over all prior public comment. The intention of this meeting is not for additional debate about the pros and cons of removal. Instead, recent events indicate the Cottersville Dam may pose a threat to our community. Federal Agent Macalister Stevens is here to discuss that threat and then we're going to decide what to do about the dam."

The room went silent. Mac stood to one side angling himself so he could speak both to council and the audience at the same time. "We have reason to believe a group is planning to sabotage the dam."

A small rumble went through the room. Tilly hoped Mac wasn't planning to trash Frank, with her sitting right there.

"This is based on recent evidence and online activity pointing to the Cottersville Dam as a possible target."

So he was going for it. Tilly wished she hadn't come. Why hadn't he been more clear about how this meeting was going to go?

Using the full depth and gravity of his voice, Mac went on: "A new op-ed, just published and allegedly written by Mr. Stone, mentions the Cottersville Dam, at least indirectly." Mac looked pointedly at Tilly. "So we're treating this as a domestic terrorist situation."

People started talking all at once. The mayor banged his gavel and then again to regain order.

Mac cleared his throat, "We want to take the dam out safely before something potentially harmful happens. All the required permits and works plans are already in place thanks to previous efforts by Ms. Stone."

Mac made it sound like they were working together. Everyone in the room was glued to what he was saying. It helped that his haphazard look and short stature had made him easy to dismiss, at least at first. That was until he'd started talking. Because that's when the crowd realized there was more to him than they'd first thought.

"If we start now, we can get the dam out by Saturday," he said.

Henry stood. "Is it the FBI's job to take out dams?"

Mac pointed to him. "Fair question. And the answer's no. But we're asking the town to approve this unusual circumstance, for the safety and wellbeing of Cottersville."

Tilly looked back at Henry with a growing sense of alarm.

Mac crossed his arms and spread his feet. "Here's the thing. This crisis goes way beyond this town. A legal and safe dam removal would be a high-profile example for this country. And that's what we need in the public domain right now because people online are portraying Frank Stone as some kind of hero. This has been going on at a low volume for years. But the dial's been turned up. And I can't overstate how serious that is. Growing numbers of people believe Frank Stone is someone to emulate. I know the people of Cottersville can attest to that, given how many have come to your community over the years simply because Frank Stone grew up here. That problem is going to get worse, and potentially dangerous."

Many were nodding their heads. Mac seemed to grow taller, his voice becoming almost preacher-like. "I just learned about a failed bombing in Oregon. The person who set that bomb was someone who followed Frank Stone online, claimed to have met him and definitely drank the Kool-Aid. Unfortunately, that person got caught in his own explosion and lost an arm when the bomb's timer malfunctioned. If the bomb had gone off later when it was supposed to, it would have hurt even more people."

This had to be someone from the violent group Mac had mentioned. Tilly felt that old shame, like she bore responsibility for what Frank did or inspired in others. Like the fear now palpable in the room was her doing.

"The most important thing right now is to put a stop to this," Mac said. "We know the Cottersville Dam was personal for Mr. Stone. It was his trigger, and we have to assume it still is. If he's resurfaced, that puts everyone in this town at risk. Taking the dam out is the one preemptive move we can take. So I'm here to ask for permission to begin that removal now. The potential danger to this town—to the country—warrants immediate action. If the dam is blown up before we can take it out, someone could be hurt or killed either by Mr. Stone or others inspired by him. And that could also set off a series of bombing from here to California. So the threat is not just here, my friends, but everywhere."

Several hands shot up.

"Hold your questions," the mayor barked. "Please continue, Agent Stevens."

Mac softened his voice so everyone in the room had to lean in to make sure they got every word they needed to protect their friends and family. "I've taken the liberty of talking to the contractors Ms. Stone lined up for the project several years ago. These people are experts in what they do and will manage the logistics of the removal itself." He nodded at Tilly and she dropped her eyes to the floor, seething that he was using her in this way. "They're willing to mobilize as soon as tomorrow and set up this weekend so work can begin right away. Thanks to Ms. Stone's previous efforts, we have everything we need in terms of permits and approvals. I've already been in contact with all the agencies that need to be involved, and they're ready to support the immediate removal, given the circumstances."

Tilly glanced at Mac hoping he was finally finished. She saw him look at a man sitting in front of him she didn't recognize. He wasn't from Cottersville. He snapped Mac's picture with his phone and wrote something hurriedly in his notebook. A reporter.

"Thank you for your attention." Mac nodded to the council and to the audience before taking his seat.

Had Frank known how this meeting would go down? Was that why he'd asked her to make sure the dam stayed where it was? Because he couldn't stand the FBI taking out the dam before he had a chance to do it himself? Tilly's head hurt. This was all so much more than she felt capable of handling.

She glanced back at Henry who appeared even more disturbed than she felt.

Finn suddenly came in searching for Henry. Henry was as startled to see him as Tilly was. Finn didn't like crowds and he wasn't in a good way right now. Still, he took a seat beside his father.

"We're open now for questions and remarks," the mayor said.

Hands went up. Tilly only half listened to talk about when exactly the dam would be removed, who would do it, and what security would be put into place in the meantime. She was instead trying to arrange what she knew into some kind of logical story.

But the pieces weren't fitting.

Henry walked to the front of the room and her mind focused. She wanted to hear what he would say. He faced the council: people he'd known his whole life who'd want to side with him if they could. "John, Alice, Jim, Margaret, Greg—I hope you aren't considering this. We're talking about *our* town. Let's make the right decision for Cottersville. How many more years do we let Frank Stone take from this community? The dam is part of our history. And not just Cottersville's history. Small dams built this country."

Henry had given some version of this speech before, and it had worked. But this time it fell flat.

"Frank Stone's a thug," he continued, trying a different angle. "By taking out that dam we're giving him exactly what he wants. For all we know, we're playing right into his hand."

The faces of the council members remained unmoved. The room wasn't with him. Henry let out a shaky breath. "There are reasons I can't say for why the dam needs to stay where it is." He stopped talking, appearing so raw and vulnerable in front of everyone that Tilly wanted to go stand with him. But she stayed where she was.

The council members shifted uncomfortably. "Can you say more, Henry?" John asked.

Henry's lips pressed into a firm line, as though he had to seal in words that might escape.

"We can only make our decision based on the information we have," John urged.

Henry bent his head and after a long, painful moment, returned to his seat.

Tilly'd pushed for this dam removal for eight years and now she wanted to delay, not for Frank, but for Henry. But if she asked for that now, it would look suspicious, especially to Mac. She wished she knew what Henry wasn't saying.

People started talking and the mayor called for order, pounding his gavel until the room quieted. "Henry, this is your last chance to say whatever you need to."

Henry shook his head. Beside him Finn, white as a ghost, stared at the side of his father's face.

Council voted unanimously in favor of removal and just like

that the meeting was over.

Tilly felt a deep sense of dread and confusion.

Henry and Finn stood and moved toward the exit. She hurried to catch up with them. Maybe together they could figure out a way to stop this. It wasn't too late.

Henry pushed open the doors to blinding flashes of light. People from outside surged in, forcing Henry and Finn back. Henry tried to close the doors, but reporters held them open as cameras and cell phones were thrust forward. Someone behind Tilly yelled her name and she looked back to see Anna Birch, trying to reach her, trying to help.

Mac took Tilly's arm and steered her forward. "We're driving you home."

chapter twenty-six

Mac threw his jacket over Tilly's head and pushed her firmly forward.

She was shoved into a car before she could rip the jacket away. Mac was beside her in the back seat. Agent Sharp was in the front beside another agent who drove slowly through the crowd of news people standing outside.

"Where did they all come from?" Tilly's voice sounded far away to her and she was vaguely aware of sweat beading on her forehead. Her heart was going like she'd just run ten miles. There were so many reporters, more than she'd ever seen in one place.

"This is what I was worried about with that op-ed," Mac said, staring straight ahead and speaking to her in a detached neutral tone meant to keep her at arm's length. Maybe because Sharp was in the car. Or because he'd helped make this happen by inviting a reporter to the community meeting, one who'd probably been tweeting a play-by-play of the whole thing. Tilly couldn't get her breath right, couldn't feel her fingers.

Mac turned to her. "Are you okay?"

She heard what he said but it was as though he spoke from the end of a long tunnel and she was on the other side.

"Slow your breathing," he was saying.

But there was no air. Didn't he know that?

"What's wrong with her?" That was Sharp's question. "Why

does she seem so upset, do you think? Maybe because we just threw a wrench into her plans with daddy? Is that what we did, Ms. Stone?"

Mac's glance at Sharp told him this wasn't the time and Tilly could tell they differed widely on this subject and probably a lot more.

But this thought was replaced by a more pressing one: that she was trapped in the car and needed to get out before she ran out of air. She reached for the door handle with fingers she couldn't feel. Locked.

"Calm down," Mac was saying to her. "You're okay. You just need to breathe."

But she couldn't. The press pounded on the car window, screaming her name. It was scary. Her worst nightmare. They'd cut her off from Finn. He needed her right now. And she was out of air. She had to get out of the car, even if that meant smashing the window and running through the reporters outside. Because otherwise she would die.

"You're having a panic attack," Mac said. "On the count of three, take a breath in. One, two, three."

"Maybe we should take her down to the station," Sharp said.

Can't breathe. She pounded on the window with her fist trying to break the glass, until Mac held her hands, which only made things worse. Flashes of light from outside meant these people were taking pictures, even now.

Mac's voice came from an even greater distance. "Tilly. Listen to me."

She broke free and tugged the door latch again. Still locked.

Mac grabbed her shoulders, turned her toward him and shook, hard. "Breathe!"

"This is ridiculous," Agent Sharp said.

"Shut up!" Mac growled before searching Tilly's eyes. "I'm going to help you get in your house. But you need to take a breath."

She did want to be in her own home, in her space away from all of this. She wanted that desperately. She sucked in air and let it out.

"Good." Mac's face came into some focus. She took another

quick breath and the darkness ebbed some. Mac nodded and handed her his jacket. "Cover your head until we're inside. I'm going to come around to your side and then I'm staying right next to you."

He stepped out of the car. The noise from all the reporters was deafening. A group of agents appeared and surrounded him as he came to her side and extracted her. Then somehow, they were in her house.

"You contact a PR person yet? You need someone now."

"I called Anna Birch."

This surprised him. "I don't think ... she's no PR specialist."

Tilly still felt light-headed and odd, like she wasn't completely there. She wanted Mac to go. "She's who I have."

His eyes flicked back and forth like he was doing some complicated math. "You need someone objective. She's not ...."

Even if he had a point, she was done with this and him. "Leave me alone, Mac."

He gave her a long look. "Keep the blinds and curtains closed. Don't come out of this house. We're going to watch your place round the clock until the dam is out." He flipped up his collar and left.

chapter twenty-seven

FRIDAY SATURDAY SUNDAY MONDAY **TUESDAY** WEDNESDAY THURSDAY FRIDAY SATURDAY SUNDAY

Voices woke Tilly well before daylight. She peeked out her bedroom window, being careful not to move the curtains. News cars and vans lined the street. Reporters gestured at her house and the dam, alongside the grind and beep of heavy equipment already at work. Mac hadn't wasted any time. Tilly's heart thrummed too rapidly as it had the night before. A Tesla pulled into the drive and Anna Birch got out wearing a pale grey linen dress. The reporters rushed her, screaming questions and Tilly figured right then Anna would get back into her car and flee. There were far too many of them to handle.

But Anna, unmoved by their efforts to outshout each other, held up her palms like a crossing guard. They quieted like school children in front of a stern teacher. Anna swung a pointed finger around in an arc saying something that appeared to strike the crowd as both serious and somehow charming.

The reporters stood and watched Anna pull a sign out of the back of her car and sink it into the ground at the edge of Tilly's lawn with an efficiency Tilly imagined Anna probably applied to most everything. Anna retrieved a second sign from the trunk and the reporters standing between her and Tilly's house parted for Anna when she fishtailed her hand at them, indicating she needed to get through.

Tilly realized only then that Anna meant to come inside the house. She should have anticipated that. It wasn't like they could talk now in the shop where Tilly took company. Tilly quickly scanned the room for anything that might say too much, but Anna was already there, knocking.

Tilly opened the door quickly, ushering Anna inside, feeling an urge to shield this woman from the reporters outside even if she didn't seem intimidated by them.

Anna held up the sign she carried. *For all inquiries about Frank Stone, call 555-484-2323. This property is monitored by security cameras.* "This one's for the backyard, in case anyone thinks they can sneak in that way."

"I don't want cameras."

"And no one will know you don't have them," she said, looking around.

She set the sign beside the back door and did a three-sixty, studying the private details of Tilly's home: the embarrassing romance novels, pillows on her couch with a repeating pattern of outstretched wings, a framed series of Finn's drawings. There was Henry's portrait, hanging, of all places, in her bedroom. Anna wouldn't go back there, would she?

"You built this place on your own, right?"

"Yep."

"On the old mill property? You were just eighteen when you bought it."

Anna wanted to show her how much she already knew, that she'd done her homework. Tilly wondered how many private details of her home might wind up in Anna's book.

"How long did it take to build this?"

"Years. The shop went up first, while I lived in a camper. The house came later."

Anna's eyebrow arched in a question.

"I had to be able to build furniture so I could pay for the house."

"Ah. And you've worked on getting rid of the Cottersville Dam, too. To carry out Frank's wishes, I assume. You must be happy about last night's meeting. Ironic though. The FBI taking out the dam. I don't think Frank would like that too much."

Tilly sat at the kitchen table, hoping Anna would follow her lead. "Is this biography of Frank part of your academic work?"

Anna set down her bag on the table and pulled out a laptop. "That's right. This book about your father makes my job matter. His story's important, and I want to share it."

She opened her laptop. "Of course, I want to hear your side of things. That's why I wanted to talk to you. Aside from the news reports when Frank went missing and some town meeting minutes, there's nothing online about you, other than the website of the gallery representing your furniture. And you're not even pictured there." She gave Tilly a coaxing smile. "Is there a reason you keep yourself secret?"

Tilly shook her head figuring if Anna had really done her research, she knew why Tilly didn't put herself out there. Too many people found her as it was, and they were only interested in Frank, not Cottersville, or how most of the community might feel about Frank.

Anna squinted, like she was trying to bring Tilly into better focus. "My editor told me the biography wouldn't be complete without your viewpoint, so I'm glad we can help each other." She smiled. "You're doing me a big favor."

Her fingers were poised above the keyboard. "Why don't we start from the beginning. What happened to thirteen-year-old Tilly after you left Cottersville? There are five years between then and your return that I know nothing about."

"I went to stay with a man Frank knew. August Travers."

"Someone you knew before you and Frank came to Cottersville?"

"Frank kept the people in his life separate from one another. I'd never met August until I showed up at his house. Just like I never met you until now."

Anna was smiling but there was something in her eyes Tilly couldn't decipher.

She looked down at her laptop and back up, somewhat shyly. "Did Frank ever talk about me?"

"Not to me." Tilly got up to make coffee, suddenly uncomfortable. Anna was about to tell her how she and Frank first met. Every woman's story was the same, more or less.

"We met in a bar where I waited tables—my first job. I was twenty at the time." She smiled, remembering him. "Back then I never envisioned anything more for myself than waitressing." She laughed. "It's embarrassing to think of now."

Anna had to know about the other women. She was working on his biography, after all. She would have a sense of how many letters and visits Tilly'd gotten from women who claimed to have been involved with Frank, each one of them sure they were the one. Most of this went back to before they'd come to Cottersville. Tilly hadn't known about any of them as a kid, just as they'd never heard of her back then. Not until the news reports of her discovery and Frank's identity as the bomber.

"Certain people you don't forget," Anna went on. "Don't even realize when they're in your life how important they are. Not until the years go by and you understand your happiest times were with them—"

Tilly's happiest times had been with Henry, she suddenly thought.

"You realize when you were with that person, everything was right. Frank had a lot of women, I know that. But I wasn't just some affair. It was special between us."

When the coffee finished burbling, Tilly set a container of milk and sugar in front of Anna and handed her a mug. She was ready to switch gears. "So, what's your plan for handling the press? I want to know you can keep your end of our deal."

Anna sat a little higher in her seat, clearing her throat, the spell broken. She spun her laptop around. "I'm sure you've seen the website I built." The header on the screen said THE REAL FRANK STONE. Tabs at the top read: ABOUT FRANK, FRANK'S JOURNAL, RECENT NEWS, BIOGRAPHY BLOG, and TELL YOUR FRANK STONE STORY.

"And besides this website I'm updating social media several times a day. Interest has surged since the Umbra Creek incident and the op-ed. Most people will be satisfied to learn what they can from the comfort of home. Our strongest tools are the ones I've already built online."

She went on now in a tone Tilly guessed she used in her academic life.

"Frank already has a strong following in the anarchist subculture. And with the recent events, he may become more mainstream. I wouldn't be surprised if national news shows up soon. And Frank's persona is complicated. Framing it the right way is critical. Terrorist or hero? Context makes the difference."

Anna pointed toward the reporters milling around the edge of Tilly's front lawn. "They're in competition with each other to get an exclusive. Those people are local, but if this does turn into a national story, the pressure on them will increase, and they won't stop knocking on your door. They'll stay outside waiting for any movement and pounce every time you or someone else comes or goes. They'll talk to your neighbors or anyone else they can find if they can't talk to you." Her phone buzzed and she looked at it and then put it down. "Anyway, the big papers and national networks aren't going to be your problem; it'll be those people out there that will be pressured to beat the national outlets. Their jobs will be on the line so they'll get aggressive, especially if the story gets big. They'll create a barrier between you and everyone else."

A drop of sweat slipped down the middle of Tilly's back. If Anna was trying to scare her, she'd done well.

Anna leaned closer. "My manuscript's due to my editor by Christmas, so I'm right up against it. I can help you if you help me. I already have everything set up online. People want to interact with Frank and that's mostly how they do it. It's clear on these sites it's me and not him. Frank's a fugitive, after all. People know he's not on X."

"But you're using his name."

"To focus people's attention. And if I didn't, someone else would. Think about it: people search for Frank by name and so they're going to my sites for their information. For the most part that means, they're *not* knocking on your door."

She was trying to sell Tilly. "Can anyone post? Like on TELL YOUR FRANK STONE STORY?"

"Yep. And there've been a lot of postings lately from people who've seen Frank in person." Anna started typing. "I want to show you the social media. And you should know I take the time to remove unflattering comments. Some stuff I can't control, obviously, if it's not on a site I manage. But I have a lot of say over how people see Frank."

"How many negative comments are there?"

She stopped typing, thinking. "Not that many. Some see Frank as a reckless, liberal type. Occasionally people question his motives or what kind of father he was. These are rare. I don't feel bad deleting them. That negativity doesn't reflect Frank's mission and what he stood for.

Tilly didn't want people saying things about Frank that weren't true but erasing people's opinions didn't seem right.

Anna was typing again, excited. "Last week, Frank reached more than two million followers on X. Same kind of expansion on other social media. If Frank's out there, he must be tracking some of this. I know how he feels about technology, but he'd also like the attention on his mission, right?"

Tilly couldn't deny that. He'd loved writing the op-eds because he'd wanted people reading about his ideas. In his mind, that meant changing minds and behaviors. She believed he'd be reading the online chatter about him. He wouldn't be able to resist. Still, it felt strange that all those people spent so much time talking and reading about Frank. "I just don't get all the interest. I never have."

"Your father's fascinating. People want to know more. Some of what he and Ted Kaczynski had to say about the evils of technology years ago now seems prophetic. I mean, how about the relationship between social media and degraded mental health or all the hubbub lately about how AI might mean the end of humanity as we know it? A lot of people are cynical and dissatisfied with modern life. They feel hopeless about the prospects for real change. They're looking for something new. That's why Frank has been able to amass a group of people to carry out his vision. Word is spreading. I study anarchists and people who disrupt systems. Extremism and violence changes behaviors, even if no one wants to acknowledge that. The more extreme, the more change. Radical tactics work. That's a proven fact. A lot of people are ready for radical change. In their minds, Frank's someone to emulate."

Anna seemed oddly animated about what she was saying, given that someone had just blown themselves up in Oregon. But she also did seem to understand Frank on some level. Tilly wanted to be able to trust her. She didn't know anyone else who could help her and Anna'd done a good job with the press outside.

"So, what questions do you have for me about Frank?"

"Can I record you on my cell? It's just to make sure I have the details right when I'm writing."

"Okay." Tilly didn't love that idea, but she decided to go along with it, for now.

Anna tapped her phone a couple times. "Can we talk about when Frank went missing? Like was there anything out of the ordinary at the time? Something you think back on now and see as significant?"

Her friendship with Henry, Helen, Frank's secret plans. Tilly shook her head. There were things she would talk about and things she couldn't.

"Interesting how the Cotters disappeared, too," Anna said.

"The Cotters left because of bankruptcy." This is what people still believed. There was no reason to suggest otherwise. Tilly realized now she needed more time to think all this through before she would be ready to talk. She made a show of looking at her watch. "I know we're just getting started, but I need to get back to work in the shop. I have an order that can't wait. Let's pick this up another time very soon."

"Did I say something to put you off?"

"No." Tilly stood.

Anna quickly put her laptop and notebook into her bag. "Next time I want you to take me to the cabin where you and Frank lived."

"I doubt it's even standing."

"Whatever condition it's in, I need to photograph it for the book. Plus, it might help bring some things back for you. And I have so little time to get your part of the story."

"Okay." Tilly'd think of an excuse later for why they couldn't go.

Tilly got all the way to the door before she stopped short. She'd forgotten about the press. She couldn't go out there.

Anna took her arm. "Look straight ahead—not at them. Don't say anything."

They walked out the door and Anna put herself between Tilly and the reporters, delivering her safely to the shop: something that had seemed insurmountable just a moment before.

chapter twenty-eight

Tilly avoided looking at the reporters and instead focused on the way the light from outside streamed slantwise into the shop, illuminating the powdered wood that fell as she worked on the doors for the sideboard.

Woodworking required keen attention, which usually provided a distraction from thinking about Frank and all the rest of it. But today she couldn't keep her mind on the work. She'd imagined Frank would show up on their birthday, privately and without fanfare, to share an hour with just her. When she'd daydreamed about what their reunion would be like she'd thought he'd explain everything in a way she would understand, even if he would tell her things that were hard to hear. She'd convinced herself that once she had the truth, whatever that was, there would be a kind of peace between them. She wouldn't be haunted any longer by all the things she didn't know. She'd be able to move on with her life.

But Frank hadn't come back quietly and so far he'd offered no answers. She was beginning to question if she even wanted to hear what he had to say. His truth was, after all, his. It would be the version he needed to justify the choices he'd made.

Ruth and Ada, the women who managed the library, knocked on the window of Tilly's shop door, their smiling faces creased like soft apples. Ruth held up a foil-covered plate to the window.

Ada gripped the leash of their Great Dane, Sunny. They showed up like this on occasion out of some sense of duty and politeness that Tilly appreciated more than she wanted to admit. And today they'd had to brave the scary line of reporters, too.

She ushered them inside and Ruth pushed the plate into her hands. "This is from the wedding reception, which was a potluck. The best kind. Figured you could use a little home cooking right about now, especially after that meeting and everything that's been going on."

"Thanks."

"There's a sandwich, coleslaw, and also some of Marybeth's blueberry crumble. You know, everyone loves that." Sunny raised her nose as though in agreement.

Ada and Ruth stood looking at Tilly, backs straight. She shifted her own shoulders to assume their stature, part of Frank's training she'd never entirely shaken. She wanted to ask them if Finn had been to the library searching for news on the dam or Frank. But what if he hadn't. That could mean Frank had contacted Finn somehow and that was something Tilly just couldn't take.

Her stomach growled. "Sounds like we came just in time," Ruth said. Sunny strained toward the plate, drool dripping from the sides of her mouth.

"We wanted to bring you something," Ada said.

These were solid women, ones who served breakfast at the firehall on Saturdays, worked for next to nothing at the library, and took care of the flower beds in front of the post office. They'd been kind to her over the years.

"How are you handling it all? The press and all the attention?" Ada asked, scratching Sunny behind the ear and looking up at her.

"Embarrassed mostly. I don't like people here having to deal with it all. That's the hardest thing."

"Well, it's not your fault." Ada shifted the leash in her hand. "We'll leave you to it. You need anything, let us know."

Tilly watched them walk back toward the group of reporters who tried to get them to talk. They got through with relative ease thanks to Sunny, who was large enough to intimidate, even though she was gentle as could be. On the way back to the house they shared, Ruth and Ada held hands. People in Cottersville mostly ignored this or referred to them as spinsters out of some misplaced sense of politeness or forced ignorance. That's how some of Cottersville dealt with Ada and Ruth, by refusing to acknowledge the obvious so they'd didn't have to acknowledge the truth. Just like how she'd been dealing with Frank.

What was she so afraid of anyway? Finding out Frank wasn't the person she thought he was? That he'd done something unforgivable? That their relationship was based on lies and deception. That she'd wasted her life waiting to find out?

Yes, all of those things. And she hadn't felt this alone since she was thirteen.

Fall 2006

chapter twenty-nine

SEPTEMBER

After Frank didn't come home, Tilly listened all through the next day, during a ceaseless downpour, for sounds of him and Helen. He'd said they would come talk to her, together.

What was keeping him away? He'd been trying to convince Helen of something down at the dam. Maybe it had been to go away with him because Tilly had told him about Henry and so he'd decided not to come back to the cabin. Maybe that's why he'd been in such a hurry. Of course he'd be back for Tilly soon enough. He wasn't going to just leave her. That much she knew.

She kept vigil, staying awake all that night and through the next day and night, imagining one scenario after another. The rain for starters. Frank was laying low until it stopped. Or there'd been some emergency, maybe at the mill, that kept him in town. His escape bag remained where Tilly had stashed it. He'd packed nothing for a trip.

On the third day, she woke, realizing she'd fallen asleep. It took her a long moment to remember Frank was gone. But when she did, a new raven-eyed part of her brain woke up. A part that wouldn't again forget Frank wasn't there. A part that would watch and wait until Frank returned, as long as it took.

His journal lay beside his cot. Tilly allowed herself to read just the last entry.

> *Action is the only form of protest that means anything.*
> *I've used bombs as a means of disruption and sacrificed*
> *my life to do something with relevant consequence.*

So his last thoughts had been about the bombs and dams, not about them, or her. She reread the last part. ...*sacrificed my life to do something with relevant consequence.* What was she, then? An irrelevant consequence?

She closed the journal and put it back, exactly as it had been.

More days and nights passed. Sounds of a football game came from Cottersville: the announcer calling the plays and the cheering crowd. *Quarterback Roy Booker, number thirty-nine, runs it in for a touchdown!*

Things had returned to normal there after the storm. People lived as though nothing had happened. Meanwhile mold grew on the blackberry pie she'd made for Frank. She hardly left the cabin now, afraid she'd miss him when he returned. She slept in her clothes with her shoes next to the cot in case he needed her to go with him right away.

When she was awake thoughts swooped around inside her head like noisy birds. It was her fault after all. She'd let Henry into their lives. Frank's own daughter, the person he trusted the most, had betrayed him. He'd been forced to find a new location for them to hide. They'd have to go even deeper underground than before. It was probably taking him a long time to find that place.

chapter thirty

With a knife Tilly scratched two lines on the wall next to her cot, one for each week she'd been on her own.

Over the next days she read all of her grandmom, Max's, romance novels and considered what it must have been like for Max reading those books with a husband lying next to her, who was not really there. Thinking about that made the love stories seem false and even painful.

Tilly's food stores dwindled, and she started rationing. She thought about leaving. Frank had given her that address. But that was before she'd seen him with Helen. There wasn't anything to hide now. He'd be back.

Outside the cabin, she split logs: maple, pine, walnut, hickory and oak. Over and over, she raised the axe and brought it down into the heart of the wood. Each time the logs splintered with a crack and the smell of sour sap. Wood chips became embedded into her cashmere sweater as she stacked the wood in neat rows capped with end pillars. Frank would see she'd been tough and even prepared them for the winter. If this was a test, then she'd prove herself.

On her second trip to the overlook, the trees along the river were covered in dying leaves. Birds flying too high above to see called out faintly. The wind-swept leaves up toward the gray sky, before dropping them suddenly to the ground. And in the valley below, Cottersville looked starkly normal. Swimming pools were covered. John Hart fed his horses. School buses went by. There was another football game going on. Roy Booker, whoever that was, made another long pass for a cheering crowd. Tilly wondered if Henry had saved her a seat in the school cafeteria on the first day. How many days had gone by before he gave up? Did he even think about her now? Why hadn't he come to see her?

Frank had been gone overnight before. Two nights at the most. Sometimes he'd come back smelling like some perfume. A couple weeks wasn't that long, not if he'd had to travel across the country this time.

chapter thirty-one

OCTOBER

September turned to October. The soybean fields yellowed, and leaves fell, leaving the trees bare-branched. Hawks migrated south on a river of wind toward a steady food supply, while Tilly's fresh food—all the eggs, milk, and apples, even the rotten ones—disappeared. She'd finished the last can of beans and raided the emergency escape bags.

In the woods, black walnuts littered the ground, some of which she ate even though they stained her hands and soured her stomach. She tried to fill herself with the last of the chanterelle and oyster mushrooms she could find in the woods, stuffing them into her mouth raw even though she knew better.

Hunger makes you slow. It makes the waiting a thousand times worse because you're reminded of every minute of every day by a gnawing that never stops. Time was now a trial to endure hour by waking hour. She made a fourth mark on the wall.

In the cupboards, all that remained were a couple tablespoons of Crisco, some sugar, and a quarter bag of flour infested with mealworms. She was down to the last three scraps of toilet paper.

She thought about going to town but didn't want to risk being seen. Frank hadn't wanted her there and she'd already done enough to betray him. It had occurred to her that maybe the FBI had him. He would have told them nothing about her.

That's what they'd agreed to. And in that case, maybe she should go to the address Frank had given her. But she just couldn't leave if there was a chance he would be back.

She decided to read Frank's journal from start to finish. Maybe that would give her clues about what he was up to.

He'd started off writing about his dad's accident. He described reading the novel his dad had given him, *The Monkey Wrench Gang*. At the time, he wanted to be like the main character, an ecoterrorist named George Hayduke. The thing he'd been most drawn to was Hayduke's biggest aspiration: blowing up big dams out west. Frank had insisted Tilly read all kinds of books, but never that one. Not even after she'd repeatedly asked him to bring it home from the library.

Frank wrote about his early days sabotaging Cotter Paper, inspired by the acts of ecoterrorism he'd read about in the novel. He described slashing the tires of the company trucks, gluing the locks shut on doors, and spraying graffiti to send a message that the company was harming the natural world and so he would harm them in return. That's when he'd met Helen.

He wrote a long section on her, describing how in the middle of the night he'd been spray-painting the Cotter Paper Mill smokestack across the river with a quote from Thoreau: "We do not ride the railroad; it rides upon us." And Helen, who'd been watching him from behind a tree, had just walked up and announced she was a reporter. Except she looked way too young and Frank figured out she was a senior in high school. He told her to get lost. But she'd stayed and kept talking to him. She showed up again a few nights later. And then again, gaining his trust over time. She'd heard the story about what happened to his pop and was outraged by it. She understood what he was doing and why.

They'd kept talking over many months and she proved smarter and more savvy than he'd first realized. She understood his actions were a political act before he did. She claimed she could help other people understand this. She'd written some stories for the school paper that eventually got reprinted in the local news. It turned out that even though people might not have agreed with his approach, they could understand this wasn't just about vandalism. At least some people were interested in the reasons for his actions.

All of this was right after Frank's dad had died when he knew he had to figure out what to do next. Helen had shown him the importance of communicating the broader picture of his actions to the public. Her articles got people talking about pollution and clean air and water in ways they hadn't before. And that excited Frank more than anything.

His adoration of Helen was clear in the pages he devoted to her. There was no mention of the pregnancy in his journal, perhaps to protect her.

The last thing Frank had written about Helen was that he wanted to keep working with her. But she had other ideas for her career. So when they parted ways, he'd written his own op-eds. But he couldn't pull off what she had, no matter how hard he tried.

His journal went on about how he'd decided he wanted to be more than a nuisance and settled on taking out smaller dams in the Northeast as his main mission. There was nothing about Tilly or their life in Frank's journal. Not one thing about how she'd been his partner. Not even her name or mention of a daughter. This was Frank's story. He'd told her that all they had was each other. But only one line near the end of his journal could have been meant for her:

If it doesn't go the way I planned, look for me at 50.

Did he really mean to stay away for seventeen years? She thought again of her green scarf dangling halfway out of his pocket when he'd been arguing with Helen. Had he taken it as a keepsake because he knew he wasn't coming back? But then why would he have rushed off that morning without a proper good-bye?

Frank knew she was done with moving from place to place. She'd made that only too clear. The more she thought about it, the more she realized he'd probably come to Cottersville to blow up the dam, to finally settle the score. He and Helen had been standing right in front of the dam when Tilly'd seen them together. Tilly made no secret about wanting a normal life instead of the one they'd shared, so Frank had been forced to make false promises and take a new partner. They'd been a team until he couldn't rely on her anymore. Maybe now he'd decided to pursue his relevant consequences without her.

She hid his journal in the cupboard beneath the sink. If he was coming back, he'd have to see her if he wanted it.

On a day in which the sunlight felt especially thin and warmthless, she went to the spring, the source of Stone Creek, near the rookery. She took off her clothes, including the blue sweater that was now filthy, snagged and torn. Sharp edges of wind lashed out as she settled herself in the cold, shallow spring water, pressing her back to the pebbled bottom hoping to feel something.

She lay back and stared straight up at the geese flying over-head, urging each other on with plaintive cries, the impulse to go rising in their chests. She nestled deeper into the water, so only the surface of her face remained exposed to the air. Water filled her ears, muffling everything around her. The cold pene-trated her limbs and seeped into her bones. All secrets were wit-nessed, and this creek and these woods were witnessing hers. Frank had left her, and she didn't know what to do. She still thought he'd come back. But if he didn't, she wasn't sure she could survive on her own for a lot longer.

She watched her own breath rise above her in white puffs, like some repetitive reminder she was still there.

The nights grew colder and for the first time the sweater plus both blankets weren't enough. She didn't dare light the wood stove since she was no longer hiding in plain sight. Boiled creek water dampened the hunger pains only to a point. She made cakes from the last of the infested flour, sugar and Crisco, and ate every bit.

The sixth mark on the wall had her feeling like she was at the bottom of a well so deep she could no longer see daylight. Her thoughts still swirled around and around reasons why Frank had left and stayed away. She talked to herself, sometimes speaking as Frank. Or Henry. One, two: all the people she knew in the world. She hadn't seen Marvel in weeks, yet there was no way she'd been able to fly south.

The grass around the cabin withered and the air had the musty scent of rotted leaves. The asters she and Frank had planted off the front porch bloomed purple. She snapped off every stem. From the cabin windows she ripped down the lemon curtains, cut them into small pieces and scattered them over the garbage dump among the other broken bits of the past near the outhouse.

When she did manage to sleep, she kept dreaming of running through dark woods, terrified. Frank was there, too, racing ahead before he vanished. Each time she woke to the realization he was gone because that raven-eyed part of her brain would not let her forget for a second.

If this was Frank's way of testing her, she wasn't sure now she could pass. She was out of food. Out of toilet paper, soap, toothpaste, and tampons, although she hadn't gotten her period over the last month, probably because she wasn't eating enough.

Late one night in week six, she pulled one of Frank's sweatshirts over her sweater, stuffed a cloth sack into the pocket, and started for town.

chapter thirty-two

The bright October moon made it easy to get down Short Mountain, but it was less welcome at the edge of town where Tilly would have to step away from the tree cover. Then the moonlight became more like a spotlight directed at her. She felt paralyzed, unable to move from the edge of the forest. Instead, she surveyed the scene around her looking for a way forward.

The cemetery and the homes surrounding it, were all aglow in pale, powdery light. Every shadow was a place where police or FBI could be crouching, watching, ready to pounce.

To the right of her stood the mill building. On the left, there was John Hart's house and horse stables with the firehall on the other side of that. No one appeared to be out. Frank had said John Hart was nice, so perhaps he would understand someone stealing out of hunger. Maybe he wouldn't call the police.

She stepped away from the trees cautiously, expecting the worst. The time it took her to walk to the Hart house seemed like an eternity. But then she was standing next to the Hart's clothesline hanging low with laundry. The extra-large white t-shirts, jeans and camo sweatshirts had to belong to John. She guessed the set of smaller jeans and shirts were his wife's.

Next to the house four bikes were dumped into a pile and she imagined the kids back just in time for dinner, leaving the bikes in a heap before running inside. In a nearby sandbox, they'd carved a racetrack into the sand with small cars positioned in different ways. A collection of action figures and Barbies watched the race from outside the track, some of them with arms raised. A small teddy bear was positioned in the center wearing sunglasses and holding a black and white checkered flag.

Tilly kept to the shadows created by the house and crept to a window. She peered inside what turned out to be the kitchen, lit by a small utility light over the stove. Crayon drawings and photos covered the outside of the refrigerator. On the windowsill above the sink, an ivy plant growing in one long piece was draped over the window sash and threaded over a series of nails framing a group of photos hanging in two columns on the wall next to the sink. The first column began with a wedding picture: John and his wife. Under that they posed with a baby. This was followed by the two of them holding a second child with a toddler nearby. Then a third and fourth baby were added. Next to the family photos, another column of pictures featured horses, dogs, cats, and what looked like guinea pigs.

No one seemed to be awake in the house. She heard nothing.

A small path led to a back door. She followed it until she stood staring at a doorknob. A bead of sweat traveled down the middle of her back. Her stomach growled, loudly, and one of John's horses neighed, stomping in its paddock. She froze, sure someone must have heard either her stomach or the horse. She imagined the horse was trying to warn the family she was there, an intruder. She strained to hear any sound, but there was only the wind.

She put her hand on the doorknob, held her breath, and turned. It was unlocked. She gently nudged, praying the door wouldn't stick. It swung open into the Hart's back pantry and she breathed more easily than she had since she'd stepped away from the forest edge.

Tilly stared at the all the food for a long while, not quite believing. She lifted a bag of rice and a can of beans and placed them as noiselessly as possible into her bag. She took bouillon cubes, chocolate drops, a canister of nuts, a box of pasta, and a container of powdered milk. She stuffed a box of baking soda into her sweatshirt pocket. That'd work as a toothpaste and soap for now. A roll of paper towels under her arm would do for toilet paper and pads if her period came back.

She picked up a pencil laying on one of the shelves. On the wall above the light switch she wrote: *Sorry about taking food from your family. I'm just so hungry.*

Closing the door softly behind her, she made her way back up the mountain feeling a great sense of relief both because she hadn't been caught and because, at least over the next week, she'd have food. She could continue to wait for Frank, at least a little while longer.

September 2023

chapter thirty-three

From her kitchen Tilly stared at the thick gray clouds hanging in the sky and watched as wind scattered leaves across the grass, piling them high against the cemetery wall. To avoid the reporters, she went out the back door, wearing a hat and sunglasses, and walked to the library the long way around.

She and Ruth were the only ones there, aside from Sunny, Ruth's Great Dane. Tilly pointed to the computer in the back. "May I?"

"Go ahead, hon," Ruth said.

If Finn had searched the library computer, Tilly wanted to use the same browser in case it made a difference. A search on images of Cotter Paper yielded dozens of photos of the mill. Most with Paul Cotter, but some with Helen, too. Tilly took a moment to study Helen's face. She was pretty, but what you noticed was a knowing intelligence in her eyes and her upturned chin suggested a fierce independence. Not unlike Frank's.

Finn would've had no trouble getting a clear idea of what his great-grandpa, Paul, and the mill might have looked like. He was clever enough to have searched the same keywords and could easily translate what he found into paintings.

Tilly turned to Ruth. "Finn Cotter been on the computer lately?"

"Not that I noticed. I guess it's possible he was here when Ada was working. I can ask her when I get home."

Tilly turned back to the screen thinking of Finn's paintings and the way his hand had shaken when she'd insisted he write out what was on his mind. She'd forced that on him more for herself than for him and she felt ashamed now thinking about it.

Ruth walked over. "You all right, hon?"

Tilly wiped her eyes but kept her face to the screen, not wanting Ruth to see what was already obvious. "I just wish sometimes that things weren't so hard." Tilly hated that her voice shook.

"You'll figure it out. Whatever it is."

Tilly glanced at her, red eyes and all.

"Although, some problems are too big to handle on your own. You can let people in to help, you know."

Tilly nodded, not willing to risk actual words.

"And sometimes you have to make peace with what's out of your hands. People have talked about me and Ada for years. That used to bother me."

"I haven't heard people talk." Tilly felt wrong as soon as the words were out of her mouth, as though this lie might make Ruth feel better. Tilly knew how it felt when people denied what you knew to be true.

"We're lesbians in a small town and people talk about us in all kinds of ways. For some we're inconvenient to the way they wish the world was. But the important thing is we live as we are, and at the end of the day, most people respect that. At least anyone worth knowing does." Ruth patted her arm. "People know you're not your father."

Tilly felt relief at hearing Ruth say this out loud.

"Did you find what you were after?"

"Not entirely. Are the Cotter High yearbooks still around?"

Ruth pointed over Tilly's shoulder to the back corner. "Next to the magazines on the left side, bottom shelf."

Tilly wanted to try to find out more about Helen. Maybe that would help her figure out why Finn was painting the paper mill office. Paul and Helen were the last people to work there. And that had been the last place she'd seen Helen and Frank together.

Tilly went to the back and pulled the yearbook from when

Helen would have been eighteen. She flipped to Helen's school photo.

"Ruth?"

"Yes?" she called from her desk.

"What do you know about Helen ..." Tilly looked at her name in the yearbook, "... Price?"

Ruth joined Tilly in the back. "Bright, curious, independent. Not many like her. She was a great writer, even back in high school. She came into the library a lot researching this and that." Ruth's eyebrows came together. "But then she took off unexpectantly right after graduation. Caused quite a stir, as you can imagine. But she was back a few months later. Although quieter. Something had happened to her, I'm pretty sure." Ruth seemed to be thinking more carefully about her next words. "Back then people handled hard things with silence. She and her parents were no different. I remember it took quite a while for her to kind of get back to herself. But she did eventually write again. Best the *Bucks County Mirror* ever had. She married Paul Cotter much later on, but a year or so after that, you know, they left." Ruth gave her a side glance.

Had Frank had known about Paul and Helen's marriage before coming to Cottersville? Either way it would have made him crazy. And what did any of this have to do with Finn's paintings? Tilly thought hard, trying to remember the details. There was the creek running so high. Tilly remembered how much it had rained before and after Frank left.

She went back to the computer and searched for news of storms around the time of the disappearances and found headlines about two hurricanes that had come up the coast and blown inland, one after another, causing heavy, sustained rain over the whole region. Maybe Finn was painting the day Frank disappeared.

Tilly stared at the ceiling, blank and uncomplicated. Her mind worked on the fabric of the past, trying to realign what she'd thought was true with what she now knew. Beside her, the dog Sunny made little huffing noises as her enormous legs and feet moved like she was chasing some kind of dream animal that remained out of reach.

chapter thirty-four

From the library, Tilly went to Henry's.

He saw her coming, because when she got to his door, he stepped outside to meet her, turning toward the racket of heavy machinery over at the dam and frowning. Thankfully most of the press had gone for the time being, probably to cover a bigger story. When Henry turned back to talk to her, the sun, low in the sky, made a glare on his glasses, hiding his eyes from hers.

"I came to see how Finn's doing after the meeting last night," she said.

"He's worse off."

Tilly wasn't surprised to hear this, given how he'd looked. "Still painting the same thing?"

Henry crossed his arms. He was angry with her: likely blamed her. "Yeah, but it's messier. Like he's having trouble 'talking,' even with his brush."

There was hurt in his voice, the longstanding kind that had been there all these years and never healed over. She wanted to explain herself. "Last night, I finally understood that, for you, there's more to the dam than the Cotter Paper legacy."

He gave her a sharp look. "You've only ever seen your side. No matter who might be hurt."

"I didn't know anyone would be hurt."

"There's a lot you don't know."

Goosebumps rose on her arms as wind pulled leaves from the oak tree above. "I just came from the library. I went to see if Finn might have been there looking up stuff for those paintings. Ruth didn't remember seeing him. She was going to ask Ada about it. But in the meantime, I think I figured something out."

"What?"

"Finn's painted the creek full of water, almost over its banks. Remember how much it rained right around the time of the disappearances? When I saw Frank and Helen together that last time, they were standing in front of the creek, and it looked a lot like it does in Finn's paintings."

Henry gave her a searching look, like he was trying to make up his mind about telling her something. But the moment passed.

"Can you tell me more about Finn?" she asked.

"He won't even look at me." He let out an anguished breath and leaned back against the house. "I just want to keep him safe. I'm afraid for him." He glanced at her. "I'm sorry if I've come off as angry. I'm just really scared."

Tilly reached up and squeezed his arm.

"Finn's going to his mom's tomorrow. Maybe that will help bring him out of whatever this is."

Thinking of Finn struggling so much made Tilly's eyes well up. She was conscious of appearing melodramatic and self-indulgent, especially now in front of Henry. This was his son after all.

"Didn't think I'd ever see that." He reached into his shirt pocket and produced a small pack of tissues.

She wiped her eyes for the second time in an hour. "You carry around tissues?"

He handed her one. "Yard mowed before anyone is even up for the day. Snow shoveled first. Enough wood split for the next two years. Don't need nothing from no one. Taking care of yourself, thank you very much." He gave her a wry smile. "It figures Finn chose you as his special person. I've wondered over that. Haven't you?"

She dropped her eyes, unsure of what to say next when so much needed to be said. The sun slipped away leaving behind a sky edged in gray and pink pearly light. She leaned back against the house next to Henry remembering how easy it used to be between them. What had it done to Finn—she and Henry against each other all these years? "I noticed when I was here before you had a hard time looking at those paintings."

He stared off into the distance for a long moment. "Finn's painting stuff he shouldn't know nothing about."

Before she could ask what he meant, Ruth and Ada came walking up the driveway. "Hey," Ada said. "Ruth mentioned you were asking about Finn. He was in the library during my last shift. He had a list written down and was searching on the computer."

Tilly and Henry glanced at each other. "Did he say anything about what he was looking for?" Henry asked.

Ada shook her head.

"Anything else you remember?" Tilly asked.

Ada thought about it. "There was a picture of a boat at the top of the paper he had with him, like from a notepad. But I'm not sure that helps."

Ruth pulled Ada by the arm. "I managed to leave the lights on at the library, so we're headed that way. But I'm glad to see you two talking together." Ruth winked at Tilly before they walked off.

Crystal stepped out onto her porch, looking ready for a confrontation. "Wish those reporters would leave this town alone. Can't do anything without one of them jumping out to accost me." She gave Tilly a resentful eye. "Ever since the meeting, I'm worried about the dam. What if Frank Stone shows up here before they get it out of there?"

Finn came out the back door and saw Henry and Tilly standing together. For a moment, a hopeful look replaced whatever dark thing had taken over. He even smiled at them. But that disappeared as soon as he noticed the heavy machinery at the dam. He retreated into the house and Henry followed.

Crystal, still in her feisty little moment, glared at Tilly expecting an explanation. But she had no response nor the energy or inclination to invent one. She left Crystal standing there, knowing she was acting rudely, and walked home in the dusk now deepening into pale black and blue. The night air, cooler than the creek, created a rising mist spreading outward. As she got closer to the creek, she could just make out the silhouette of a great blue heron lifting from the water, its flight, slightly irregular, made her think of Marvel for the first time in a long while. Was it possible she was still alive?

Fall 2006

chapter thirty-five

NOVEMBER

The eighth scratch on the wall meant it was November. Tilly's next trip to town was almost as easy as the first. It took a few tries to find an unlocked door and this time she had to go all the way into the kitchen to find the food, but the place was quiet as sleeping cats. The people who lived there organized their mail by the front door in slots labeled: Bills, Letters, Catalogs, and Outgoing. Letters and envelopes were addressed to either Ada Parks or Ruth Harper or sometimes both. Their paychecks suggested they both worked at the library. Two jackets hung by the door: one denim, the other tweed. The living room was all shadow and silhouette, but Tilly could see the books were neatly shelved. On closer inspection, she found them ordered alphabetically by author. On top of the shelves were photos of Ruth and Ada, who were roughly the same age. Tilly thought at first they might be sisters, but they looked too different.

She scored another bag full of food. And this time real soap on the sink.

After that she walked to town after dark even when she didn't need supplies. She was interested in how people lived and took to watching from outside windows trying to imagine her own life in Cottersville.

She visited the Hart family most often, coming after dark when they were all still awake, but not yet in bed. Frank had been right about John. He kissed his wife often and listened carefully when his children spoke. From the mail in the box in front of their house, Tilly figured out his wife's name was Mary. They had two boys and two girls, all below the age of about ten. Besides the horses in the paddock, the Harts had a dog, who apparently didn't bark, three cats, and several guinea pigs the kids liked to play with before bed.

Tilly also enjoyed visiting Ruth and Ada's house, with all their books. Those two laughed a lot and often talked late into the night, way past the Hart's bedtime. Tilly realized after a while they were in love. They and the Harts represented the way she'd imagined Cottersville to be: a loving home.

But she saw other things, too. People who were probably well-behaved or seemed normal until they got behind their own doors. Like the man who beat his wife. Or the woman who ate cereal for dinner every night in front of the television, shoving in huge spoonsful of the stuff while she cried.

There was the couple who had dinner together without speaking and went to bed in separate rooms. And a woman who started each evening with one bottle of wine and then another before passing out on the couch. Her daughter, who was close to Tilly's age, sometimes couldn't wake her. At the house beside Henry's, Tilly'd never found anyone home, but after seeing the shrine on the mantle covered with photos of a boy in a football uniform and R O Y spelled out in block wooden letters next to a framed jersey, she realized this was the quarterback, Roy Booker's house.

Back up the mountain at the rookery, yellow flowering stalks of mullein leaned heavily over ground cracked with thin ice. Snow would be coming before long. When that happened, she'd be easily tracked. She had to stockpile enough supplies to get through a few weeks in case snow lay for a while.

Tilly tried to build up her supplies, but found doors locked in town. Almost everyone had a light on outside. They were onto her. She tried the garbage at Fredrick's, the town store, and lifted a lid on one of the cans. A large rat-shaped creature, bewhiskered, with a shaggy coat and button-eyes bared a large number of sharp teeth. She stifled a scream and it fell on its back. She stood gaping when a moment later the opossum climbed out of the garbage can and waddled away.

This reminded Tilly of the baby opossums she and Frank had rescued before they'd moved to Cottersville. What had happened to them? Had they survived?

She looked into the garbage can for other opossums but found only a discarded newspaper, with this headline: **No Trace of Paul and Helen Cotter, Missing Now for Eight Weeks.**

Tilly stared at the words for a long time. Her brain felt slow, like it was full of mud. Only little by little was she able to take in the meaning of that headline: *Paul and Helen Cotter had disappeared at the same time as Frank.* She turned this over in her mind, struggling now to remember the details of her last conversation with Henry, when he'd tried to tell her about Frank and Helen, and she'd pushed him away. So Frank's disappearance was related to the Cotters? But how? And what did it mean?

She tucked the newspaper under her arm and walked to the cemetery. Henry's house was darker than the others on the street. There were no lights on, not even the outdoor light above the garage. She'd avoided even looking at his house as she'd wandered around Cottersville over the last weeks. She'd been too afraid of finding him living happily, going to school, having forgotten about her. She'd been thinking if she got to know other people in town she wouldn't need him anymore. But now she saw no one was even living at his house.

She held the newspaper up to the glow of moonlight to be able to read the story. Paul and Helen Cotter had disappeared with only the clothes on their backs, Helen's purse, and Paul's wallet. Their car had been found at the bus station ten miles away. The story said Cotter Paper faced bankruptcy and the police thought they'd left to escape the consequences and responsibility of the company's failure. There was nothing about Frank.

So Henry hadn't said anything to the police about Frank, or her. He was mentioned only once at the end of the news article. He'd gone to live with his uncle. Tilly didn't know where the uncle lived, but she knew where Henry went to school.

chapter thirty-six

Tilly got to the school before light and hid behind a wall where she could watch the buses arrive unseen. All at once a throng of noisy kids showed up.

Two girls walked past, shoulders hunched, speaking in hushed tones. One of them was the girl whose mother drank herself to sleep every night on the couch. John Hart's oldest son walked behind them.

She scanned the crowd and realized some of these kids stood out from the others. Tilly couldn't put her finger on why exactly. It was as though the more invisible ones tried not to be seen even as they watched the others—not full on, but kind of sideways, like they were interested in learning the secret but didn't want anyone to know.

Tilly understood she was watching a game she knew nothing about. Or maybe it was like poker. Some of them were better than others at using what they had to get what they wanted. This is what Frank had been talking about. There was a code under which these kids spoke or didn't speak to one another. Rules Tilly could see were in place but didn't understand. This was part of the system he'd been talking about and why he hadn't wanted her in school.

Henry now walked toward her, head down. He was thinner, like something essential had been sucked out of him. He'd probably wondered why she hadn't come before this.

She whistled an oriole call, which was all wrong for the season, but he didn't look up. She whistled again, louder, exaggerating the notes and he stopped abruptly, searching around. When he saw her, his eyes widened in utter surprise. He got a hold of himself and tilted his head toward the direction of the fort up the mountain, mouthing *after school.*

When Henry emerged from the trees, Tilly ran to him, throwing her arms around his neck. It took her a long moment to realize he wasn't hugging back. She stepped away, embarrassed and hurt. "I thought they took you with them," he said.

"Who?"

"Frank and—" He squinted at her. "You look terrible. Are you even eating?"

She glanced down at the mangled, filthy blue sweater he'd once thought pretty. "I saw a newspaper that said your grandpa and Helen are gone, too. Do you know what happened?"

Henry's face turned more shadow-eyed and distant. He'd been essentially alone, too, all this time. Probably as scared and confused as her. Heartbroken, too.

"I saw Frank and Helen together at the mill, right before they disappeared. They were fighting about something." She said this to confirm what he'd told her the last time they'd talked. That Frank had been seeing Helen. "And I found out something else." Tilly swallowed hard. This had to be related to whatever had happened. "I think Helen's my mother."

This made Henry pause. His drawn look yielded to something more alarmed. He took her by the shoulders, squeezing too hard. "What do you mean you were there? What else did you see?"

"They were fighting, like I said. And Frank saw me and said something to Helen that made me realize she's my mother. That's what I'm trying to tell you."

Henry shook his head like he didn't believe her or that her news wasn't the important thing. "But what did you see?"

She was suddenly scared of what he knew. What did he think Frank could have done? What had *he* seen?

She pulled loose from his grasp and ran back in the cabin.

She'd leave Cottersville at first light. Henry's eyes told her what Frank probably already knew. That he'd be blamed for whatever had happened to the Cotters. And there was no way he could come back.

chapter thirty-seven

Someone pounded on the cabin door in the middle of the night. *Frank. Finally!* Tilly jumped out of bed and ran to the door.

"Police! Open up!"

She froze.

"Tilly Stone, are you in there? This is Officer Williams. State Police."

Tilly quietly slipped on the shoes by her cot. "I'm not dressed. Don't come in!"

She slid open the back window, climbed out and landed hard on the frozen ground outside.

"Check the back. Move!"

She sprinted toward the heron rookery. *Don't get caught,* Frank's voice said inside her head. *You'll be in the system.*

"Stop! We're here to help!"

She ran for the thickest part of the woods. Flashlight beams crisscrossed the ground, reaching her ankles.

"There!" A voice yelled behind her.

Heavy footsteps and grunts of exertion, her own and theirs, punctured the quiet. But she knew these woods. They didn't. She pushed herself faster even as her lungs and legs burned.

To stay together we have to be free.

A break in the tangle of vines lay just ahead. She jumped a log and ducked through the vines into a dark hole in the brush.

She sat there, still as a rabbit, slowing her breath into silence.

Tunneled lights bobbed and weaved in the woods around her. "Where'd she go? You see her?"

She was too far in for their lights to reach. She settled in to wait.

Hours passed. They kept searching and calling, trying to talk her out. "Little girl, we're here to help."

Little girl. That was funny. She wondered how long it would take them to give up. As soon as they left, she would get her stuff and go. She shivered and crouched into a ball to try to keep warm.

The police didn't go. She had a thought they might bring in dogs. She wasn't sure what she would do then. Her stomach growled and she willed it quiet.

A thought bubbled up. *What if she walked out and gave herself up?* She quickly dismissed the idea, scrunching herself into a tighter fold. She stayed in that position, listening to footfalls in the woods as they kept searching. Weren't they getting tired by now?

Her feet were numb, and her legs began to cramp. She switched position and sat on the ground for a while. It was too cold to keep doing that for long. She returned to the low squat, rubbing her hands up and down her arms to get the blood moving. Overhead the moon crept slowly across the sky as the minutes ticked by, one by one.

When light broke through the trees, the cold had sunk deep into her bones. She felt slow and could hardly stay awake. She trained her eyes on the sun and watched it climb the sky willing it to warm her. In those hours the thought of giving herself up came back and formed into a more solid possibility. Because what if she could find a way to stay in Cottersville and have some kind of life? She probably didn't have to go to school if she didn't want to.

She heard dogs in the distance. She waited until she was sure they were getting closer, that they were coming for her. She couldn't hide from dogs. And she wasn't going to let them trap her. If she was going to be caught, it would be her choice, not theirs. And maybe this was how it was supposed to be. Maybe she was supposed to stay in Cottersville. Frank had brought her here. She listened to the barks and bellowing getting closer. Blood hounds. They weren't far away now. She crawled out of her hiding place and stepped through the vines out into the open. There was sudden yell and a rush of footfalls.

And then everything went black.

chapter thirty-eight

Dead flies lay at the bottom of the long fluorescent light hanging above Tilly. Her head ached. She turned her face away from the brightness of the light. A woman in a flowered dress sat on a chair beside her.

Tilly, feeling slow and fuzzy, squinted at the tag hanging around the woman's neck: "CRYSTAL BOOKER, FAMILY SERVICES."

This woman, Crystal Booker, forced the kind of smile Frank used with people to pretend a friendliness he didn't feel. Tilly had a growing awareness of machines beeping around her. She was in a hospital.

She closed her eyes, wanting to retreat back into sleep to escape a fear now rushing up inside. She hadn't thought this through very well.

"Tilly?" the woman said.

The police had come. She'd allowed herself to be caught. She tried to work out how she'd gotten from that moment to this one. But that didn't really matter. She'd been foolish.

"Tilly Stone, I think you can hear me." The woman's voice sounded like rusty hinges forced open. "I need to ask you some questions. And I'm not going anywhere until I get answers, so we might as well get started."

"How do you know my name?" A sharper pain stabbed her head when she spoke.

"From the police."

Tilly reached up and touched her head. It was bandaged.

"You fell and hit your head. You were knocked out. When you came to, I understand you were confused. That's what the police said. But you did mention your name and your father before you passed out again. Where is your father?"

"On ... a trip." Each word was a new shot of pain.

The woman, Crystal, looked at Tilly like she was some pitiful thing. "After a certain amount of time, if a parent leaves, we have to consider they may not come back."

Tilly turned away from her and stared straight up into the light above her, hoping the throbbing the light caused would make her pass out. She didn't want to talk to this woman.

"No matter how you feel right now, Tilly, you're not alone." Crystal Booker sounded like one of those prerecorded commercials Tilly heard on the radio all the time.

When she realized she wasn't going to be able to knock herself out, Tilly flung back the covers, and stood. A dizziness hit, and she grabbed the edge of the bed.

"Lie down!"

A needle in her arm, taped in place, was connected to a long tube attached to a bag full of liquid. *Hospitals pump people with poison.* Tilly's head spun and she swayed. She had to get out of this place.

"You've got a concussion. Get back in bed." Crystal stood and pressed a button. "Nurse!"

They'd taken her clothes and dressed her in a thin gown. Where was her sweater? "Give me my clothes."

Crystal pushed the button again. "Nurse!" Tilly ripped the needle out of her arm.

"Tilly! Do not ...."

She reached for the door handle.

"...open that door. Don't!"

She ran down the hall, past nurses who looked up in surprise. Tilly stopped only when she was blocked by a crowd of people. Lights flashed and everyone spoke at once. She covered her eyes with her hands as they yelled questions. It was like too many animal paths to follow and she couldn't understand anything they were saying. She sank to her knees, overwhelmed.

"Nurse! Help me." Crystal pulled Tilly to her feet. "Get these reporters out of here!"

Tilly let Crystal drag her back down the hallway and into the room where Crystal pointed to the bed. "Lie down," she said, as though Tilly were a dog.

Stumbling over to the rumpled sheets and pillow, sucking for air, Tilly fell into bed. She'd have to find another way out. But right now it was like someone had sunk a knife into her brain, slowly and methodically, and wedged it there just when she needed to think. She couldn't breathe right. Crystal didn't seem to notice.

Someone else came into the room. "I'm Nurse Connie, honey." This woman ran a warm hand gently over Tilly's arm and gave it a reassuring squeeze. "I'd like to put the needle back in your arm to give you something for the pain and help you relax. This is all a lot to take in, I know. I'm sorry about all those people out there. They're gone now. Would it be okay if I put the needle in? I promise to be gentle."

Her head hurt so badly that her eyes teared. This nurse didn't seem like she wanted to hurt her. Tilly nodded.

"Lie still."

Afterward it was quieter. Her head didn't hurt, and she could breathe again. But when Crystal started asking questions, it took her a long time to turn in her direction.

"Was your dad holding you against your will?"

Tilly lay there wanting to answer, but the words were out of reach.

"How did you survive all these weeks?"

"He's. On a trip."

"And your mother?"

Tilly tried shaking her head, but it had grown too heavy. Her eyes closed now against her will, even as she fought to stay awake. She couldn't trust Crystal. She'd already blabbed her name and told them she had a father. This was a hospital. She was in the system. She'd done everything wrong.

"What are you going to do now that your dad's gone?"

Had Crystal said this, or was it her own thought? Either way she didn't have any idea.

chapter thirty-nine

Tilly opened her eyes sometime in the night. Her face was wet with tears she didn't even know she'd been crying.

She got up to find a way out of the hospital. But then fell. Nurse Connie was there and helped her back to bed before giving her another shot of blissful still darkness.

Tilly woke next to the television blaring and, beside her, sat Crystal Booker. Thirsty, Tilly reached for a pitcher next to a vase of sunflowers. Crystal quickly shut off the TV. "Nurse Connie brought those flowers. You'll have to thank her." Tilly didn't like the way she talked as though it was her job to correct and instruct.

On the windowsill, Tilly saw Teddy bears, flowers, and cards lined up.

"People have sent you things."

"Why?"

"Well, they feel bad for you."

Every repeating blip of a machine in her room reminded Tilly where she was and what she'd gotten herself into.

Crystal folded her hands in her lap and cleared her throat. "Now that you've had a couple days' rest we need to talk about what comes next."

Tilly gave her a blank look. She was leaving this place. That's what was coming next.

"After you leave the hospital, you'll need a place to stay. So we need to discuss foster parents."

Tilly set the glass on the table beside her. "Foster what?"

Crystal regarded her with wide eyes, rattled that she might not know what this meant.

"Like ... substitute parents. Sometimes it's for a short time. Sometimes longer."

Tilly stared past Crystal out the window, watching sleet fall. It weighed down branches with a sluggish heaviness. For some reason it made her imagine Marvel, standing with her broken wing while predators circled. "I don't need foster parents."

"Well, I'm just mentioning it, for now. But we'll have to talk seriously about it soon."

Crystal's cell rang and she answered, her voice transforming from artificial to something warm and real. "The playoffs! That's wonderful, Roy! I'm so happy for you sweetheart!"

Roy. Tilly looked at the tag around Crystal's neck again. Crystal Booker. Her house stood next to Henry's: the one with the shrine for Roy Booker, the quarterback.

Outside, the sleet turned into tiny, hard pellets that hit the window in rapid clicks. Tilly wanted to be out there rather than trapped by floor to ceiling mauve and beige smelling of ammonia and piss. Maybe Frank had figured out where she was by now. He could have been watching from somewhere close by this whole time. Maybe he would come and get her now that she really needed him.

The next morning the gray sky was so blank it looked bleached. Short Mountain was just a low dark smudge against the horizon on another boxed-in November day that made Tilly's insides feel like cardboard.

Crystal dozed in the chair beside her bed. The television was on again; this time it was the news.

"... Tilly Stone, rescued after living on her own in the woods for nine weeks. I'm here with young Henry Cotter, the boy who discovered the girl's whereabouts. Henry, tell us how you found her."

The reporter thrust the microphone at Henry. He stood outside a house Tilly didn't recognize. His uncle's place most likely. "I was walking in the woods."

"And that's when you saw her?"

He hesitated.

"Son?"

"Yeah, that's right."

"Anything else you can tell us?"

"No."

"Well, you're a real hero. You know that?"

Henry looked off, away from the camera. "It's not a big deal."

"It's a very big deal. We need more young men like you." The reporter patted him on the back and Henry walked off suddenly. The reporter turned to the camera. "Back to you, Peter."

Crystal cleared her throat and snapped off the TV. "Glad you're awake."

So, it had been Henry who'd called the police. She should have realized that before. His friendship had meant everything to her. She'd lied to Frank for him. Chosen to be loyal to him *instead* of Frank. And he'd ratted her out. It was only a matter of time before he told someone about Frank and Helen. Everyone would assume, like Henry, that Frank had done something terrible.

"How's your head?" Crystal asked.

Tilly kept her eyes straight ahead, refusing to acknowledge her. It was strange how parts of her brain could continue to function when other parts had come to a complete stop.

"You need to know, in case you haven't already figured it out. Your story's on every major news channel. People want to know how you survived. Everyone's talking about Tilly Stone."

Crystal said this with a strange excitement in her voice. Tilly shifted, uncomfortable, unable to relax. Where was Nurse Connie?

"At least the attention is making it easy to place you."

"Place me?"

"A family right here in Cottersville is ready to take you in. Nice couple. Older, stable, with good values."

"I take care of myself."

"But they want to take care of you. Maybe you should let them."

Tilly ended the conversation by closing her eyes. She wasn't going to any foster family. Frank had given her an address. She should have gone there from the beginning. Now she just had to figure out how to get out of this hospital.

chapter forty

Later that day the police found Frank's journal where Tilly'd hidden it under the pots and pans in the cabin. So now they knew he wasn't just the father who'd left her, but also the bomber the FBI apparently really had been looking for.

News reports blared from the television in her room because Crystal had left it on when she'd left the room abruptly after her cell phone started ringing when the news broke. Now Tilly didn't know how to turn the TV off. Reporters talked about the similarities between Frank and Ted K.—the bombs, the manifesto, the belief system—and speculated about connections between the two of them.

The ceaseless noise in the hospital had already worn Tilly down. She'd lived all her life with only one person and always in the woods and so being in the hospital was too much and all at once. And now any small moments of quiet she'd had before Frank's journal was discovered vanished. Her name was mentioned while the television showed old photos of Frank from back when he was still probably in high school and fake drawings of what he might look like now. At least those drawings didn't look like him.

Nurses and doctors came in an endless loop not only to poke, prod, and question her the same way multiple times a day as they had since she'd arrived, but now also to stare, like she was some kind of hospital sideshow. It seemed the world was riveted and she wasn't sure which story people were most excited by: that of her as a feral child living in the woods or that of Frank, the insane bomber.

The hospital staff whispered in the halls with Crystal and each other, plotting her future, without asking what she wanted. Frank had trained her to be invisible but that was all over. The preparation and drills—he'd known how it would go from the start. With so much attention on her now, she'd have to put off leaving the hospital.

After Crystal finally went home, Tilly hoped Nurse Connie would come. Instead, a big man in a Carhartt jacket showed up. Tilly realized this man holding a dish covered in foil was John Hart.

"I'm John." He smiled at her. "My wife Mary would have come, too, but with her mother away right now, there's no one to watch the kids. But she sent this lasagna." He put the dish on the table near Tilly's bed. "Mind if I sit?"

Tilly shrugged, trying to keep her face blank, like she hadn't watched him and his family for weeks or stolen their food. She wasn't supposed to know him.

He sat. "The lasagna's vegetarian. Hope you don't mind."

His face had a friendly openness reminding her of why she'd visited the Hart home so often. "Vegetarian?" That was a stupid question out of her mouth before she'd thought it through. It had to do with vegetables, obviously.

He looked down like he was the one that was embarrassed. "I get asked that a lot. Most people are pulling my chain. But do you really not know?"

She shook her head since she was stuck with seeming dumb and didn't see a way out of it.

"Wish more people were curious like you," John was saying, like he wanted to explain. "Vegetarian means I only eat vegetables. No meat, not even fish."

"Oh." She wondered why someone would choose to not eat certain things.

"It's because I love animals." He looked at his hands. "We've got horses and a dog. Also, two cats and three birds upstairs. The kids each have a guinea pig."

Tilly thought of those animal photos hanging beside the ones of his family in his kitchen and how his children loved to play with the guinea pigs.

"Anyway, I can't stand the thought of animals being hurt. I mean we wouldn't eat any of our own animals, of course." He laughed at himself. "But I can't see any difference between my horse and a pig or a cow. I've been this way since I was ten or so. I don't hold it against anyone who wants to eat meat. It's just not for me."

He watched her face and seemed to decide he needed to explain more. "Mary and the kids eat everything, so I make my own food most of the time. But Mary did make this lasagna." His brow creased like he was worried about what she thought.

"Why are you here?"

"Oh, well ..." He cleared his throat. "My house is the one with the horses, next to the firehall."

She gripped her sheet in her fist. So he was going to confront her. About the stealing, or about how she'd been looking in his windows?

"Mary and I got your note," he said quickly. "We're happy we had food to get you through while you were on your own. In fact, this whole community feels that way. I'm here on behalf of the town to tell you we understand you were hungry and needed supplies."

Tilly relaxed some. "You knew my dad, right?"

He sat back. "Grew up together. Headstrong that one. And surer about right and wrong than most people, even when his right and wrong didn't match up with what others believed. I admired his courage back then. Still do." He chuckled to himself. "Now that I'm thinking about it, he's the one who told me I should be vegetarian when he learned how I felt about eating animals. He even decided to be one with me for a few years to make it easier. You know, so there were two kids instead of one asking for a school lunch with no meat." He crossed his arms, remembering. "He never minded agitating. Didn't make him uncomfortable like it would most people. And I don't mean that in a negative way. He followed through on what he believed." He glanced at her. "Although maybe that hasn't always led him down the right path."

"I miss him." Tilly's voice wavered.

"Course you do." He wanted her to know he understood. "That's the other reason I'm here. You need anything, you can come to me and Mary. I owe your dad that much."

Tilly peeled back the corner of the foil on the lasagna. It looked like the regular kind she'd had in restaurants with Frank from time to time and it smelled good, too.

John stood. "Let me get you a piece." He cut a slice big enough to feed three people, put it on a plate he'd brought with him and handed it over. He produced a fork and napkin from his coat pocket and set those in front of her.

"What do you mean you owe Frank?"

He gave her a look she couldn't interpret, maybe thinking they'd already left that subject. "Well, after his dad's accident I could have been a better friend."

Tilly forked a piece of the lasagna. "I know about the accident, but not much about what happened after. What do you remember?"

John linked his big hands together in his lap. "I shouldn't have brought it up."

"But I want to know. Please."

He thought for a while, then shifted forward, elbows on knees. "When Max, your grandma, lost the house and she and Frank had to move to the hunting cabin with Frank's dad, people kind of forgot about them up there on the mountain. Did he tell you that part?"

She nodded.

"The only jobs were at the paper mill. So having to face Frank and Max made people feel bad about going to work. They knew what happened wasn't right, but it had been an accident. And people still had to make a living. I was a kid, but I'm as guilty as the rest for not doing more to help. Out of sight out of mind, I guess they say. But that's not right and I knew it back then."

She chewed her food, hoping he'd keep talking. "So did anyone see Frank and Grandmom after they moved?"

John looked out the window and Tilly sensed this was an

uncomfortable conversation for him.

"Frank stopped coming to school after about a year after they moved. You know, I would see him sometimes in town, but mostly he stayed away." John had his eyes fixed on Short Mountain. "Probably taking care of his dad took a lot of time. Occasionally I would see him do odd jobs for people. But nothing consistent. I don't really know how Max and Frank got on caring for someone who should have been in a nursing home. They didn't even have a functioning bathroom. That place was good for a few days during huntin' season, playing cards and drinkin' beer, but it was never meant to be a home."

Tilly put down her fork. *Never meant to be a home.* She swallowed, holding off a sadness inside that felt too big to contain. "How come Cotter Paper didn't do anything to help?"

John crossed one leg over the other. "Paul Cotter offered money. He'd wanted the dam fixed because he was interested in preserving history, but he never expected things to go the way they did. He felt responsible. He tried to make it right, or at least as right as it could be."

Tilly ate another piece of lasagna, chewing and considering this. "What money?"

"It was right before Frank and Max moved up the mountain. I was there helping pack boxes while Frank was out in the garage getting some tools together. Paul came to the door and handed her an envelope. He said it was enough for her to keep the house in town and care for Frank's pop. She had a temper and could hold a grudge and she refused to take the payoff, as she called it. Plus, she was already furious with people in town who kept saying it had all been an accident and she needed to forgive. I think that the money seemed like a slap in the face to Maxine when the community had already turned their backs. She held Paul responsible for ruining her life and your dad's. In some ways there was no way she could take the money. I kind of understood that even then."

The late day sun broke through the clouds changing the color of everything outside. Frank must not have known about the money. Because if he had he wouldn't have hated the Cotters so much.

"Anyway," John was saying, "that's why I say me and Mary will help you if we can."

"Could I come live with your family? I mean if I stayed here? Maybe you and your wife could be my foster parents?"

The look on his face told her he hadn't expected this question and was only pretending to consider it out of politeness.

"Let me talk to Mary, okay? We've got a houseful. But there might be a way." He scratched his ear and checked at his watch. "Mary and the kids are waiting. So I need to get back home." He stood but hesitated like he felt bad about leaving. "I'll visit again in a few days." He pointed to her plate. "Try to eat."

That night Tilly snuck out of her room to scope out the nearest exits so she'd be ready when it was time to leave. She couldn't count on John Hart.

Fall leaves made from paper hung from the hallway ceilings. Pictures of turkeys and Indian corn decorated doors. A magazine on a waiting room table had her face on the cover with the headline: FUGITIVE'S THIRTEEN-YEAR-OLD DAUGHTER SURVIVES ON HER OWN FOR NINE WEEKS. The photo of her, thin and dirty, had been taken the night the police found her. She was conscious in the picture but had no memory of it. Maybe that's when she'd blabbed. The accompanying article described her as a victim of neglect, raised by a narcissist, and a product of manipulation and abuse. The cabin, the home she and Frank had made, was referred to as *a miserable shack with no running water.*

The Cotter's disappearance was mentioned but the article said that so far the FBI had found no direct evidence connecting the two events. Henry, apparently, had still said nothing. The story continued to be that the Cotters had left town to avoid facing impending bankruptcy.

chapter forty-one

The next morning, a short man, chubby and rumpled, came into Tilly's room wearing a tag around his neck similar to Crystal's. He smelled strongly of cigarettes. She assumed he was also from social services. He extended his hand, and she shook automatically, mostly because it was so unexpected. "FBI agent Mac Stevens. Good to meet you."

She snatched her hand away. He took this in without comment, sat in the chair beside the bed, and opened a small notebook on his lap. "I need to ask you a few questions. Let's start with when your dad went missing."

She would not show how scared she felt.

"Has he been in touch?"

"No."

This man closed his notebook and sat back. "Do you know your father is wanted by the FBI?"

She didn't answer.

"Where were you living before Cottersville?"

"In the woods."

"Were you in school?"

"No."

"Do you know about the dams?"

She turned her attention to the window. This man would arrest Frank if he showed up. As unlikely as that now seemed, Tilly scanned the fields in the distance in case Frank might be striding out of the corn, refusing to be kept away from her now that the FBI was here.

Agent Mac Stevens was back the next day and she pretended he didn't exist. The sooner he realized she wasn't going to tell him squat, the better. But he didn't seem frustrated. At least while he was around, Crystal stayed away, along with everyone else. That meant she got some kind of privacy.

When Mac left that second day, she went to the window to watch him walk to his car. In the parking lot, he pointed angrily at some reporters. Then he chain-smoked three in a row, glaring, until every one of them had driven off.

The following day Mac didn't ask more questions. Instead, he lit a cigarette and puffed away even though she'd seen the no smoking signs. He told her about his wife, who he said was far too classy for him. He said his dad told him the secret to marriage was to treat your woman like a queen. He didn't even have to try because it turned out his wife was a queen. He'd been lucky to marry her, to catch her before someone else did. He talked about his two daughters. His older, a teenager, was smarter than him and had her whole life already planned out. The other one was just two. A surprise baby he called her. He talked a lot about this younger one, Amelia. He explained her favorite stories were ones with Knuffle Bunny and Ferdinand, whoever they were. Tilly learned Amelia hated peas, but loved tomatoes fried in butter and that Mac had driven to the hospital in a snowstorm on the day she was born.

Tilly listened but kept her eyes to the wall.

Mac showed up at the same time over the next days to tell her about growing up in North Philly, naming streets and corner stores as easily as Frank named trees and warblers. He talked about his part of the city with the same reverence Frank had for the land and water.

On that last day he was still lighting one cigarette after another, stubbing them out in a potted plant in the corner of the room before adding the butts to a plastic bag kept in his coat pocket. He told her about his mother and father; his four sisters; where he'd gone to college and how he'd met his wife, Maggie, in a record store. He talked about what was wrong with the boys his older daughter dated and how he tried to tell her she could do better, a lot better. Sometimes Tilly caught herself looking at him as he spoke, forgetting to stare at the wall. Occasionally he'd slip in a question about how she'd grown up, not about Frank, but about her. Sometimes she thought about answering.

Mac told her a story about taking Amelia grocery shopping the night before. He'd been busy searching for a special kind of eggplant his wife needed when the produce manager tapped him on the shoulder and pointed. Amelia, clothes and diaper discarded on the floor, happily ran around the sweet potato display. Mac laughed as he told this story, his cigarette jiggling up and down. His wide-open manner seemed so genuine. "That girl is the light of my life."

Tilly found herself crying in loud embarrassing sobs she had no control over. Mac jammed his cigarette in the plant and fumbled around for a tissue box sitting next to him. He held a tissue out. "I'm sorry. I am. Better days are ahead, Tilly. I promise you that."

She dabbed her eyes, wanting to believe him, even with Frank's voice in her head reminding her Mac was FBI and this was all part of his plan to get her to trust him. But Mac seemed like he wanted to help her. "Why do you work for the FBI?"

He set down the tissue box, thinking about how to answer. "To make the world better."

"By breaking up families. That makes things better?"

"I'm sorry about what's happened to your family. You have every right to feel as you do."

She balled up the tissue he'd given her and threw it into the trash can next to her bed. "I'm going to tell you about Frank now."

He sat back. "All right."

"It's my fault he had to leave."

"Your fault?"

"I broke his trust."

"Any other reason you think he didn't come home?"

"He would never hurt anyone."

"Okay."

"He didn't say goodbye because he's protecting me."

"Protecting you from what?"

"And I'm going to protect him, like I should have all along. So that's all I have to say about Frank. I don't want you to waste any more of your time thinking I'll tell you more. Because I won't."

September 2023

chapter forty-two

Tilly spent hours remaking knobs on the lathe when previous attempts failed. This was a task she'd easily done hundreds of times. But for some reason the shop felt cramped, nagging, and full of orders she couldn't make any headway on. She needed a break and took off her eye and ear protection.

Her cell rang and she checked to see who it was. Charlie Vans. She pictured him sitting at his desk in the furniture gallery in a snappy suit, blissfully unaware of anyone named Frank Stone, and impatient she hadn't picked up by the second ring. If it wasn't happening in New York City, it wasn't happening for Charlie, which was the primary reason Tilly liked having him in her life. All they'd ever had between them was furniture and that's all he would want to talk about.

"Tilly, darling?" he said when she answered.

"Did the table make it to Alberta, okay?" She worried something had happened with the last order.

He paused for a moment, like he had to think about this. "Oh, yes. They're thrilled."

Tilly put Charlie on speaker so she could have her hands free to make coffee. "I'm working on the sideboard for the New Paltz person. I got a perfect match on the wood I used for the dining room table a few years back." She hoped to sound more competent than she felt.

"Right. Good. But I'm not calling about that."

"Oh?"

"I just got off the phone with a woman from California. She stopped by the gallery about a month ago during a visit to the city to look at your furniture. We talked for like thirty minutes about proportions and harmony and how important it is to have clean lines at home so she can think at work. She manages a gaming design company something or other. Thought for sure she would buy one of your pieces, but she left empty-handed. But she called just now to say she wants your furniture in the new home she's building. Yours exclusively. And she's incredibly wealthy."

Charlie's excitement was catching. "How many pieces?"

He paused. "Are you sitting down?"

"Yes?" she lied, feeling the corners of her mouth turn up.

"Sixty."

Good god. She could make twenty-five large pieces in a good year if she worked really hard.

"She hasn't even built the house yet," he rushed on, without missing beat. "It's on track to be completed in two to three years. So there's plenty of time. And a designer, a famous designer, has already worked on the specs of the spaces and laid everything out. He gave me a list of everything you'll be making. Best of all this woman is willing to pay half up front. And I'm talking gallery prices, Tilly."

Charlie talked fast, perhaps afraid she wasn't up to this and he had to convince her. But that wasn't the case.

"Think of the people she'll have in that house. Your furniture will be featured in magazines."

"Is there a contract?"

"She's having one drawn up now. I'll send it to you as soon as I get it and we'll go over it together." The sound of a single hand clap came through the phone. "I knew this would happen for you one day, Tilly. I knew it from the day we met."

chapter forty-three

Tilly finished rounding off the front edges of the drawers for the sideboard and looked outside as the late afternoon sun lit up silky milkweed seeds drifting skyward. A murmuration of starlings shifted in unison through a series of organized shapes against the bright blue sky.

Those shifting shapes felt like her own thoughts about Charlie's proposal, which were changing from excitement into something more cautious. Frank hadn't slipped into her life as quietly as she'd expected. Instead he seemed intent on creating questions and calling attention to himself. Could she sign a contract with a client, especially such an important one, when so much was unresolved and potentially unstable? That wouldn't be fair to Charlie or this woman. As far as both of them knew, Frank didn't even exist. And that's the way it should be.

Mac's car pulled up. Agent Sharp was with him again.

"You didn't stay in your house, like I asked," Mac said, when he came into the shop, this time with Sharp at his heels.

She turned the drawer she'd been working on so she could see it from a new angle. "Still have to make a living."

Mac sat on a stool next to her workbench while Sharp, who struck Tilly as not very intelligent in a silent, incurious way, stayed by the door, scanning the place like he might see some clue Mac had overlooked. "Anna Birch been to see you?" Mac asked.

"She was here this morning."

"What did she want to talk about?"

The problem with Mac was Tilly never knew what he wasn't saying. This seemed truer now than ever.

"Did she mention the timing of the Cotters' and Frank's disappearances?" Agent Sharp asked this as though he'd decided to cast a line and see what would happen.

Mac shook his head like the question was for him. "I've looked at that. Frank wasn't violent. Not a kidnapper. I don't think he would have run away with them either. That doesn't make any sense, given how he felt about the Cotters."

"Did you ever figure out where Paul and Helen went or what happened to them?" Tilly asked.

"That case is unresolved. Most people turn up. That's what the law expects. The Cotters never did." Burnt jumped into Mac's lap and made himself comfortable. Mac ran his hand over the cat's back. "There's no evidence to connect the two cases, except the timing, which is obviously significant. And the fact that Frank might have wanted to avenge his father. But I'm not sure what any of that has to do with what's going on now. The thing I wonder about ..." He let the thought trail off.

"What?" both Sharp and Tilly asked in unison.

"Well, it's probably nothing, but ..." Mac glanced at Sharp. "I wonder what Henry Cotter knows. There are things he's never said."

"What do you mean?" Sharp asked.

"It's more of a hunch than anything. My guess is he's protecting someone."

"Who?"

"That's the question." Mac turned at the sounds of a loud rumble outside. A truck unloaded stone near the dam. "Listen," he said, turning back to Tilly. "I understand why you're working with Anna, given her connections on social media, but her priority is her book and she's not objective. You should find someone who's trained for the kind of PR you might need. Especially given your panic attack the other night."

Tilly picked up a broom and swept sawdust into a pile, trying to read between the lines. He wasn't here to give her PR advice again. She couldn't afford a real PR person anyway. Mac knew that. "Anna's shown me she can handle the press."

"You gonna ask her some real questions? Or should I?" Sharp suddenly said. "You can't keep dancing around it."

Mac put an unlit cigarette between his lips, flipping Sharp an eyebrow.

Sharp glared at him. "Go take a smoke break."

It was a directive, but even so Mac hesitated. Tilly could feel him staring, wanting her to look at him. But she didn't do that. He stood and went outside.

Sharp sat where Mac had been. "I was assigned to this investigation because Agent Stevens is too personally involved. He's bent a lot of rules when it comes to you. So I'm looking at this case with fresh eyes and I have questions."

"Like what?"

"You helping your father?"

"No."

"Been in contact with him?"

"Nope."

"Because you do realize if you're not telling the truth you'll be charged with aiding and abetting a domestic terrorist." He looked at her sharply. "That's a federal offense."

Outside Mac puffed away on his cigarette, trying not to seem like he was watching them.

"You think it's possible Frank killed the Cotters? Maybe even accidentally?"

Tilly shook her head. She didn't want to think that was possible.

"That would explain a lot. Like why they've never been found."

She swept the pile of sawdust she'd collected onto a dustpan and dumped it into the trash. Sharp was getting on her last nerve. "I don't have anything to say to you."

She glanced outside looking for Mac, wondering again what he knew. But he was sitting in the car and she couldn't see his face. Maybe she should tell him about Frank. Because what if Frank wasn't who she thought he was? What if he was right now planning something terrible and she was standing by and letting it happen? He was capable of inflicting great suffering. She knew that personally.

Fall 2006

chapter forty-four

NOVEMBER

Tilly left the hospital barefoot and still in the hospital gown since she'd never been given her old clothes. She walked up the mountain along Frank's path, thick now with cold leaves. The opening of tree cover overhead revealed a river of stars.

She retrieved her escape bag and went to the fort where she changed clothes and pulled on a pair of boots. She stowed pretzels she'd brought from the hospital alongside a water filter, plastic bottle, hammock, tarp, compass, her radio, and map already inside. From the bag she pulled the piece of the paper with the address Frank had given her and stuffed it into her pocket.

She put the bag on her shoulder and caught a glimpse of Henry's painting on the wall. Tilly now thought it looked like some naive version of herself, one that watched and disapproved of this plan to leave Cottersville. Tilly walked out and didn't look back.

She stuck to country roads, stopping briefly for more food and supplies, before heading north until she reached the Appalachian Trail. For six days she followed the trail southwest alongside bare trees, some of them snaked with red and orange bittersweet vine. Each night she slept off-trail in her hammock.

Near Hagerstown, she stole more food and some duct tape. The sole of her right boot had peeled away and she used the tape to secure it back in place. Before heading out, she stopped at the library to take the only copy of *The Monkey Wrench Gang*, the novel Frank had never brought home, the one his dad had given him at the time of his accident.

Outside of Hagerstown, she turned west onto the Chesapeake and Ohio canal path and walked two more days to Cumberland, Maryland, reading *The Monkey Wrench Gang* each night in her hammock.

George Hayduke, the main character, pulled up survey stakes for new roads, pipelines, and construction sites; he plugged waste discharge pipes at landfills and industrial outfalls and poured sand and water into the fuel tanks of heavy equipment at construction sites. That was similar to how Frank had started out at Cotter Paper.

But some things about the book didn't sit well with Tilly. Hayduke, frustrated with corporate greed and corruption, believed, like Frank, that people needed to rise up and take action against the industrial machine. But Hayduke was a slime ball when it came to other people. His relationship with the main female character in the book was revolting. And now that Tilly thought of it, Ted K., Frank's other hero, was a loner and a loser, too, when it came to other people. He'd killed three people and injured twenty-three others, some of them permanently. What did Frank see in these men who thought of no one but themselves and had no close family?

Still, Frank had cared for her and raised her to be strong and to take care of herself. He'd trusted her with secrets and responsibilities like she was an equal. He'd respected her. They'd been a team. Maybe this novel had been a phase from his younger days? Something he'd loved because it had been a gift from his father.

At Cumberland she left the trail and headed west into the woods, with the compass and map as her guide. She hoped Frank would be waiting at the address he'd given her, the one for a Mr. August Travers. That glimmer kept her putting one foot in front of the other when walking away from Cottersville was starting to feel like the opposite of what she should be doing.

chapter forty-five

When she finally arrived at August Travers' place, which lay deep in the woods of western Maryland, she stood for a long while at the edge of the forest watching him chop wood, trying to get a sense of what kind of man he was. But all she could tell from his skinny frame was that for an old guy, he could still handle an axe.

She approached. The duct tape repair on her boot had split open miles ago so now the sole slapped the ground with each step. When she came to stand in front of him, he kept on chopping as though he didn't notice or didn't care. Despite the late fall chill, sweat traveled tracks down his bare dusty arms.

"Frank Stone, my dad, told me to come," she finally said.

He raised yellowed eyes to her, stared at her face for a long moment, before turning and spitting over his shoulder.

"Frank had to go away." She looked at the trailer next to where they stood, hoping Frank might be in there.

August spit again, closer to her feet this time and shook his head slowly, smiling as though this was a joke he'd just been let in on. "Shit," he said, stringing out the word. "You can't stay here."

She stared down at her busted boot. Frank wouldn't be able to find her if she went anywhere else. Plus, there was nowhere else to go. Her eyes stung. Somehow in the last week she was expressing more emotion than at any time in her life, while simultaneously feeling almost nothing.

August set his axe into a nearby stump with a whomp and reached for the pack of cigarettes in his shirt pocket. "Oh, for fuck's sake." He lit up, took a long pull and blew the smoke out fast, looking at her, shaking his head. "Fucking Frank."

He turned and walked off. "Come on then."

She woke up on August's beat-up couch, starving. She'd been too tired before to notice housekeeping wasn't something August concerned himself with. The kitchen floor had spills no one had bothered to clean up for years. Stinky garbage overflowed the can and made Tilly retch. In the filthy fridge an ancient container of yellow mustard sat beside three cans of Coke. The cupboard above the sink held a box of Ho Hos, a half a bottle of grain alcohol, and a large container of powdered cherry Kool-Aid. A few crumpled bills of money sat in front of the alcohol. Tilly stuffed those into her pocket before eating four Ho Hos and washing them down with a Coke.

She found August sitting outside on the front steps, sipping from a paper Dixie cup, a forgotten cigarette burning down in an ashtray beside him. He took a long, slow sip from the cup.

She sat beside him, taking in the land around the trailer. They were surrounded by forest. A dirt road off to the right ended at August's place. Just beyond where he'd been chopping wood sat a large pole barn.

The liquid in his cup, alcohol mixed with Kool-Aid from the smell of it, was the color of red crayon. He regarded her with a glassy stare, while sucking on his cigarette and tilting his head back to blow out smoke rings.

"Let me tell you about the first time I met your daddy." He tapped ash but left the cigarette where it was. "Worked security back then. Night shift at a fancy development going up down state. This was right after I got out of the army." He checked to see if she was listening. "That development wasn't even a mile from where I grew up. When I was a kid, I played in the woods that was there then. But they had cleared those trees for the houses."

He took a long drink from the cup. "Anyway, I was doin' my rounds and there was Frank pourin' sand in the tank of one of the dozers." August smiled, drained his cup and poured another from a plastic pitcher sitting next to him. "At first, I thought to myself, let him do it. But I remembered my job and pulled my gun." He chuckled. "Course I was never gonna shoot nobody. Never even had the gun out before that. When Frank heard me, he turned. That's when I seen you was asleep in a pack on his back."

Tilly coughed on the HoHos and coke now in the back of her throat. August laughed at her reaction.

"I said to Frank, 'That a baby?' Then I asked what he was doing out there with a tiny child."

August smiled wide at the memory and drained his cup. "I've thought about that many times."

Frank had never mentioned knowing August, not until he'd given Tilly the address and told her the only thing she knew about this man. "Frank said you taught him explosives?"

August looked off in the distance. "He could tell I'd been in the military since my hair was clipped back then. And you know, he figured out pretty quick I grew up near there and didn't like my job. It turned out we thought the same about a lot of things. We went out for a drink that night—you were there, too. Anyway, that's when he found out I worked explosives in the military."

Frank would have taken all that as a sign he was, once again, on the right path, living the life his father would have if he'd been given the choice.

"We spent a lot of time together for a few years when you were little. I did the first bombs for him." He took a long drag and tossed back another gulp. "Until he started doing them. But, you know, he'd still show up here now and again and check in. Bring me some bottles, sometimes a case. Keeping loose ends tied, you know what I'm sayin'." He poured himself another and lit a cigarette even though there was already one sitting beside him.

Tilly was glad to hear Frank still visited from time to time.

"I figured out over the years that Frank cared most about three things," August was saying. "His work. And you." He glanced at her. "But those things aren't compatible. That's why you're here and he's not."

"You said three things."

"You came from Cottersville, where Frank's from?"

"Yeah."

"He go there to blow up that dam? Or for her?"

"Helen?"

"Yeah, that's the third thing."

"He told me we were going there to live a regular life. That we were done with the bombs."

August looked at her like she'd just said donkeys flew. "Frank wasn't made to stay in one place. He's always doing something different than he's sayin'." He picked up his cigarette and pointed the incandescent tip at her. "When you think he's coming for you?"

She lifted her shoulders and let them fall. He tried standing, dropping his cigarette in the process and grabbing the railing to keep from falling. He stumbled inside the trailer, lay down, and passed out before he even got the door closed.

She stared at him for a long moment, at first thinking he might have died. But she saw his chest rise and fall. He was too heavy for her to move on her own, so she decided to leave him.

She walked over to the pole barn and tried the door. It was locked. She cupped her hands and looked inside. It was some kind of wood shop with a bunch of furniture piled up on one end.

From her pocket, she pulled the bills she'd found in August's kitchen cupboard. She grabbed her backpack and followed the dirt road until she came to a town not much bigger than Cottersville. It was the same in many ways: one main street, a church, a cemetery. The only real difference was she felt nothing for it.

At a little grocery, she bought eggs, milk, cheese, and some apples, stuffing it all in her backpack. Outside the grocery, she watched a couple men walk out of the Goodwill Store across the street carrying a small table. They loaded it into their pickup and drove off.

The first days with August turned into weeks. He lived like a hermit with no interest in what was going on beyond his place. Tilly had no idea whether news of Frank had died down or if her disappearance from the hospital was in the papers.

She figured Frank would come to get her in the night. So she slept in her clothes. She'd taped up her boots again and kept them next to the couch. She figured they'd travel west maybe, where she pictured the woods to be more vast; somewhere they could stay completely out of sight, even more than they had before.

She spent most of her time in those first weeks waiting for him on the trailer steps. She imagined Frank had somehow tracked her progress. She daydreamed about how he'd watched her survive on her own at the cabin. He'd probably been frustrated when she'd given herself up to the police and disappointed that she'd wound up in the hospital. It had taken her much longer to get to August's place than he'd counted on. That had probably messed up his plans. He'd wanted to come sooner, but she hadn't done what he'd asked of her.

She did miss Cottersville even if she didn't want to. Or maybe she just missed Henry. She wondered how John and his family were. She liked to think about them around the dinner table. Tilly tried to imagine what a vegetarian ate night after night. Sometimes she thought of Ruth and Ada up late, with so much to say to each other.

Weeks turned to months, and it came to her slowly that maybe Frank wasn't coming anytime soon. Maybe she would have to wait a lot longer than she'd first thought.

2007-2013

chapter forty-six

2007

August, it turned out, was prone to long drinking binges. He didn't like people, either, and only went to town for liquor. Even though he'd said quite a bit about Frank upon her arrival, he wasn't normally interested in talking. He didn't have a phone. Lived on booze, Ho Hos, and pork rinds. And the only mail he opened were his checks from the government.

Tilly learned to take money from his wallet when he passed out. He never asked how the food got in the fridge. When their power was turned off and August couldn't be bothered to do anything about it, she opened letters marked Passed Due to pay those bills even when that meant taking most of what August had in his wallet.

Sometimes, even for weeks at a time, August could be sober. That's when she discovered his other side as a hard worker with a single-minded dedication to building beautiful furniture in the pole barn he kept neat and tidy in ways he never bothered with in the trailer.

Tilly also had no interest in cleaning the trailer or trying to make it nice. She'd taken to sleeping outside on her hammock unless it was raining or too cold. When she couldn't sleep outside, she slept in the pole barn which smelled of wood and polish.

She loved the Shaker style furniture August made, even if most of his work was covered in dust and crammed into one side of the barn.

It was thrilling to watch him make a table from start to finish, witnessing how he turned the rough boards into beautiful pieces for a home. She loved the idea of trees living a whole other life from the one they were born to.

After months of watching August build a cabinet and another table, Tilly began to anticipate which tools and supplies he'd need. One day she got up from the corner where she'd been sitting and handed him a clamp. He took it, after some hesitation, checking first to make sure it was the one he needed. She sat back down, watching and getting up only to retrieve what she thought he might need next. After a week of this, he got to the point of holding out his hand so she could place the right screw or mallet there.

One day he started with a thick plank of wood and cut it down to size. As it took shape and he hollowed out the center by shaving off wood with a special tool, she realized it would be the seat of a chair.

"This here's a hand plane," he suddenly said. "The chair seat has to be comfortable. So the hollow is deeper toward the back to give the sitter a slight backward lean."

She saw what he meant.

"You have to leave it thickest where strength will be needed to join the legs, spindles, and rails."

He shaved off more wood and held the planer out to her. "You try. Make small changes, not big ones. We're after simple and elegant."

She took the hand plane from him and held it like he showed her. She shaved off a thin strip of wood. He nodded and she shaved another.

In the months that followed she worked on more projects with August and came to understand how thoughtfully he'd set up the shop. There was a strategy to it. Wood was organized by type and stored away from windows or doors that might let in the damp. The hand tools he used most often hung together above his main work bench stacked with organized bins holding screws and fasteners. There was a shelf for glue, clamps, and squaring braces.

For the larger pieces of furniture, where access to all four sides was needed at one time, there was a bench in the middle of the barn near the table saw. The table saw was part of a machining area used for sizing, jointing, and planing. It was set into a kind of work triangle so August could move easily among the jointer, planer, and table saw. The nearby workbench doubled as a way to feed boards into the machine area.

Other shelving and cupboards held extra jigs, hold downs, miter gauges and blades as well as sanding and finishing supplies. The space had been organized over a long period of time by someone with a lot of experience. Frank must have known about this woodworking side of August. That's why he'd sent her to live with him.

Tilly brushed off one of the small tables August had made a long time ago now, considering the amount of accumulated dust. He stood watching her, hands on his hips.

Over the last weeks, he'd kept less and less cash in his wallet. Either he was spending more or he didn't want her taking it when he was too drunk to know better.

"So, what now?" he said. "You want to sell that down at Goodwill?"

"The electric bill is overdue, again. I'll give you whatever money is left over, okay? We need the room in here anyway."

He scrunched his face. "I don't like to go to town. And I'm not going to Goodwill."

"Then don't. Just help me get this table in the truck. I'll drive in. Can't be that hard."

August stood and picked up one side of the table so they could move it to the bed of the truck. After they slid it into place, he fished the keys out of his pocket and handed them over. She got into the driver's seat, put the key in the ignition and turned it like she'd seen Frank do. August ducked his head in the window. "There's the gas and there's the brake. That's all you really need to know."

She started off down the road, testing out the brake and gas, jerking the truck forward and back, and then, when she mostly had the hang of it, headed to town.

chapter forty-seven

2011

As the years went by Tilly made enough from sales at Goodwill to make sure the essential bills got paid. She never got too friendly with anyone in town. The last thing she needed was some social worker snooping around.

She thought less of Cottersville, not because she forgot about it, but because it hurt less to put it out of her mind. Because when she did think about Cottersville, she thought of Henry. And that led to remembering how upset he seemed the last time they'd spoken. The more she'd thought about that the more it seemed to her he'd really been scared. Scared of what she might have seen when Helen and Frank had been arguing at the dam. Her mind ran back and forth over that like a tongue over a chipped tooth.

Days after Tilly turned sixteen the transmission blew on the truck. Fixing it required more money than she had stashed away or that she could make at Goodwill, at least over the next month. She reserved a booth at an arts-and-crafts festival in a nearby town, hoping to sell enough to cover the repair. She borrowed a truck from the Goodwill manager and hauled what furniture she could fit in the bed.

When she arrived at the numbered tent, there was no one to help her set up. Tilly climbed into the truck bed and pulled the sheets off the furniture. It was a hot day and by the time she un-loaded the chairs her t-shirt was damp, and she felt flushed. She climbed back into the truck and stood facing the cabinet, think-ing about how she would have to leave it since it required more than one person to lift. Two men walked past and took stock of the situation. "Where you need that, honey?"

She pointed to her tent, and they unloaded the cabinet and placed it there.

"We're Tent 38. You come find us when you're ready to go. We'll help you load up."

The festival was crowded but people walked by Tilly's tent without stopping. They were interested in cotton candy, hotdogs, and little crafty things, not furniture.

She was thinking about leaving early when a young man wearing a tan suit and straw hat showed up. He didn't look like anyone she'd ever met before. He stood, arms crossed, studying the cabinet. He turned to her and offered his hand. "Charlie Vans."

Tilly used a firm grip the way Frank had taught her. "I'm Tilly."

He ran his hand across the outside of the cabinet, then opened a drawer and examined the joinery.

"August Travers made these. And I helped," she said.

"Never heard of August Travers." He sat in one of the chairs, crossing his leg one way and then the other. He stood, picked up the chair, and flipped it over. "Remarkable." He squinted at her. "I'm sorry, you are, again?"

"Tilly. August Travers is my ... uncle. My aunt's husband. They adopted me, but my aunt died, so now it's just me and August." Frank would have hated the complexity of that explanation, but it was the best she could come up with in the moment.

Charlie Vans was examining another chair and didn't seem to have heard what she'd said anyway. "I was driving by on my way to see an old friend and needed to stretch my legs, so I stopped. What can I say? Perhaps it's serendipity." He grinned in a way that made her wonder if he was joking. There was still a lot she didn't understand about the way people were with each other. At least she knew enough to recognize that his suit was tailored. Shoes polished, too. Maybe he'd buy something.

He handed her his card: CHARLIE VANS, FURNITURE GALLERY, NEW YORK CITY. "I specialize in Shaker pieces."

"You should buy some of these."

"I'm thinking about it, Ms. Tilly. Besides the quality and craftmanship, there's something special about this furniture." He gave her a sideways look. "They're Shaker, undeniably, and yet ... who did you say made these?"

"August Travers. And me."

"Yes, right. Mysterious Mr. Travers, the world-class craftsman no one's heard of." He bent to study the legs on the cabinet.

"The subtle ornamental details are artful. But this ..." He pointed to the legs. "This tapering evokes connection and continuity, qualities fundamental to the Shaker style. And it's mighty elegant."

Charlie seemed too young to talk the way he did or own a gallery in New York. He stepped back and slipped his hands in his pockets. "Tell me about August."

"Not much to tell. We live up on the mountain. But he can make anything. He's teaching me."

Charlie tilted his head, studying her now with the same intensity he'd given the chair. "And where does this furniture get made?"

"In the shop next to our trailer. August has been making stuff like this for years, but never sold any of it so I'm trying to help him. I sold some at Goodwill. But there's a lot stacked up."

"How old are you, Ms. Tilly?"

"Sixteen."

He crossed his arms, leaning back a little. "Can I meet August? Is he here somewhere?"

"No."

"He's not here or I can't meet him."

"Both."

"Why can't I meet him?"

"He doesn't like people."

"Oh." Charlie crossed his arms and leaned against the cabinet. "You know what sells furniture, Ms. Tilly?"

She thought of the things August talked about. "Craftsmanship?"

Charlie clasped his hands together in front of him. "That should matter more than it does. But no, that's only part of it. A good story makes art valuable. And pretty little you and August who doesn't like people, both living up on the mountain in a trailer in western Maryland, making furniture of this quality, well ... that's a story I can work with."

"We keep to ourselves."

He held up a hand. "Of course, and that's just fine. I'm going to make a phone call and have a couple people from my gallery drive out here." He checked his watch and nodded to himself. "From the city they can be here in five hours, give or take. So, expect them at around six. You're here until then?"

"I guess I can be."

"Good. I'm going to ask them to pick up this cabinet and two of these chairs. I'll display them as floor models in my gallery. People will want to buy them. I'll get you their orders, and you and August will make the pieces. When you're finished, you'll let me know and I'll arrange delivery to the customer. I take forty percent of all sales, which is what any gallery would charge. So, we need to price accordingly."

She'd sold a cabinet the week before at Goodwill for three hundred. They'd only taken fifteen percent. "You're taking almost half?"

"That's standard. But Shaker is a style people want. Your furniture will sell, and I suggest we start by asking between eight and nine thousand for the cabinet. Chairs might start at eight hundred each. Sound reasonable?"

She tried her best to look unimpressed.

"I'll need your phone number."

"We don't have a phone." She could tell he was ready to change his mind. "We do business by mail."

"All right," he said slowly. "What's your address then?"

She wrote it on the back of his business card.

By five o'clock most of the other vendors began packing up to go home. Those two young men from earlier in the day came back wanting very much to help her get the furniture back in the truck so they could all go get a beer after. She was glad to have an excuse for why she had to pass on that. But by six-thirty, she was left standing alone in an empty field. They'd taken every tent down, including hers. By seven she figured Charlie had been pulling her leg and began loading the chairs into the truck, re-signed to leaving the cabinet sitting in the field until she could get August to help. But just before she drove off, a man and woman showed up in a white van looking for her.

When Tilly got home that night August didn't seem to care one way or the other that she'd let the furniture go with no money down. A week later the first order came in the mail for two cabinets and twelve chairs. Charlie had included half of their sixty percent up front.

She and August bought a truck at the used-car lot in town. After pulling a few chairs and one cabinet from August's store of furniture, they got to work making the remaining pieces.

Three weeks later she went to town to call Charlie to say the order was ready.

"I'm sending two trucks: one to pick up the order and an-other to collect a couple other examples of whatever you have, which I'll also display in the gallery."

Just before the trucks were due to arrive, Tilly led a stum-bling, drunk August to the trailer and helped him inside where he collapsed on the couch.

"Stay in here until they leave. You hear me?" He didn't an-swer and she realized he'd already passed out.

Shortly after that, a huge white truck came up the drive, fol-lowed by another. The man and woman who'd picked up the chair and cabinet from the festival were there, along with a younger guy wearing a camera around his neck. "You must be Tilly." He smiled down at her.

"Yep."

He looked around the place and nodded to himself as though what he'd heard from Charlie was really true. "Charlie wants me to put together a little catalogue of the furniture. That's why I'm here. People will buy from a picture."

chapter forty-eight

2012

Tilly took charge of the furniture orders, making sure pieces were finished and shipped on time, even when that meant filling in for August more and more. At eighteen she'd become more accustomed to dealing with people, at least in the business sense. She'd even rented an office with a phone in town so she could put in the long hours vetting wood and tool suppliers and arranging repairs to power tools and, occasionally, the ventilation system. Not to mention having to work through the details of sales with Charlie, which was an evolving process as demand for the furniture grew and they needed to adjust pricing.

August was oblivious to most of it and tolerant of the rest since it meant he had a full wallet most of the time. He had no idea how much money they were making. Tilly kept that to herself, stashing the cash in a duffel she kept hidden in the pole barn behind some old solvents they never used.

The photographer came back several times to take more photos for Charlie. He returned on his own to take Tilly to the bar in town. They drank and danced to songs on the juke box. It was the first time Tilly had ever done something purely for fun and she fell for the photographer simply for showing her a joy she'd never considered hers to have.

He and other men watched her in ways she was still growing used to. It didn't feel the same with the photographer as it had with Henry. She preferred this kind of relationship, one that she could keep at a distance in her head and see it for what it was. There were no surprises. She could take this man or leave him. It was her choice.

One evening the photographer asked her to take her clothes off so he could take her picture. His attention and the way he watched her through the lens made her feel beautiful and special. Enough that she took him to bed. After that he made the trip from the city to see her again and again.

When August got sick with a cough that didn't go away, he drank even more. As the months went by, she spent more time taking care of him since he refused to see a doctor. He got winded just on the walk to the barn. Tilly hid his cigarettes and threw out his bottles, but he got angry and used energy he didn't have to drive to town and get more. The photographer stopped coming as much when August couldn't get out of bed for days at a time and Tilly wouldn't leave him.

By winter August was getting up and spending at least parts of his days wrapped in blankets, smoking on the trailer steps.

And that's where she found him, still and cold. Somehow, she hadn't really thought he'd leave her, too.

Tilly hired a backhoe from town to dig a grave next to the shop. She was the only witness, besides the backhoe operator who helped her lower August into the hole before covering him up.

Tilly thought Frank might show up for the burial, but, of course, he didn't.

chapter forty-nine

After August's death, Tilly lived in the trailer with not much more than a hazy awareness of the passing days and nights. She stopped working in the shop. Stopped opening the mail from Charlie. Sometimes she went to the bar she'd been to with the photographer to work her way steadily through one beer after another ignoring the men who tried to pick her up. At least until one of them offered her a joint to go with her beer. She liked the way it softened the edges more than the beer alone. She took that man home for the night.

From then on, she stayed high and in the company of men because it turned out that feeling both numb and wanted was how she could get through the days. Otherwise, there was no more holding off the grief she'd held at arm's length since Frank left, and the weight of it threatened to crush her.

FBI agent Mac Stevens showed up at the trailer door one day, a cigarette dangling from his mouth.

"You found me." It was all she could think to say.

She stayed in the doorway while he took a seat on the trailer steps, blowing out thick streams of smoke, not even looking at her. "You know I'd only been on the job a month when I came to see you in the hospital that first time."

His cigarette made whistling noises every time he took a drag.

"You were my first real case. You were tough back then, you know that." He turned to get a response, which she didn't offer.

"I don't know where Frank is," she told him.

He'd stubbed out his butt and flipped open his pack, reaching for another. "I got an anonymous note last week saying this was where I'd find you."

So, Frank had been watching out for her after all.

He tilted his head to light another one. "Sorry I didn't do more for you back in Cottersville. I knew that social worker pushed the foster parents way too soon. I should have intervened."

She was tired of standing and sat on the step above where he was.

He watched the smoke from his cigarette drift upward and disappear, then fixed his eyes on her. "You need to get out of here. Start fresh."

They watched a flock of sparrows scratch the dirt. "How about I take you back to Cottersville?"

Tilly shook her head. That was done with.

"I'll help you get settled. Other people will, too. John Hart for instance. We've been in touch. He asked me to tell you you're welcome to stay at his house for as long as you like. He and his wife want you to come."

Tilly didn't know why, but even as part of her resisted the idea, she wanted to be in Cottersville again. Maybe it wasn't too late for her.

chapter fifty

2013

John Hart helped Tilly unload the lumber from his truck.

"You sure you want to live in that camping trailer while you work on this place? You can keep staying with us if you want."

"I'm used to being on my own."

She hoped he understood. He and Mary had lent her a room for the last couple weeks. But when she'd realized the property was for sale where the Cotter Paper Mill office building had once stood, she'd used the money from furniture sales to buy the land and materials for a shop. All that was left now of Cotter Paper was a mix of crumbling concrete, overgrown grass, and, of course, the dam. The town had taken ownership of the dam, but she had the rest of it. And the land needed a new life, just like she did.

Once the shop was up and running, she hoped to earn enough making furniture to build a house.

A few days later Tilly nailed part of the wood shop's frame together when a shadow blocked the sunlight warming her back. She looked up and saw Henry. He'd grown taller, of course. A man now.

He leaned against a stack of lumber and crossed one foot over the other. "So, you bought this place?"

"Yep." She shielded the sun with her hand as she peered up

at him, wondering if this upset him. "I heard you went away to college."

"Came back to work for the post office."

"Oh." She was glad to hear he was in town.

"I didn't think you'd come back here," he said.

"I didn't know I would."

Henry looked at her for a long moment. "I didn't think I'd ever see you again."

"Well, my being here just kind of happened."

He held up his hand to show her his ring finger. "Just got married and my wife's expecting."

She kept her face passive or tried to as she pulled a nail from of the box and pounded it into the frame. It annoyed her how much she was affected by this news. It had been years since they'd seen each other. Of course he'd fallen in love with someone.

When she finally looked up again, he was staring at the old dam. She followed his line of sight to the tire trapped in a continuous eddy created by the spillway.

"Listen," he said, turning his eyes back to her. "About what happened at the end of that summer—it wasn't what it seemed."

What was the point of talking about that now? Maybe they just needed to move on with their lives. Henry was certainly doing that.

"I'm interested in building my own life, starting with a shop. Then my house. After that I'm taking the dam out so the creek can go back the way it was. I want to restore things. For myself, for this land. That's what I'm doing here."

His face grew stern. "Build whatever you want but leave the dam alone."

She stood, angry that he thought he could tell her what to do. Like just because he'd found his family, he knew better than she did. "You live your life and I'll live mine, okay?"

September 2023

chapter fifty-one

Tilly texted Anna asking her to get rid of the reporters once again camped at the edge of the lawn. Between them, the prospect of Frank either suddenly appearing again or never coming back, and the growing mass of rubber hose, erosion-control matting, and heavy stakes sitting beside the dam, she felt crowded and in a dark mood. Anna replied saying she'd be there soon, followed by another text: *intvw tbc afterward?*

Minutes later Anna was there getting rid of reporters. Then she came into Tilly's house without knocking as though they were past that formality.

"I have something to show you." Anna sat at the table and reached for her laptop. She typed quickly, the glow of the screen on her face. "In the last twenty-four hours, there've been more sightings of Frank and they've been closer to Cottersville."

Tilly's hand went to her throat. All of this was considerably more than she was prepared for. She needed time. Why was Mac fast-tracking the dam removal? Couldn't he let up? Give her some breathing room? She didn't know how to stop the dam from coming out nor did she want to. She also didn't have a clue what Frank would do when he realized she wasn't going to help him.

"Look at this post from a day ago." Anna clicked the tab labeled, TELL YOUR FRANK STONE STORY.

Anna scrolled through pages of memes and messages, some with pictures and hash tags like "anti-civ," "freedom club," and "primitivist."

"Here." She clicked on a slightly blurred photo of a man wearing a blue jacket with the bird insignia on the upper arm.

"That's not Frank."

"How do you know?"

"Because I know."

"The post mentions you."

"Where?"

She pointed to the screen and read aloud, "Talked with him about his daughter. He went on and on about her."

Tilly studied the photo again, less sure it wasn't him.

She handed Anna a copy of the local newspaper she'd picked up from the store that morning. "The front page is about how the dam removal has been taken over by the FBI."

"They want to make sure Frank knows," Anna said.

Tilly nodded. "The dam comes out on Saturday, just three days from now. Those details are also in the article."

"Because they think he'll intervene and can bring him in."

"That's what I figure."

Anna closed her laptop. "I want to visit the cabin today."

Tilly was annoyed that Anna's main priority seemed to be her book. "It's a long walk."

"Oh." Anna looked down at her shoes. "How far?"

"Couple miles and it's steep. There's probably nothing there anymore, like I told you before."

Anna stood, stuffing her phone and notebook into a bag. "I want to go anyway."

Anna wasn't going to be put off. Tilly got her boots from beside the door and pulled them on. It was possible Frank was at the cabin or whatever remained of it. Maybe he was hiding out there. At least then she could get some answers.

chapter fifty-two

Short Mountain blocked the morning sun and cast Anna and Tilly in shadow as they climbed toward the cabin. Anna fell behind almost immediately. Tilly stopped and waited, studying the trees on the slope. She traced the massive limbs overhead down to the root-crossed ground. The trunks were straighter here with less branching than if they'd grown all alone in a field. Those straight trunks were the prize of furniture makers since lower branches caused complications in the wood. The straightness was a result of the battle being played as each tree reached for sunlight. Weaker fallen trees like the one under Tilly's foot disintegrated and returned to the soil, feeding those still standing. She tilted her head back, searching for the highest branches. Those were like Anna who sounded like an expert on Frank, making it clear to everyone she was happy to speak about him, reaching for attention like a tree reached for sunlight. On one hand that had taken the pressure off Tilly. But she'd also started feeling a bit like a rotten log on the ground. How much of her own story did she want to feed Anna for her book?

Anna came huffing up behind her. She bent, hands on her knees, to catch her breath. "You and Frank walked up and down this mountain every time you needed to get to town?"

"He walked it every day. I didn't. At least not until he disappeared and I ran out of food. Then I didn't have a choice."

Tilly started walking again, but more slowly this time, until they reached the cluster of hemlock trees standing near the cabin. Through the boughs of the trees, she could once again see the place that had been filled with so many of her expectations.

Tall, pale grasses still surrounded the cabin, making it look remarkably like the first day she'd seen it. She'd had no idea about real disappointment back then. Or how hard a person could come crashing down. Her eyes followed a trail through the grass. Maybe from a deer, or a person.

She cupped her hands to her mouth and made their old screech-owl call. What if he was in the cabin right now? She waited for a return call, expected it.

But there was nothing.

Anna was calling her name. Tilly turned to her, sensing Anna'd been trying to get her attention for a while.

"What are you thinking right now?"

Tilly eyed the tattered remains of the tarp she and Frank had put on the roof, visible now as patches of stringy blue plastic, rattling in the wind. They'd worked so hard together that summer to make this place nice. Those lemon curtains. Why had he asked her to make them if he'd planned to leave?

"Let's try to get inside." Anna walked on ahead.

Tilly stayed where she was, eyes fixed on the moss growing next to the cabin. It was like an old ruin, haunted and protected by spirits better left alone. It was enough for her to see it from the outside.

Anna came back for her and grabbed her arm, tugging her toward the cabin door. Tilly let herself be pulled as far as the front porch before shaking free.

Anna cupped her hands to the cabin window. "Can't see anything." She reached for the doorknob which turned, but when she pushed, the door held fast. Anna tried again, putting her shoulder into it, and the door budged. "We can get in!"

Fledgling swallows swooped around their nests in the porch rafters, agitated by the sudden presence of people. Tilly picked up a long stick lying next to the porch and cleared away cobwebs from the porch corners, which did little to settle the birds. "I'll wait here," she told Anna.

"But you have to come inside. I need to see you reexperience the cabin firsthand."

Tilly didn't move and so Anna took a seat on the porch step, deciding, apparently, to switch back into interview mode.

"How about the bombs? What was the technique Frank used? I mean I know he used dynamite, but can you talk specifics? Those are the kinds of details I need for the biography that I can't find in the public record."

Tilly threw her stick into the distance and watched it break into pieces when it hit the ground. She was tired of answering questions. Tired of talking about Frank.

"Or if you don't know that, maybe you can tell me how Frank explained it to you back then. I mean about the bombs. Did you know he was blowing up dams? Or is that something you learned later?"

Tilly stepped off the porch and into the yellowed grasses blowing in the wind before turning back around. "Of course I knew. But I had no reason to think what Frank and I did wasn't normal. I knew we lived different, but I didn't understand how much. Not until Frank left and the rest of the world told me so." Tilly walked back towards the hemlocks.

From behind her, came Frank's voice. "*I love you.*"

Tilly spun around, trembling. Anna held up a small tape recorder.

"*I love you, too.*" That was a woman's voice. Anna's, Tilly realized.

The tape hissed and crackled. "I'm going away for a while," Frank's voice said.

Anna pressed stop. "I had a feeling I wouldn't see him again for a long time. That's why I made this recording. To keep him with me."

Those purple asters, the ones Frank had planted and she'd tried to kill all those year ago, bloomed beside the porch. She hadn't noticed them before.

"I would have helped him," Anna said, "if he'd told me what he was doing."

The cabin, crouched there, was like something alive and dangerous.

"I'm going in there with or without you," Anna said. "Avoiding this place doesn't erase the past."

The wind pushed against Tilly's back, and she returned to the porch, brushed past Anna, and shoved the rusty hinges until the door stood wide open.

chapter fifty-three

The cabin had a remote, stale air, as though satisfied to have resumed its abandoned state. It was clear no one had been in there. The sharp must of damp earth and rotten wood took Tilly back to the early days she and Frank had slept with the door and windows open, trying to air the place out. His voice and face were suddenly so clear to her she expected to see him step from the shadows, just as he had in her shop.

A fall of weak light coming through the dusty windows lit up powdery strands of cobwebs hanging over the table where they'd eaten their last dinners together. But now the table, along with everything in her former home was filthy with animal droppings.

Anna swiped away cobwebs a little fearfully with the corner of her notebook as she made her way to the cupboard door above the sink. She reached in and took out a plate, caressing it before setting it on the counter and reaching for another dish. "I can't believe this is all still here."

Tilly went to the window, covered her hand with her sleeve and rubbed at the windowpane until she could see the place where Frank had walked through the hemlocks on his way down the mountain each day to meet Helen. Why would he have kept that from her?

"Where did he sleep?" Anna's eyes seemed over-wide and bright.

Tilly tilted her head toward the overturned cot. "There, and I was there."

"How about his journal? Where did he keep that?"

"Under his cot."

Cobwebs were of no concern now as Anna walked toward Frank's cot tracking footprints through the dust with her camera clicking away. "I can't believe this place hasn't been vandalized. It's just as he left it."

Tilly had never been back to the cabin. The police and FBI had sealed this part of Frank's file. Henry must have kept the place a secret, too.

Tilly bent to examine the nine scratches she'd made on the wall. She felt a deep well of loneliness from that time. That feeling had never entirely left her. She'd just gotten better at living with it. Or ignoring it.

Anna eased herself onto Frank's cot even as the tattered, rotten fabric ripped in places. Somehow it still held her. "I did love sleeping next to him." Anna turned her head to inhale, as though the moth-eaten fabric could still smell of him.

Tilly went back to the doorway, having seen enough of the place. And Anna.

"How did Henry know you were here?" Anna asked. "When he called the police? Did he really just happen to find you that day like he said? I never bought that story."

"We knew each other back then." Tilly stepped onto the porch and took a long, cleansing inhale she hoped would ease the headache she felt coming on.

"What do you mean you and Henry knew each other?" Anna now stood beside her having given up whatever fantasy world she'd been in.

Tilly had closed her eyes for a moment against the bright outdoor light that caused a sharp pain in her head. "We were friends that summer." That came out without the usual premeditation. But she was tired of secrets. She stepped off the porch toward the tall grass. Anna followed her down the mountain.

When they reached Tilly's house, the generator next to the dam roared to life and Anna jumped at the noise. They watched as men set the last of the hose in place: the hose they'd use to divert the creek so they could remove the dam. "Think Frank'll show before they take it out?" Anna asked.

Tilly didn't answer even though she felt certain he wouldn't stand by and let the FBI take out this dam. Not if he could do it himself.

Despite the headache, Tilly tried to work in the shop. Joints for the sideboard required exacting precision since any small space would show. Pieces had to be measured to one one-thousandth of an inch. The work was slow and painstaking and, it turned out, impossible with her head hurting the way it was. And anyway, work wasn't going to tame the restlessness inside her, not this time. She had an undeniable feeling something big and unstoppable was rolling toward her and she wasn't ready for it.

She walked outside into the cool night air. Moths fluttering and whirling against the outdoor light by the shop door were pushed by a gust of sharp wind that cut through her sweater.

She looked across the cemetery to Finn and Henry's house remembering now that Finn was away visiting his mom. It wasn't that late, and she couldn't go back into her house by herself, not yet. Maybe she and Henry could have another look at Finn's paintings.

chapter fifty-four

As Tilly walked to Henry's, moonlight glinted off black granite stones along the cemetery path until a thick cloud folded and closed over the moon. Then all she could see were different densities of darkness around her. The lit windows around the cemetery seemed suspended in nothingness. She patted her back pocket for her phone, but she'd left it back at the shop. The wind gusted again, and the way it was honed toward her face felt somehow personal. She slipped her hands into the sleeves of her sweater as she walked on.

Halfway to Henry's she tripped on something and fell. She lifted her hand to see the blood she could feel trickling down her palm, but the darkness was so complete her hand hung in a blackness that looked the same with her eyes open or closed.

She got to her feet, set her eyes on Henry's lit window and kept walking. At the edge of the cemetery, something hit her hard at hip level. "Damn it!"

Her hand met the rough texture of crumbling mortar and stone. The wall around the cemetery. The one that had always been there. The moon broke through the clouds, illuminating a cluster of ferns growing on the wall. Now she could see that stuck to her hand were rotten crumbs of the mortar that once held the stone wall together. She kicked the wall, sending more crumbs flying.

When she knocked, Henry didn't answer. Not even on the second or third knock. Crystal's bedroom light came on and her curtain peeled back. Tilly picked up a handful of stones and pelted them at Henry's window.

A minute later he was there opening the door, pulling down a shirt he'd just put on, eyes puffy.

In his kitchen Tilly got a look at the blood smeared across her sweater where she'd tried to wipe it off.

Henry blinked, suddenly more awake. "What happened? Are you all right?"

"I wanted to see Finn's paintings again, while he's at his mom's ..." she held up her hand, "but I tripped on my way here."

"Come to the sink." He turned on the water, tested the temperature and then held her palm under a gentle stream, while she pretended it didn't hurt.

"I know it stings," he said.

She could smell the mintiness of his soap. He turned off the water and pressed a fresh towel to her hand. "Keep pressure on it and go sit," he said, gesturing toward the kitchen island before leaving and returning with the largest first-aid kit she'd ever seen.

"Good grief."

"I have this for Finn. And it's a good thing because you need more than a Band-Aid."

He removed the towel and seeming satisfied with what he saw, dabbed ointment on the cuts. He pressed a nonstick pad to her hand and then began wrapping her hand in gauze to hold it in place. It was too much fuss, but he was determined and worked slowly, taking his time.

"You know what I've wondered?" He wound the gauze around and around.

"What?"

"Why you always wait until I walk away before getting your mail. I'm halfway to the Hart place before you ever open your door."

She glanced at him. "I figured it was easier if we didn't have to see each other face to face."

"Easier for you maybe."

She could feel heat in her cheeks and didn't dare meet his eyes as he secured the last of the gauze in place.

"I went back to the cabin today." She wanted him to know this. He was the only one who could understand what that meant.

"And?"

"I thought the place had collapsed or burned. That's how I imagined it anyway. But it's still standing."

He looked at her closely. "I think about that summer sometimes, when I can't sleep."

So he did think of her then, and at night.

He wanted to kiss her. She was pretty sure of that. But she didn't know if that was a good idea. She stood. "Maybe we should go check out those paintings?"

chapter fifty-five

Tilly and Henry studied the first few in the series of Finn's paintings, the ones more carefully composed and less abstract. "Look at this dot of red paint here." Tilly pointed to the mill window. All the paintings had this detail. She just hadn't seen it before.

Henry leaned in and then stepped back, considering. He scanned the other paintings. "There's a person there," he said. Tilly saw it now, too. A shadowy shape stood in the window. The relief she felt at finally figuring this out was quickly followed by a thorny feeling.

Her head throbbed. The blinking light on Finn's answering machine wasn't helping. "Does anyone ever check those messages? I mean aren't they from Finn's mom? That's what he told me once."

"Sometimes. But it's mostly junk calls. That's probably what those are."

A pencil and pad of paper lay next to the phone. On the notepad Tilly noticed a small canoe printed near the top. She walked over, picked up the notepad and studied it before turning it toward Henry. "Didn't Ada say Finn had a paper with him at the library? One with a boat on it?"

"Yeah."

Tilly picked up the pencil and rubbed the lead lightly against the paper, revealing what had been written there most recently: *Frank Stone, Paul and Helen Cotter. Picture? Flood?* She turned the notepad toward Henry.

He walked over and pushed *PLAY* on the answering machine.

A message from a home insurance company promising lower rates was followed by another from someone running for state senate.

Tilly leaned against the wall when a wave of dizziness came over her. She needed to go home soon. She was overwarmed. Felt fevered.

Another beep on the machine was followed by: *Henry? Are you there? I need to talk to you. It's Helen. Your ... grandpa's wife.*

Henry and Tilly looked at each other, then at the machine. There was a long pause on the tape.

Henry, can you pick up? There are some things you should know, now that ..." She paused, as though trying to figure out what to say next. *"There was a man named Frank Stone. I guess you know who that is. Anyway, we had an argument in front of the mill office. He had a picture he was going to show your grandpa, which I didn't want him to see. I threw the photo into the creek. Frank went in after it.*

Henry and Tilly waited through another long pause.

Right as Frank went into the water, your grandpa pulled into the office driveway. I didn't want him to see me there, you see. So I ran into the mill office, and ... I saw the rest from a window. Her voice went shaky. *The creek was a torrent. You have to understand—*

The tape stopped with a sharp click.

Henry wasn't looking at Tilly. His mind was probably like hers, full of too many thoughts at once. Helen was alive. She was talking about the morning Tilly'd seen her with Frank. He'd been trying to get her to take something from his hand. That must have been the photograph she'd mentioned. And this is what Finn was painting. He must have been in his room when the message came across. And the person she'd seen in the car that day, the same one in Finn's painting, was Paul Cotter.

Tilly turned to Henry. "I ... I don't know what Frank did. I'm sorry."

"I have something I want to show you," he said. "Downstairs."

Tilly sat at Henry's kitchen island while he went to get whatever he wanted to show her. All of this felt very important, but she definitely had a fever and wasn't sure she could manage the walk home on her own.

Suddenly Henry was beside her, holding a scarf. "I found it on the stream bank, in front of the mill on the day they all vanished. The same day Helen is talking about in that message. The same day you were there."

Tilly took the scarf in her hands studying the uneven knit of green yarn. She'd last seen it in Frank's pocket when he was outside the mill building arguing with Helen. She swallowed past a rawness in her throat.

"I thought you were with Frank that morning and dropped the scarf," Henry was saying. "That's why I figured you went with them and why I never came looking for you."

Tilly lay the scarf down and rested her head in her hands trying to keep the thread of this conversation. "With who? Who's them?"

"Frank and Helen left Cottersville together, not my grandpa and Helen," he said slowly, waiting to let this sink in.

"But if your grandpa didn't leave with Helen, where'd he go?"

Henry didn't answer that. Instead he pressed his hand carefully to her cheek. "You're not well. I'll take you home. We'll talk about this later."

chapter fifty-six

Tilly woke, unsure of where she was and struggling for orientation. This was her bed. Her house. It was night. But noises were coming from the kitchen. She sat up, suddenly alert.

Henry appeared in the doorway.

"What are you doing here?" Her voice sounded gravely, as she tried and failed to remember how she'd gotten there.

"You passed out on the drive here. Then you came to and refused to go to the hospital. Insisted two aspirin was all you needed. I couldn't leave you alone. So here I am."

"I just have a cold or something." She put her hand to her head remembering the fever. That was gone now. "I do feel a little better, now that I've slept. I'll be all right. You can go."

His eyes went to the floor and then back to her. "I'd like to stay, at least for a while, to be on the safe side."

"Okay." She didn't really want him to leave anyway.

He stepped into the bedroom to look at her portrait hanging on the wall. "You kept this."

"I've always loved it."

He moved a chair from along the wall to sit beside the bed.

Neither of them said anything but it was a companionable silence. She now remembered what they'd heard on Finn's answering machine. Sharing this new revelation with Henry made her feel closer to him, like she could ask him what she'd never been able to. "You never said anything to the FBI about Frank and Helen's relationship or that Helen's my mother. Why?"

"You weren't saying anything and so neither was I."

Tilly closed her eyes, thinking about the summer that separated her life into two parts. It was the same for Henry. Why had they never spoken of it? "That September you went to live with your uncle. How was that?"

He thought about her question. "He was good to me. People around here helped. It wasn't as hard as it could have been had I been on my own. What about you?" He looked guilty, she thought, as though whatever she'd been through had been his fault.

"The worst part was being left with so many questions no matter how hard I've tried not to care about the answers."

"What kinds of questions?"

She thought about that and gave him a sad smile. "Maybe there's really just one. Did Frank really care about me? Because having to wonder about that hasn't given me a lot of trust. Not in other people. And certainly not in myself. I loved him. Still do. But maybe I'm a fool."

"It's hard to know who people really are. Especially family."

Tilly wasn't sure she entirely agreed. Many people had families they relied on. "I'm sorry about not telling you who Frank was when we were younger."

Henry rested his forearm on the edge of the bed. "How do you feel about Frank now?"

She thought about this. "Mixed up. He had a lot of secrets. I think it must have been lonely to carry them around, to never lay them down in front of anyone."

Henry studied his hands. "I have a secret I'd like you to know. It's about my grandpa."

Here it was. Tilly was afraid of what Frank might have done, even by accident. "Okay."

He sat, gathering his thoughts. "The morning you saw Frank and Helen together—"

She nodded.

"—I was in my room, Finn's room now. I happened to be at the window when Grandpa, dressed in his business suit, went into the creek and head directly for the spillway. He walked in with a purpose." Henry stopped talking for a long moment. "And he didn't come out. That photo Helen mentioned in her message had to have been of Frank and her. Frank must have fished it out of the water and shown it to Grandpa. He was already down about the bankruptcy. And he loved Helen so much. I think an affair on top of everything else would have crushed him, especially when he realized Helen was going to leave him."

Tilly couldn't believe Paul Cotter would have taken his life, if that was what Henry was saying. There'd been so much love between him and his grandpa.

"I created all kinds of reasons for why Grandpa went into the water." Henry was back there in his mind. Tilly imagined him, fourteen years old, watching from his bedroom and trying to make sense of what he was seeing.

"I couldn't see part of the dam from where I stood. I figured he was over that way. I expected at any moment he'd walk home through the cemetery, sopping wet with some story. But, you know, if I'd run to him as soon as he went in, instead of standing there ...."

"Henry ...."

"I didn't realize how high the water was. How powerful it could become." He clutched his hands in front of him. "But when I finally did go down there, I found no one. Just your scarf. That's when I saw the water up close and began to piece together what happened." Henry stood and went to the window. He parted the curtain and looked out into the night. "But it didn't really solidify in my mind until later when Grandpa and Helen didn't come home. Then all the reasons I could come up with for why they might have left for a day, or two, or three didn't bear out. Slowly, I realized there could be no other explanation other than Grandpa'd gone into the creek not planning to come out. And after that, Frank and Helen left together so they wouldn't be blamed."

Henry let the curtain fall and returned to the chair beside the bed. "It was days before I told anyone. I reported them missing, but that was it. I stayed quiet about everything else. I mean, how could I explain it had taken me days to figure out what I'd seen with my own eyes? And really I didn't want anyone to know. Not about what Grandpa had done or that I'd done nothing to stop it. So I let people believe Grandpa and Helen left because of the bankruptcy. That seemed better than him being remembered for giving up."

Henry sat quiet for a moment. "I've thought about setting the record straight. But after Finn was born it became important he never know I'd just stood there and let that happen. Or that his grandpa was capable of such a thing. Finn paints like him. He reminds me so much of Grandpa that I don't want him to know about the suicide. Because what if ...."

Tilly lifted the covers. "Come lie beside me." He climbed in and she put her arm around him. "Maybe there's more to all of this than we understand." She wanted this to be true.

He locked his hands behind his head. "I know what I saw. I thought I knew my grandpa. But you can't really know anyone."

She propped herself up so she could look at him. If there was one person Tilly did know it was Henry. And he knew her. At least in the ways that mattered. Inside, they were still who'd they'd always been.

His eyes turned from hers to the ceiling, like he needed some distance to say the next thing. "I think his body, whatever's left of it, is stuck in the spillway, like that old tire. Things get trapped there." He glanced at her. "Bones too maybe. I know that sounds crazy. But I've had nightmares about it." He closed his eyes. "That's why I fought for the dam to stay where it is."

She took Henry's hand and held it to her chest.

He turned to her. "Do you think Frank's coming back? Is that why Helen called my house?"

The fear in his voice made Tilly's throat close for a moment. She swallowed hard. "I don't know why she called."

He stared at her for a long moment, his face revealed nothing of what he was thinking. "I want you to know why I called the police on you that night."

"Okay."

"I thought Frank and Helen took you with them. That's the only thing that made sense to me. When you showed up at my school half-starved and without even a coat, I had to go to the police. It was almost winter, remember? I didn't know how you'd make it through. I couldn't do nothing. I'd already done too much of that."

She touched his cheek.

"I planned to warn you, but the police went in the middle of the night instead of waiting until morning. I didn't think it through. I'm sorry about how things turned out. You took a tremendous risk being my friend back then. But I only understood that later."

They'd both risked so much for each other.

His lips brushed hers. She kissed him back with a sudden, deep need held back for far too long.

chapter fifty-seven

Tilly woke to the sound of voices outside. She slipped out of bed where Henry still lay sleeping and wrapped a robe around herself, scanning the curtains in the house. All closed, thank god. She peeked through a small parting of the curtains. The press had gathered again, only there were more of them now.

She checked her phone. There'd been an explosion just after midnight at a dam only fifteen miles away. A man had been injured. He was in the hospital, unconscious.

Tilly dialed Anna and got voicemail. Surely, she would've heard about this by now. Maybe she was already on her way. Tilly looked again at Henry. Anna couldn't find him here. And neither could any of the reporters outside. Not right now. Henry and Finn couldn't be tied to whatever Frank had done.

Henry's sleeping face was so blissfully unaware that she waited another minute before shaking him awake.

He opened his eyes, giving her a warm smile she couldn't return.

"There's been a bombing, at a dam close to here. A man's been hurt. Reporters are outside. I tried calling Anna Birch, but she's not answering. She might already be on her way so, she could be here soon. You should go."

Henry sat up and swung his feet to the floor. "The man—is he okay?"

Her throat tightened. "I don't know."

"You think it's Frank?"

"Maybe."

Henry rubbed his eyes. "Did you say Anna Birch?"

"Mac Stevens told me to get a PR person to handle the press, so I hired her."

He ran his hand through his hair, still trying to wake up. "She's writing that book about Frank, right?"

Someone banged on the front door. "Ms. Stone! John Stipe from *The Philadelphia Inquirer*. I have some questions."

"When's Finn due back?" she asked Henry.

He stood and pulled on his pants. "This morning. He and his mom drove most of the way last night. They stayed in a hotel. They're supposed to arrive around seven. And she's usually right on time."

Tilly checked her phone. It was a quarter till seven. "If Anna doesn't show up in the next few minutes, I'll go talk to the reporters." She reached for a shirt and a pair of jeans.

"You should be back in bed."

She did her shirt buttons. "While I have their attention, you slip out the back and go around the long way to get home. Finn shouldn't come back and find you gone, not in the state he's in. Not unless you can call his mom?"

"She doesn't use a cell anymore."

Tilly went into the bathroom and pulled her hair into a ponytail while Henry checked his phone for news of the bombing.

"*Jesus*," he said.

"What?"

"You talked to Anna Birch about me and my family?"

"I ..." She couldn't remember what she'd said to Anna.

"Look." He turned his phone toward her. "Anna posted this on her blog last night. It came up when I searched for news of the bombing."

Biography Update and <u>My</u> <u>Visit</u> to Frank's
Cabin!!!!

I've been to the cabin where Frank lived
right before going into hiding. Many details
will be included in my biography. Out soon!
There's an intriguing connection between
Tilly Stone, Frank's daughter, and Henry
Cotter, as in <u>Cotter Paper</u>, the same company
responsible for the Cottersville Dam! Pre-
order my biography now to get the whole story.

Henry regarded her with sudden distance. "That woman has tried to get me to talk to her plenty of times, but it's not any of her business what was between us. Or how our families are connected."

Tilly finished tying her shoes and stood. "Anna insisted I take her to the cabin. That's why I was there. Seeing the place brought up a lot. I think I only mentioned we knew each other as kids."

A storm of emotions played across his face. "What are you going to say if you go out there and talk to those reporters? Or if you send Anna out there?"

"What do you mean?"

"You're gonna do whatever you can to stop the dam from coming out, right? For Finn?"

She wished she could see inside Henry, measure the proportions of love, fear, and anger. "After last night don't you think things need to be laid out in the open, Henry? So many people have been hurt because of that dam and all the secrets it holds."

A thud against the back door and a muffled groan made them both turn. Tilly went to the back door with a sinking feeling about who was there.

Frank, pale and sweating, leaned against the doorway, his right hand wrapped in dirty, bloody rags. She pulled him into the house, and closed the door, glancing at Henry as a visible tremor of what he was seeing ran through him.

"No one saw me," Frank said, as though this was what

mattered. Sweat dripped from his temples. She reached for his bandaged hand, and he jerked away. "You don't want my blood in your house for the FBI to find."

"What's he doing here, Tilly?" Henry said.

She grabbed Frank's wrist, held firm, and started to unwrap his hand. He'd done the bandage himself with strips of rags torn from the shirt he wore. She pulled the last piece of cloth free. Three of his fingers were missing.

"I need to know what he's doing here," Henry demanded again.

"I can't explain it all right now, okay?"

"What is it you were saying about secrets?" Henry stepped past Frank to the back door. "Stay out of my life. And away from Finn. Both of you need to get the hell out of Cottersville."

Then he was gone.

Frank stared at his hand, his breath coming too rapidly.

"The news said someone was in the hospital. That wasn't you?"

Frank shook his head. "I was there at the dam." He glanced at her. "But this isn't what it looks like."

Only bloody, raw stumps remained where his fingers had been. She checked around for her phone. "You need a hospital."

"There's nothing they can do now." Frank gathered up the old rags laying on the floor with his good hand and stuffed them into his coat pocket. "It was Anna. I followed her. Mac Stevens was there, too. I didn't see him at first, not until it was too late. I tried to wave him off, but ...."

Tilly sat back. She couldn't connect all the parts. Didn't want to. "What do you mean Mac was there?"

"He must have suspected Anna, too. Followed her, like I did."

"Mac's the one in the hospital?"

Frank nodded.

Tilly sat unmoving, thinking of Mac's family. "Tell me what's really going on here, Frank." Was he actually trying to shift the responsibility to Anna? Did he expect her to believe that? She wasn't a thirteen-year-old child anymore.

It hit her then—the full magnitude of his self-centered arrogance. He wouldn't even look at her now. She checked the time. It was just a few minutes till seven. She could still be a distraction for Henry to get home to Finn. She could do that at least.

She left Frank sitting there and walked out the front door.

chapter fifty-eight

As soon as Tilly closed the door behind her and stepped outside, she knew she was in over her head. She hadn't realized how many people there were. Her heart pounded against her rib cage as she became their sole focus. Their faces blurred in front of her eyes. She turned to go back inside but was blocked by cell phones now jutting toward her face from every direction. They all spoke at once, calling her name, trying to overpower the person next to them. Lights flashed. They pushed in, taking all the air.

"Ms. Stone! Ms. Stone! Tilly Stone …."

There was no space for her. She needed to say something but didn't know what. Wished she'd thought about that before she'd left the house. She fought the urge to crouch and cover her head. She wasn't up to this.

Get it together she told herself. She'd made a decision to come out here. She had to walk this tightrope because it was too late to look down now. Tilly tried to think of what Anna would do if she were there. She held up two hands like a crossing guard and put everything she had into pretending she wasn't about to crumble.

The crowd quieted some. Enough that she could take one breath, let it out and take another. She stood on her tiptoes to make herself taller. "I just learned about last night's bombing."

234

They could hear the quiver in her voice as well as she could.

Questions flew at her like shotgun spray. At least she could make sense of some of them now. She raised both palms again and tried to crank up the command in her voice. "*If* you stay quiet, I'll take three questions. But raise your hand and wait until I call on you."

Hands went up and she searched the crowd for a kind face. An older man, with a tape recorder instead of a phone stood nearby. "You in the green tie."

"Will your father get to the dam before the Feds do?"

Anna had warned her before to say as little as possible. "No comment." She wasn't here to answer their questions anyway. This was to help Henry get home. "Next." She pointed to a woman in her twenties. "Have you seen your father?"

Tilly thought of the bloody stumps where his fingers had been. A loud whistle coming from the direction of the cemetery made everyone turn.

It was Henry. What was he *doing*?

"Shouldn't you all be talking to Frank Stone?" he yelled, hands cupped around his mouth. "I understand he's not that hard to find."

"That's Henry Cotter," someone said. A rumble ran through the crowd.

Tilly reddened as the press wheeled around to catch her re-action. It seemed they'd all read Anna's blog. Was Henry about to tell them Frank was in her house, for god's sake?

Blood pumped audibly through her ears and she knew she wasn't going to be able to keep up this façade. *You can't breathe*, a voice inside insisted. Tilly tried to suck some air in, remembering how Mac had helped her before. Except now Mac was in the hospital. Tilly swayed as she watched Henry turn and stride toward home.

"You all right?" asked a woman to her right.

"No more questions," Tilly managed to say, but too softly to really be heard. She would faint in front of all these people. And was Frank still in her house? She tried to ignore the growing tightness in her chest, while her vision narrowed to pinpricks.

"You said three," a woman in a red scarf yelled. Tilly blinked, trying to understand. "Three questions." *You're out of air.* "I have just a quick one."

"I have to get inside," Tilly managed.

The reporters, apparently seeing the situation, parted so Tilly could get her hand on the doorknob, which helped calm her enough to be able to turn back to the crowd for a moment. That's when she noticed Agent Sharp. Maybe he had news of Mac.

"What will you do if your father shows up?" the reporter beside her asked.

Tilly could feel her hand tremble on the doorknob. She blinked, biting her lip to keep herself there. Voices swelled around her as she turned the doorknob and slipped inside pulling the door shut behind her.

chapter fifty-nine

Frank was gone. And it was a good thing because Agent Sharp came through the door right after Tilly closed it.

"We need to talk."

She hoped against hope. "How's Mac?"

He regarded her with cold distance. "I'll assume you learned about Mac from the news that just broke." He didn't believe that, and he was letting her know it. "His brain's so swollen they had to put a hole in his skull. He's unconscious. No one knows if he'll wake up."

Tilly thought of Mac's wife and daughters. His granddaughter. He loved them so much.

Sharp cocked his head, studying her as though he could see through whatever bullshit she would offer up next. "That bombing last night was different from the way Frank did things. Not the kind of set-up he used. What do you know about that?"

"Nothing." She wanted to know more about Mac, but she wasn't going to get anything else out of Sharp on that. She wasn't even sure he cared much about Mac's condition. Rather it seemed he was ready to use him to get to her.

Outside a truck dumped another load of riprap next to the dam. A few men worked to drop an intake hose into the creek. They were almost ready to start pumping water to reroute the creek downstream. As soon as that section was dry, they'd take the dam out. "It's about to happen," she said to herself.

Sharp crossed his arms and stepped to the window. "Dam comes out the day after tomorrow. If Frank shows, we think it'll be tomorrow night. Law enforcement from all over the country are mobilizing right now. We're going to sweep this entire area of press and people tomorrow by dusk. I've already talked to everyone on this side of the cemetery and told them to find another place to stay the next couple nights."

Tilly thought about her neighbors. They'd be afraid for themselves and their property. Where would John and Mary go? Would they be able to find a place for their animals, too?

Sharp stepped to the door. "We'll keep the Frank followers away, given the potential danger. But we need you at home."

It started raining outside but the workers at the dam continued as though nothing had changed. "You mean you need me to act as bait?"

"Frank will expect you at home."

chapter sixty

After Sharp left, Tilly was too exhausted to do anything but turn off the lights and go to bed even though the day had just started. Everything was ruined anyway.

She stayed in bed all day and through the night, feeling a strong disinclination toward everything. By Friday morning the weight of what had happened over the last week felt so heavy she half expected the floor to crack beneath her. This life she'd made, the people she cared about, her home, her business; all of it was slipping away. She'd never deserved any of it anyway. She'd put Henry and Finn in danger, as well as the community she'd so wanted to a part of. People in town were fed up. She had no answers from Frank and no idea what he would do now. Then there was poor Mac, so badly injured.

Morning turned to afternoon and all she could think about was how she'd let Frank back into her life, because some old feeling of allegiance still bound her to him. For seventeen years she'd closed herself off and waited for him to provide some explanation that would make everything understandable, some storyline in which she wasn't a fool. Henry was right: the only thing she could do now was leave Cottersville and hope Frank followed her.

It was dark again when her cell rang, stirring her from the deep place in her mind. She answered with a croaking hello.

"Tilly?"

She tried to make her brain work. She looked at the caller ID. It was Charlie, from the gallery.

"Are you sick?"

"I'm fine." She wished her voice sounded less heavy.

There was a long silence. "You don't sound fine. Is there someone I can call?"

"No."

"You're sure?" He wanted to believe her.

"Yes."

"Okay, well, I'm calling because I wondered if you'd had a chance to look at that contract?"

She tried to think. Then it came to her: that woman in California with the new house who wanted the furniture. Tilly turned her head toward the mail scattered on the floor under the mail slot. "I have to go away," she told him. "You'll have to find someone else."

He was quiet for a long moment. "I'm coming to see you."

"I'm leaving," she said. "It's too late."

She could hear his chair squeak as he shifted around. "Stay where you are. I'll be there in—"

She hung up and got out of bed. It was time. She didn't want any part of whatever Frank was up to. But it was possible he'd follow her out of town and spare Cottersville and the people she cared about from any more harm.

chapter sixty-one

FRIDAY SATURDAY SUNDAY MONDAY TUESDAY WEDNESDAY THURSDAY **FRIDAY** SATURDAY SUNDAY

Tilly tossed her pack on the truck seat and decided to stop by Henry's one last time before she drove off.

A black car was parked outside his house. Through the kitchen window she could see Sharp, paying close attention to everything Henry was telling him. Sharp was doing his job well. Tilly could almost hear the confidential note in his voice. If that had been Mac, he'd be telling Henry about his granddaughter by now and Henry would be thinking he was a good person, which he was. But Sharp just played the part. Henry loved Finn so much. He would protect him from whoever he had to, including her. Henry'd tell Sharp about Frank showing up in her kitchen, about Helen and her phone message. He'd reveal how she'd betrayed his trust and Finn's, putting them in danger. He'd talk about how difficult she'd made things for Cottersville.

The night seemed to reach its deepest point and she put the truck window down to listen to the sounds of her town one last time. A white cat stepped across the road in front of her, taking its time. The cat stopped and stared at her for a long moment before walking off, unhurried. A breeze came through the window smelling strongly of creek water. That made her think of the creek in Finn's paintings and then of Helen's phone message. Helen had called Henry for a reason they didn't yet entirely know.

She knew what had happened to Frank and Paul that day. She'd been there.

Tilly looked back at her home and noticed something white near the dam. She was pretty sure it was a person. She started the truck and drove back to her place.

chapter sixty-two

Anna sat in a long white dress at the edge of the creek next to the dam. Tilly thought about what Frank had said: that he and Mac had followed her to the other dam. Maybe he'd been telling the truth after all. Mac had never liked the idea of Tilly working with her. And Tilly remembered now what Anna had once told her: that violence works.

Tilly sat beside her, pulling her knees to her chest, and wrapping her arms around them. Anna turned to look at her with the same brightness that had been in her wide eyes at the cabin when she lay on Frank's rotting cot. Only now, Tilly saw it wasn't excitement, but more like something unhinged. "What are you doing out here?"

Anna seemed surprised by the question. Her hair, done in a French twist, was starting to unravel in the wind. "Waiting for Frank, just like you."

Sharp told Tilly they'd clear everyone away, but here was Anna in plain sight and, despite what Sharp had said, there was no sign of law enforcement.

Moonlight reflected off the fine, dark sediment in the empty creek bed beside them. Roots in the stream bank dripped onto the layers of sand and mud-covered river stone. The absence of running water gave the sense of something interrupted, yet the smell of the creek was still strong. Wind whipped strands of hair against Anna's cheek, making her appear young and vulnerable. Frank had haunted her, too. Tilly could see that now.

"So it's been you," Tilly said.

Anna turned her eyes to the woods and Tilly had the feeling she wished to go there so she could sit and think about how she'd gotten to this point, somehow justify it better than she could right now. She turned back to Tilly and her face showed how much her insides were yanking her around, tormenting her. She'd found herself in a place she'd never meant to be.

"Frank made promises to me, too. And I figured out how to prove myself to him," she said. "I've done the research. I know what works to get results. Sometimes violence is necessary for the greater good." She held up the two sticks of dynamite in her hand. "We can take this dam out together. He'd like that."

Anna'd gone and done desperate things. As desperate as waiting for Frank for seventeen years. "What if he's not coming back for you?"

Anna shook her head as though this were impossible.

"I've wanted to believe he'd make things right. Just like you," Tilly said. "But maybe that's not up to him."

The whites of her eyes showed all around as she stared at Tilly. "Do you have any idea what I've been through?"

Tilly did understand, at least some of it. Anna needed Frank to tell her he loved her best and that she'd been the most important thing. That she counted. They'd both waited for him to tell them they were worth something. They'd given him that power. "Tell me how it's been for you." Tilly wanted to keep Anna talking while she tried to think of how to get the dynamite from her. But she also genuinely wanted to know.

Anna took a deep breath, letting it out slowly. "You don't even think Frank loved me." She was angry. Tilly sensed she was putting a lot into trying to keep her temper. "His only daughter, the one who knew him best. Why won't you say where he is? Why pretend you don't know?"

For years, Anna'd probably turned every memory with Frank over and over in the hope there might be a future in which things would be different. Deep down they'd both waited for him to step through the door ready to love them again and explain why he'd stayed away so long. They'd waited for answers they thought they deserved. Thought they needed. They'd locked all their hopes on a man who'd proved to be as solid as smoke.

Anna gave her a swift sideways glance. "I, for one, haven't stopped believing in him." She pulled a lighter from her pocket and stood.

Agent Sharp stepped out of the shadows. "Hands in the air, Ms. Birch. You, too, Ms. Stone."

It wasn't just Sharp. They were suddenly surrounded by all forms of law enforcement, pointing their guns.

Slowly, Tilly raised her hands and rose to her feet. An officer took the dynamite from Anna.

Out of nowhere Finn came running, his hair sticking up in all directions. He let out a wild yelp. Henry was right behind him, trying to catch Finn, grabbing for the back of his shirt. Finn bolted through the line of officers to stand in front of Tilly. "She ... hasn't done ... anything!" His untested voice sounded tinny and fractured.

"Finn!" Henry shouted.

"Go back to your dad," Tilly said, gently, her heart breaking at the courage he'd just shown.

Sharp motioned to Henry who came forward. Henry glanced at her and their eyes met before he steered Finn back to the edge of the lawn.

"Search the property," Sharp barked. Officers went off in every direction while Sharp bent Tilly's arms painfully behind her back and handcuffed her. Henry and Finn stood watching while Tilly and Anna were put into separate cars.

From the back of the police cruiser, Tilly watched Henry blowing on Finn's hands trying to warm them. She couldn't stop thinking about the fear she'd seen in Henry's eyes when he'd come for Finn. Fear for her or of her—she couldn't tell which.

chapter sixty-three

It was now two in the morning. Anna was in another room at the police station. Tilly hadn't seen her since they'd arrived hours ago.

Tilly'd been left to sit alone, intentionally, she thought, in a room smelling of sour coffee and old sweat, lit by a single flickering fluorescent light.

When Sharp finally came in, he sat across from her with an angry confrontational air. He turned and hit PLAY on a recording machine in the corner of the room, speaking aloud the date and time. "So, let's start at the beginning, before you and Frank arrived in Cottersville, back in 2006. At that time, what was your involvement with the bombings?"

Sharp saw people as good or bad. He wasn't like Mac whose mind and heart worked together to understand. Mac was interested in the hows and whys where Sharp only wanted someone to blame.

"I built the bombs. And set them off."

One eyebrow rose. Sharp hadn't expected that answer. "Starting when?"

She thought about this, trying to remember. Her chair was hard and she shifted around for a more comfortable position. "I was about six when I built my first one, although I had Frank's help in the beginning."

Sharp put both hands flat on the table. "So, you were directly involved in *all* the bombings from the time you were six until you were thirteen? For seven years?"

All she'd known was Frank. That's what no one seemed to consider. She'd grown up indoctrinated with the idea that she and Frank were fighting to make a difference in the world while others stood idly by. She might have questioned their lifestyle, but she had believed in what they were doing because that had been her entire world. Trying to explain this to Sharp would be useless.

He clasped his hands together on the table, as though this required all of his patience. "I'm going to be up front with you. Because I want to do us both a favor since," he looked at his watch, "it's late and we're tired. Why don't you just admit what we already know anyway. You set the bomb that injured Agent Stevens. Maybe it was an accident that he got hurt. Maybe you even feel bad about it. But it wasn't Frank." He shook his head as though he expected her to join in. "Because if Frank was alive, we'd have found him by now. I've heard the rumors about people seeing him out in the woods or whatever, but I don't believe it. No one stays on the run for seventeen years. It's too hard. Agent Stevens has been tracking thin air this whole time because, in fact, it's been you. And then you involved Anna Birch."

Sharp seemed to be waiting for the slightest flinch of tension or withdrawal.

He tapped his pen on the thick file in front of him. "I'm gonna lay the evidence out for you, okay? Because that says everything." He gave a quick nod to himself. "You built your house and business on the Cotter Paper property. You wanted to be right beside that dam because you enjoyed the attention that brought. Frank's fame meant that you, too, were famous. Then you thought you'd try to get rid of the dam because that's what Frank wanted, and it would bring you even more attention. But no matter what you did, Henry Cotter stood in your way. You sure as hell weren't gonna let that happen. So, you decided to resurrect Frank and blow it up while you were at it. You recruited Anna Birch to help you, manipulating her into doing your dirty work."

Tilly didn't even have to try for the blank look she gave him.

Sharp moved the file aside and leaned in, pissed or playing pissed, she wasn't sure which. "Domestic terrorism is a federal offense. Not to mention what you'll face for Agent Stevens' injuries, especially if he doesn't pull through. Do you understand how many years you'll be locked away?"

She didn't react to his bullish glare. Oddly, she felt nothing.

Sharp sat back and tilted his head, studying her. "Why did you decide to involve Anna? Was it some money-making scheme tied to her book? Thought you could capitalize a little more on Frank's fame? Is that what you've been up to?"

Her sense of calm, if that's what it was, started grinding down and shifting toward something else.

"I mean let's look at how it was for you when you were younger. Frank took you out in public. He left you alone. You never ran. You could have left at any time. You could have told someone what was going on."

He had no idea what it had been like.

"People could have been killed. You should have reported Frank to the authorities. Except you didn't because you believed in what he was doing, didn't you? And now you're trying to finish what he started."

She wondered for the first time if this man could keep her here. She hadn't been charged with anything.

Sharp leaned toward her, so close, their noses were almost touching. "You've just admitted responsibility for every bomb for seven fucking years. You were old enough to know right from wrong. Don't try to tell me you never considered the possibility someone could have been killed or maimed."

The overhead light flickered again, and Tilly felt that old shame and guilt bubbling up. "Frank never wanted to hurt anyone. Neither did I."

He laughed at her, meanly. "If someone had been there when one of those bombs you built had gone off, what then?"

Tilly pushed her chair back suddenly to get away from him. She hated this man for asking these questions. Because the truth was she hadn't thought people could be hurt, not back then. Not herself, not Frank, or anyone else. But certainly, as an adult she'd thought about it, felt responsible for so much of it. People had been hurt. Henry and Finn. Anna, Helen, Paul Cotter. John, Ruth, and Ada. All of Cottersville, in fact, had been harassed and terrorized. And she'd still been willing to help Frank, maybe not with the dam, but she'd protected him with silence.

Sharp let out a waft of sour air. "Guilt. Was that it? You felt guilty for blowing Frank's cover when you were thirteen? Is that what this is about? Some kind of restitution?"

He was trying to get to her to admit things. To be done with her as quickly as possible so he could go home to his orderly life where, she was pretty sure, he got to be right all the time. But he wasn't right about this. And she wasn't going to jail. She'd made mistakes. She'd done things wrong. But she wanted to make it right. She belonged in Cottersville. She loved Finn. And Henry. Maybe she wouldn't be able to gain their trust again. She might not deserve that. But she wanted to try.

She sat up and pulled her chair back to the table. "I helped Frank when I was a child. I was too young to understand what I do now. It's as simple as that." She stood. "Are you going to charge me? Because if you're not, I think it's my right to leave."

He wavered his head noncommittedly. "We have enough to charge you, or we will as soon as Anna talks."

He meant to put her in jail. And he would find a way to do it. That's what he was saying.

There was a knock on the door. "Sit," he said. But she remained where she was as he went out the door. She watched his shadow against the frosted glass of the door window, head bent, talking to someone. A third person joined in.

Sharp came back in the room, shoulders bent, his lips pressed into a thin bitter line. He didn't say anything for a long moment like he had to work himself up to it. "Agent Stevens woke an hour ago. He had his wife call the chief to tell him Anna was responsible for the bomb that injured him. Said you had nothing to do with it and Henry Cotter could vouch for your whereabouts. An officer checked with Henry, and he confirmed you were with him." He looked at the floor. "And Anna just confessed to the recent bombing, the op-ed, Umbra Creek—all of it. She's been leading a group of Frank's followers, one that's preparing for more violence." He shifted from one foot to the other as though it pained him to have to tell her any of this. "Chief says we can't charge you with the other bombings since you were un-derage. So," he opened the door, "I guess you're free to go."

She went to move past him, but he grabbed her arm.

"One more thing." He wasn't looking at her, even now. Couldn't do it. "Agent Stevens wants you to come by the hospital on your way home."

chapter sixty-four

Mac lay in his hospital bed surrounded by his family and a forest of flowers and balloons. His wife and daughters laughed at something he'd just said. Even from outside the room where Tilly stood watching, the love among them was palpable. His wife, Maggie, as elegant as Tilly had pictured her, sat beside Mac holding his hand. His granddaughter bounced at the foot of the bed while his daughters stood, heads bent together, deep in conversation.

Maggie looked up and saw Tilly. She said something to the rest of the family, and they began a quick goodbye and filed from the room. Tilly wanted to tell them they didn't need to leave, not because of her. But then Mac's oldest daughter held the door open for her without even a hint of annoyance and invited her inside. "He's been waiting for you."

"We need some coffee anyway," Maggie said. "You'll stay here with him until we get back?"

"Of course." Tilly was grateful Mac had these people on his side. She sat in the chair beside him, swallowing hard at the sight of him up close. One eye was still blackened and swollen.

"I'm fine," he said in a voice stronger than he seemed capable of.

"What does the doctor say?"

"That I need to quit smoking. But I need a cigarette."

She laughed, thinking he was joking, until she saw his face. "You can't smoke in here."

"My jacket's over there. There's a pack in the left pocket." He pointed to the back of the door. "And get me one of those cups on the table. We only have a short time before the family comes back."

"They'll smell the smoke."

He sat up higher, wincing. "Get me a damned cigarette."

She fished the pack and a lighter from his coat pocket and handed them over. "I'm only doing this because I feel bad for you."

He lit up, took a deep drag and sank back onto his pillow. "Thank. God." He puffed again as she tried fanning the smoke to get rid of the smell. She hoped this wouldn't trigger a fire alarm or the sprinklers.

Mac tapped ash into the paper cup. "Was Sharp hard on you?"

She gave up trying to disperse the smoke. "He helped, in a way."

Mac raised an eyebrow.

"He asked questions I needed to answer for myself. Not so much for him."

Mac still looked doubtful.

"And what about you? Tell me how you ended up here."

He glanced at the door and took another long drag. "Anna's been on my radar for a couple years. I thought she was part of that online group planning to go extreme. I followed their activity and eventually suspected Anna was the leader, but I wasn't positive. Anyway, that's how I ended up at the dam with the bomb. The leader was going to be there, so I showed up to see who it was. I needed proof because they had bigger, more dangerous plans and I had to convince Sharp the group was a serious threat. He thought they were too disorganized. And his suspicions were on you. He also had the ear of the department, more than I did anyway. So I went to the dam to get evidence and walked in at the wrong moment."

He stubbed out the cigarette into the cup and held it out.

"You better get rid of this. And get me my breath mints. Right coat pocket."

Tilly dropped the cup in the trash and covered it with some crumpled paper towels. She retrieved his tic-tacs and spilled a few into Mac' outstretched palm. "Was Anna meeting Frank?"

Mac tossed the mints back, crunching them in his teeth.

"I don't think she expected to. My guess is Frank was looking at the same online conversations I was."

"So he was there?"

"Yes, and I haven't mentioned that to anyone. I'm not planning to." He waited to say more until Tilly looked at him. "I got hit in the head by some debris after the explosion. I would have taken a direct hit if Frank hadn't grabbed the dynamite and thrown it out of the way."

Mac shifted around and picked up a notepad on the small table beside him. "Sharp filled me in on what he discussed with Henry. I know Helen left that message on Finn's answering machine."

Mac ripped off a page from the notepad and handed it to her. "I had the call traced. Helen lives under another name in New Paltz, New York. Here's the address. Go talk to her. Get some closure. She's very ill, so you should go soon."

chapter sixty-five

Before it was light the next day, Tilly got on Anna's website and clicked the TELL YOUR FRANK STONE STORY tab. She posted a message about her plans to visit a house in New Paltz, NY. Frank would know what that meant. She waited until dawn, walked to Henry's and called his cell.

He answered in a sleep-slurred voice. "Are you okay?"

"I'm at your front door."

There was a rustling and then, Henry was there, holding the door open.

Tilly hadn't realized how cold it was outside until she stepped into his warm kitchen.

"How's Finn?" she asked.

"With his mom. We thought it would be best for him to get out of town for a few days. This has been hard on him. Obviously. But he's also a lot stronger than I've given him credit for. He'll be happy to know you've been released."

Henry kept his distance. Which was understandable, but hurt nonetheless.

"And how about you?" he asked. "They aren't trying to charge you with anything are they?"

"I won't be charged. I just came from seeing Mac at the hospital. He's gonna be okay. And I found out Frank was telling the truth about Anna."

"Oh?"

"Listen, I'm sorry about Frank. He showed up in my shop on his birthday. I didn't say anything because I just wanted to get the truth out of him about what happened that summer he left. I thought he would come and go. I should have told you. If you can see a way to forgive me, I promise that will never happen again."

He was listening carefully, but she could tell he wasn't ready to give her an answer on that. Not yet. She decided to press on. "We still don't know the truth about that summer. Or at least I don't. I'm going to see Helen. And I think you should come with me."

"Helen?"

"That's right. And you should know that Frank might be there, too."

He stepped back from her and she considered how all this must sound. "I'm not in direct contact with him. I left him a message on a website he may or may not read. But I think it would be good if he was there. They know what happened. They can tell us and then we can deal with whatever that means. Even if you don't want me in your life, I still think knowing the truth will be better for both of us. And for Finn."

He wiped the sleep from his eyes thinking about what she was proposing. "I've looked Helen up before. There's no record of her anywhere. Not any I can find."

She reached into her jeans pocket and held up the piece of paper Mac had given her. "I have her address."

chapter sixty-six

Helen opened the door of her small clapboard house. And Tilly realized she wasn't prepared for this meeting. She'd been so focused on finding resolution she hadn't considered what it would be like to see Helen in person. She hadn't expected to feel anything. They didn't know each other. But now the urge to flee was strong.

Helen invited them inside, seeming to know why they were there.

Tilly forced herself to step into the house, concentrating on Helen's home to buy herself time to settle enough for a conversation. The walls of the living room were decorated with a few journalism prizes she'd won. Photos of her and what Tilly assumed were colleagues were displayed on a few bookshelves. Tilly recognized one of the bookshelves and the desk in one corner of her living room as well as the dining room table. The wood for the sideboard she was now working on matched that table. Helen, it turned out, was the anonymous New Paltz customer who always paid in cash.

Helen took a seat in an armchair and motioned for them to do the same. Tilly finally looked at Helen straight on. They resembled one another, more so than she and Frank did. Weird she'd never noticed that before in old photos she'd seen of Helen.

Sitting there face to face seemed to suddenly require some

familiarity between them that didn't exist. Tilly felt instead the blankness of this mother in her life. It was a feeling of missed opportunity more than anything. She glanced at Henry. His feelings about Helen were also complex and difficult, just in other ways.

The sun coming through the sheer curtains cast Helen's face in a soft light as she looked down at her hands folded in her lap. Her eyes moved from Tilly to Henry and back to Tilly. "I've wanted you both to know the truth. But I didn't feel it my right to intrude. At least until I heard Frank had resurfaced." There was nothing at all melodramatic or apologetic about her manner.

A sudden noise at the front door made them all turn. Frank walked in. Henry stood. Helen's face registered utter surprise.

"I invited him," Tilly said. "Henry and I are here to find out what happened all those years ago."

Frank turned to Helen. "Don't go baring your soul now. You have no right."

Tilly saw the fear in Frank's face. This, whatever it was, was the thing he'd really been running from all these years.

"We came for the truth and we're going to have it," Tilly said.

"Paul didn't know anything about me and Frank," Helen said to Henry, in an attempt to reassure him of this at least.

Henry, who was still standing, sat down slowly.

Frank leaned against the wall, arms crossed, resolving himself to the conversation, for now. He cleared his throat, maybe intending to try to steer this story the way he wanted it to go. "When we moved to Cottersville, I did mean for us to stay, Tilly. I knew you wanted your mother in your life. I wanted to give you that. It sounds naïve now, but I thought we could live as a family. I thought she'd leave Paul."

The mix of hurt, anger, and regret on Frank's face as he looked at Helen suggested he was still in love with her.

"All I could see during that summer was the life I'd envisioned for us." Frank looked down at his bandaged hand and winced. "Everything seemed possible, at least at first."

Helen's eyes stayed on Henry, her face growing sad. "There was a time that summer when I planned to go away with Frank. It wasn't that I didn't care for your grandpa. But I wasn't in love with him. And by the time I understood that, I'd also realized I wasn't meant to be in Cottersville either. I wanted an escape and I thought for a while that was Frank. I had dreams of working for a bigger paper. I was interested in a more challenging career."

Tilly put her hand on Henry's arm and squeezed. It had taken a lot of courage for him to come here with her and now to face Frank.

Helen turned to Frank, giving him an unrelenting look. "It didn't take me long to realize Frank wanted a different life from me, one that mostly involved me helping him write a book about him." Color rose in her face. "And then I found out about you, Tilly. Frank was supposed to have given you up for adoption. That's what we agreed on before you were born."

Helen said all of this in her matter-of-fact tone.

"I was eighteen when I had you. I'd spent six months during my last year of high school hiding the pregnancy. It was completely overwhelming to me at the time. My dream was to be a reporter. Frank convinced me the dream was still possible if I moved to the cabin and had the baby there. He said no one would have to know. So I left a note for my parents about taking a trip across the country and I went to the cabin. Frank hid my car. We'd agreed that after you were born he would take you to be adopted. Then he was supposed go his way and I'd go mine."

Tilly imagined what it had been like, when Helen, just eighteen and pregnant, had been living alone with Frank in the cabin. She'd have been dealing with an outhouse and a place prone to cold and damp. She'd had no family, no friends to turn to.

"After the birth he took you in the night and I figured he was doing what we agreed. I thought at the time he wanted to spare me the goodbyes. After that I went back to Cottersville to try to pick up my life again. It was harder than I thought it would be, giving you up like that."

Tilly recalled now how shocked Helen had been to see her the morning she and Frank were arguing in front of the mill.

"I figured once you were born, she'd change her mind," Frank said as much to Tilly as to Helen. "Anyway, I couldn't give you up. Especially not when you were born on my birthday, the anniversary of my dad's accident. That meant everything. We were meant to be a team."

Tilly glanced at Henry wondering how he was taking all this.

"I knew he was going to blow up dams," Helen said. "He'd been talking about it for months. And if we were going to stay together and keep a baby, I would have had to agree to living a life on the run. A life in which no one had a real say except Frank. I didn't want that for me. And I didn't want that for my baby." She turned to Tilly. "I wanted the adoption so you could have a life with choices."

Frank shifted uncomfortably in the doorway. His face told Tilly this conversation wasn't going his way.

The sound of a vacuum came from next door. There were voices of children playing on the street, another world away from the one in this room.

Henry let out a frustrated sound. "And what about my grandpa? What happened to him?"

Helen and Frank looked at each other. Frank opened his wallet and pulled out a small picture. He handed it to Tilly, swallowing so hard she could see the muscles move in his neck. The photo was faded and warped, but she recognized a much younger Helen and Frank. He was holding a baby.

"That was taken the night you were born. I showed it to Helen the day you saw us together arguing at the dam. But when Paul's car pulled in, she threw it into the creek."

Frank shifted position as though he couldn't get comfortable. "I wish I could explain what the photo meant to me. It was the dream I wanted, the reason we'd come to Cottersville—the three of us were supposed to be together."

Tilly put her hand on Henry's arm again. Despite everything he'd heard so far he was still sitting here with her. But she sensed this story was not going to end well for his grandpa.

"I wanted to write a book with Helen," Frank was saying. "She's right about that. She could have taken my journal and turned it into something people remembered. We could have changed the world, the three of us." He paused. Tilly hoped he was listening to himself and realizing how he sounded. He went on more quietly. "So I couldn't let that photo go. The very last thing I wanted to do, Tilly, was tell you we were leaving Cottersville. In that moment, saving that photo meant saving us."

"And my grandpa?" Henry asked again, his tone revealing how little of his patience remained.

Frank wouldn't look at Henry and instead he stared past him. "I misjudged him. The water was so powerful. I realized almost immediately I was in trouble. I turned back but I'd already been swept up. And no matter how hard I swam, I kept getting pushed toward the middle of the creek and closer to the dam. My legs cramped and I panicked. All I could think right then was about my dad trapped underwater all those years ago. Paul came in the creek to save me." Frank's voice broke. "Didn't even know who I was. Just got out of his car and came into that churn thinking nothing of himself. His hand touched mine just before I went over."

"Paul went over, too, right after," Helen whispered. "I was watching from the office and expected to see them come out of the water."

"But Grandpa didn't," Henry said.

Helen wiped away tears.

"So it wasn't suicide," Henry said.

"God, no," Helen answered.

Henry stood, trembling with anger and probably sadness, too. "And neither of you say any of this until now? Someone dies and then, what? You leave people wondering and questioning for all these years?" He went to the door and slammed it behind him as he left. Helen flinched as though he'd slapped her. Good, thought Tilly.

"We couldn't bring Paul back," Frank said, trying to justify to Tilly what they'd done.

Helen took a moment to collect herself. "Frank told me he was going to run. He said you knew where to go, Tilly, and that he'd join you there. I didn't want anything to do with him at that point. And I knew Henry would be better off with his uncle than with me. I was barely his family anyway. And there was nothing for me in Cottersville. No future. So I left. And that's how I ended up here. I'm not saying that was the right decision, but it's the one I made."

Frank knelt in front of Tilly, scared, and readying some explanation that would allow him to remain blameless. She wondered how he'd held so much sway over her for so long.

"I had to leave," he said. "We expected Paul's body would be found that day. And they'd have blamed me. You'd seen me and Helen together. You'd seen Paul's car. I knew how it would look."

Frank had wanted things his way. Helen hadn't cooperated. And Paul had died trying to save him.

"I planned to meet you at August's place," Frank was saying. "But then the police found my journal. Once they knew who I was it became impossible to come to you. The FBI was watching."

Tilly stood, suddenly fueled by a lifetime's worth of suppressed rage and ready to burn everything to the ground.

Frank stayed where he was, kneeling and looking up at her. "Helen was right, okay? I admit that. We weren't living a life that was fair for you. That's what I was trying to fix. And I messed everything up. I knew you didn't want to live on the run anymore. So I did the kindest thing I could think of. I let you find your own way. I'd been wrong about Paul and a lot of other stuff. But when I made the decision to leave you in Cottersville, I made it out of love."

"That's what you thought?"

"I was holding you back."

"You left me alone. I could have died."

"But you didn't."

"Not physically, I suppose. But for seventeen years I haven't been living. I've been too afraid." Even as she said this Tilly also knew Frank had made the only choice he could see. The same was probably true for Helen. But that didn't make it right.

She pointed at both of them. "You could have said something before this. Henry has suffered. I have. So many have been affected. So don't try to sell me this tidy little rationalization you've concocted to make yourselves feel better. You don't get to make the choices you did and not deal with the consequences. Because while you were out there living your true, free, authentic selves or whatever, Henry and I have been trying to live our lives with the hands *you* tied behind our backs."

Helen appeared contrite, at least. And Tilly could forgive

Helen on some level. But Frank was stone-faced.

"I came back to warn you about Anna," he said. "I knew she was up to something."

"I'm going to walk out that door now, to find Henry. From now on we have separate lives."

Frank nodded and Tilly left.

Tilly found Henry waiting for her in his car. She got in and sat staring straight ahead out the window, not ready to risk looking at him. She'd asked too much of him.

"Well, that sucked," he finally said.

"Yeah, it did." Tilly tried to digest everything they'd heard, composing her thoughts. "Listen, I've done a lot of things wrong lately. I'm so sorry." She glanced at him, but he was staring down at the steering wheel. "I needed to know what happened. Up until this point I didn't know where Frank ended, and I began. I do now. I told Frank and Helen to stay out of our lives."

"He's not going away, Tilly. He'll still be out there. People will continue to believe in him. That's not going to stop."

"I know. But I can move on. I hope you feel that way, too, at least a little bit?"

Henry finally met her eyes. "I'm pissed at everything that went down in there. But I know what you're saying. I feel relief, too. And even some peace now that I know my grandpa's death wasn't something he chose."

"He died trying to do the right thing. That's something you can be proud of."

"Yeah." He wiped his eyes.

"Listen, I love Cottersville. I love Finn, and I love you. But I'm willing to leave town if you think that would be best. With everything that's happened, I would understand if that's what you want."

He shook his head. "I want you to stay. Finn will be home tonight. Let's go home and see him, okay?"

chapter sixty-seven

That evening in Henry's kitchen Tilly and Henry told Finn about their visit with Helen and Frank and tried to explain everything they now knew.

"I couldn't look at your paintings," Henry said. "I was afraid of what you might think if you knew he died by suicide as I'd thought. I was mostly afraid of what you'd think of me."

Finn opened his mouth to say something. But whatever had allowed him to speak on Tilly's behalf the night of her arrest seemed to have gone. Henry and Tilly waited. Seconds passed. Then minutes.

Henry reached for Tilly's hand and Finn stared at their entwined fingers. He swallowed, gearing himself up. "I was ... scared, too."

"Of course you were," Henry said.

Finn took a deep breath. "I was ... was ..." he croaked, "... worried about ... what Frank did. You were," Finn looked at Henry, "hiding things. I didn't know why."

Finn's voice gained strength, "I was scared to play you the message ... because I didn't know what would happen. Then ... when you and Tilly started talking more, I figured I'd keep painting. I thought ... you might figure things out together."

"And we did," Tilly said.

263

"So ... everything's going to be okay?"

Tilly looked at Henry and smiled. "It's going to be better than okay."

three months later

chapter sixty-eight

On a Sunday morning, Tilly joined Finn and Henry at the edge of Stone Creek, for the dedication of a monument they'd commissioned.

After an excavator tore the dam apart, the debris was loaded into trucks and hauled away. No bones were found. Henry was relieved, but also disappointed not to have some part of his grandpa to say goodbye to. They'd decided to put up a monument, next to Stone Creek, to remember Paul.

Swallows plunged through the first light coming through the morning mist, curling off the creek like something holy. Finn read aloud the words of a blues ballad from one of his great-grandpa's records. John and his family, Ada, Ruth, and Mac came to stand with them.

At the end of Finn's reading, a great blue heron took off from the creek a short distance from where they stood. As the bird rose over them, Tilly reached for Henry's hand and closed her eyes. She listened to the creek, now running unfettered over rock and capable of cutting through mountains. At last, they were free.

a c k n o w l e d g e m e n t s

Dear readers, thanks for reading! I so appreciate your time and attention on this story. I hope you've enjoyed it.

I'm grateful to Nancy Cleary at Wyatt-MacKenzie Publishing for the surprise email on New Year's Eve expressing interest in publishing this book. That felt like kismet. Thanks for all you and your team do to support writers and books. It's been a pleasure working with you on this novel.

I'm indebted to the many who read drafts of this book and offered feedback over the seven years of its gestation. These fine writers and friends include: Kathryn Craft, Jenn Rossmann, Maryann McFadden, Ruth Setton, Janice Bashman, Tori Bond, Eileen Schmidt, Abby Reed, and Joyce Hinnefeld. Each of you helped shape this book and for that I'm truly grateful. Thanks, too, to my Brigadoon writing community. It takes a village!

I owe a huge thanks to the Weymouth Center for the Arts and Humanities for offering me a contemplative place to write for extended time periods that were essential for this story's development.

Thanks to Kristin DeLorenzo for listening to me talk about the various and many iterations of this novel, including the screenplay foray, over years of runs and bike rides. And thanks, too, to each and every one who asked me about this book over the last seven years. Sometimes that question is all the writer has to keep going on the long journey that is the novel.

I'm grateful to my beautiful homeplace, Riegelsville, Pennsylvania, the tiny town along the river that inspired the setting of this book. And thanks to the wonderful Riegelsville community that I'm lucky enough to be a part of. (Special shout out to the Riegelsville Enhancement Committee!)

And finally, thanks most especially to my family, David, Owen and Sam, for the time and space required to bring this novel into the world. I love each of you beyond words.

Printed in the USA
CPSIA information can be obtained
at www.ICGtesting.com
JSHW020944090724
66076JS00004B/13

9 781954 332522